COWGIRLS AND RUSTLERS

Wild Cow Ranch 4

Natalie Bright
Denise F. McAllister

Cowgirls and Rustlers
Natalie Bright
Denise F. McAllister

Paperback Edition
CKN Christian Publishing
An Imprint of Wolfpack Publishing
5130 S. Fort Apache Rd. 215-380
Las Vegas, NV 89148

Paperback ISBN: 978-1-63977-011-3
Ebook ISBN: 978-1-63977-010-6

COWGIRLS AND RUSTLERS

Dedication

*To my co-author Denise. Thanks for your
patience, friendship,
unwavering faith, and creative mind.*

-Natalie Bright

*Thank you, Dear Readers, for telling us how
much you've enjoyed
the Wild Cow Ranch series. It's a dream come
true for us and
we will strive to keep good stories coming your
way.
May God bless each and every one of you.*

-Denise F. McAllister

Chapter One

Rafter O Ranch, Texas Panhandle, Present Day

Carli Jameson shifted to relieve pressure from a rock that dug into her hip bone. Lying on her stomach, she peered over the side of a low cliff. Her friend Angie Olsen of the Rafter O Ranch was prone next to her. Even though Carli was a little older, Angie was the bolder of the two. Carli had been fending for herself most of her life but felt empowered being around Angie.

The sun had just appeared in full over the flat, treeless High Plains not more than an hour ago. Since it was mid-May, the breeze still carried a chill this early in the day, but the grass had a welcoming green tinge.

They had been in the saddle before first light, riding in silence, swiftly making their way across the Wild Cow Ranch towards the isolated back of pasture six, or P6, as Carli had learned it was called. She was still trying to get her bearings on the 20,000-plus acres she had inherited the previous year.

Grazing Angus had stopped to raise their heads, staring transfixed in the direction of the two riders. The place swarmed with frolicking baby calves this time of year and their mommas were ever vigilant. Angie had previously mentioned to Carli about getting an early start anyway, so here they were on their stomachs in the dirt.

"There they are," whispered Carli as she pointed into the washed out, dry riverbed. "I knew I'd seen a vehicle light pass headquarters and aim in this direction after midnight, but I didn't want to approach them in the dark. Everyone else was in bed. Since we had already planned to ride fence line today, I thought we could investigate together."

A wide grin spread across her face as Angie turned to look at Carli. "You know me so well. I'll never turn down a chance to ruin a doper's day. They're cooking meth for sure."

Carli stifled a giggle as they hid. Life was never dull around Angie. They watched two men emerge from a beat-up camper trailer. One kneeled alongside the campfire to stir the ash and another set a coffee pot above the flames. A third stumbled from the backseat of the pickup truck, a faded green blanket clinging to his shoulders, and walked to the other side of the vehicle to relieve himself. Carli felt her cheeks warm. She and Angie clamped their hands over their mouths and averted their eyes.

He ambled towards the fire, stretched, and looked around, his gaze passing over the girls, but not seeing them. "Told you this place was perfect."

"Yeah, it's out in the middle of nowhere. Want some coffee?" the other man asked.

They continued talking in low murmurs, but Carli could not make out all the words.

"Can you believe these guys? What should we do?" Angie whispered, frustration and a tinge of anger in her voice.

Carli hated to admit they didn't have a plan. She wanted to find them, and now here they were, but she had no idea what to do when facing a criminal element. The blanket slipped off the guy's shoulders as he reached up to remove the elastic holding his ponytail. Smoothing his dark hair, he corralled the stringy mop and replaced the band. Carli squinted. He looked familiar.

Stiff spikes didn't come from the top of his head like other punkers, or whatever they were labeled nowadays, and he wasn't wearing the silver rings on every finger, but Carli recognized that jet-black hair and confident swagger.

"I know him! That's one of my riding student's old boyfriends."

Carli's stomach clenched with nerves. Raven had been a problem for her before. Who were these guys and why had they set up their camper on her ranch? She knew she should call Sheriff Anderson. Slowly slipping the cell phone from her pocket, it didn't surprise her to see no bars. It was next to impossible to get any signal out here. Staying put would be the best thing, and don't let them see us.

She turned to tell Angie not to make a sound until she could figure out their next move.

"You're trespassing, fellas!" yelled Angie as she sprung to her feet. "We've got you surrounded."

"Surrounded? By who?" Carli asked in surprise and then hopped up to stand next to her friend.

"Just go with it," Angie said from one side of her mouth as she stepped closer to the edge of the washout.

Without thinking, Carli yelled. "Raven! I see you. Does your mother know you're out here?"

All they had to do next was sit and watch the comical show below. The three guys came alive, like scurrying chickens in a hen house running for their lives from a racoon. They grabbed folding chairs, a cooler, and plastic tubs, tossing them in the back of a pickup truck as fast as they could. Never once glancing over their shoulders to see Carli and Angie standing on the edge above them.

The three men all jumped into the vehicle. The driver gunned it out of the low washout, spraying gravel and sand in their wake before roaring across the pasture towards the dirt lane that would take them to the main county road.

The only problem, they forgot to re-hitch their pickup to the camper trailer.

Carli and Angie doubled over in a fit of giggles as a dust trail rose over the pasture grass behind the fleeing truck.

"Should we chase after them?" asked Angie, her eyes wide and bright. "Please. Can we?"

"On horseback? Are you nuts?" Carli had learned her friend was always game for anything; she was the one who usually maintained a cooler head and reined in Angie's enthusiasm. "Let's check out their campsite."

They walked back to their horses where they had left them tied in the middle of a plum bush thicket, mounted, and took the easy way around into the washout. Dismounting they surveyed the camp.

"Were they really cooking meth?" Carli kicked over an empty can of beans. In their haste, the trespassers hadn't exactly cleaned up their paraphernalia. Instead, it was like a tornado had tossed everything around to create a debris field.

"Yep, I'm sure they were. Unfortunately, it's a problem around here in the more remote parts of the county." Angie moved some trash with the toe of her boot.

"Should we go inside the trailer?" Carli was apprehensive.

"You're durn right we should."

Carli hesitated. "Will we be destroying evidence?"

"Just don't touch anything."

Both stepped inside the small camper trailer. Not much was left outside, but inside the compact space they found all sorts of supplies. Packages of coffee filters, bags of kitty litter, paint thinner, and bottles of Drano.

"What do they do with all this stuff?" Carli wrinkled her nose at the smell. Angie punched her shoulder.

"Owww," Carli grimaced. "Why'd you do that?"

Angie answered with a sharp, "Shhh" and pointed to the sleeping quarters where a pile of blankets and pillows covered the small bed.

Carli's heart skipped a beat. Was there someone else still asleep? The girls froze. All sorts of options ran through her mind. The only immediate thing she could think of was to run, but her feet refused to obey the command. Instead, she picked up a large metal spoon from the counter.

"We have you surrounded," Angie called out and stomped with purpose towards the bed. Her spurs jangled and her booted feet rocked the little trailer. She tugged on the coverlet and threw it back over her shoulder. "Nothing. They're all gone." Disappointment filled her voice.

"Again, with the surrounded bit?" Carli laughed and then grew serious. She shook her head and let out a whoosh of air. She hadn't realized she'd been holding her breath. "What if someone had been lying there?"

"I guess you were going to stir them to death?" Humor sparkled in Angie's eyes as she stared at Carli. "But there wasn't anyone, so no worries. We need to put that campfire out. Do you see a container or shovel?"

Carli opened a tall cabinet next to the shallow sink. "Found one. I don't know how to tighten ranch security to keep these people off my property. I'm sure you have the same problem on the Rafter O."

"Through the years I've heard stories," Angie said. "Rustlers mainly, but here lately the drug scene seems to be encroaching more and more. I guess we could set up a stakeout."

Carli laughed. "What night? When? Across tens of thousands of acres, where would we start? And you have twice as much acreage as I do."

"It's just so aggravating." Angie grabbed her horse's reins and swung a leg over the saddle. "I guess we should come back in the truck and pick up this trash."

"This mess makes me furious," Carli said. "I wonder if the sheriff needs this stuff for finger-prints?"

Angie's expression was no-nonsense. "I say let's take it to him and ask."

"That's one thing I like about you, Angie. Your directness and lack of fear to face things head on. I need to be more like you."

"My grandpa used to say, no sense in wanderin' around like a pony with the bridle off. Figure out what needs doin' and do it."

With sand dumped on the campfire and one final check that the flames were out, Carli swung a leg over her saddle. The prairie was fully awake now and the meadowlarks provided surround sound as they rode their horses back to Wild Cow Ranch headquarters.

"What'd you say your full name was?" Angie asked as they loped side by side.

"I've never said. I don't like mentioning it so you

have to promise to keep it to yourself."

"Promise." Angie held up two fingers. "Scouts' honor."

"We're not Girl Scouts, but I'll tell you anyway. My legal name is Carlotta Jean Jameson."

"Oh, named after your Grandma Jean, right? But where'd they get that first name?"

"Carlotta is the name of Jean's mother, my great grandmother. They called her Lottie. She moved back to Europe when my grandmother was young. Abandonment seems to run in my family. My birth mom was kind of flaky too. Ran off as a teenager when she got pregnant with me."

"Yeah, the whole town heard the story of your mom, Michelle, leaving town on the back of some guy's motorcycle. That must've been rough for you, huh, Carli?" Angie watched her friend's face.

Carli steered her horse around a clump of yucca. "Truth is, I didn't know the details until I moved here. Lawyers found me in Georgia, said I'd inherited the Wild Cow Ranch from grandparents I never knew. That my birth mom was dead and no one was sure who my father was.

"My guardians didn't tell me much when I was growing up. I met Michelle once when I was a teenager, and I've struggled to deal with the fact that my own mother did not want me to be a part of her life. I guess it made me stronger since I've had to make it on my own."

Angie kept her horse at a jog. "Well, talking about names, wait till you hear mine. Angelina Christine

Olsen. Our roots are Swedish and religious, therefore the Christine, close to Christ. There was a great-great-grandmother named Angelina. I think it has to do with our proximity to New Mexico and Mexico. Maybe one of my ancestors came through Texas and married an Olsen. My dad used to call me his 'Little Angel', again the religious aspect."

"He doesn't anymore?" Carli asked.

"Not as often now that I'm older. I don't want to be his little angel. I want him to see me as a capable rancher, and to take me seriously. I'm a better hand than most of the guys around here."

"I know you are, Angie. Your brother Nathan used to say that all the time to me."

"Hmpff, Nathan. Firstborn, in line to take over the ranch. And what does he do? Hightails it to Santa Fe to become an artist."

"He had to follow his dream," Carli added.

Angie was quiet for a minute before answering. "He did have some talent. I realize that now. I always thought he stayed out in that shop of his to avoid the work."

"Nathan was more passionate about his art than you'll ever know. He wants to be respected. He'll have a successful career, I'm sure."

"Maybe. I'm trying to wrap my head around it. Nathan had everything. Even you."

Carli felt her cheeks warm thinking about her hesitation with Nathan when she couldn't tell what her heart wanted. Heir to a ranch, the nicest people she could ever meet who had turned into the family she never had, and then there were a few cowboys that muddled the entire thing. Nathan had turned into one of her best friends during a difficult time while she tried to find her way around the drastic changes she had made in her life.

"Your brother, Nathan, will always mean a lot to me."

"My dad is a stickler for tradition, and operations of the Rafter O always pass to the oldest son. It's been that way for generations. The middle daughter was out of the question, so I never dreamed I'd have a shot, but Nathan just walked away from it all. If my dad skips over me for my younger brother, Travis, for the job of running the ranch, I'll be mad."

Angie sighed and continued. "When my older sister, Janie, joined the Army, I thought that was my chance to prove what I'm capable of. Working all hours and doing everything I can so that maybe one day he'd take me seriously. I want to be his right-hand cowman. I wish he would see ME. Just once."

"I hope he does, Angie. Maybe it's time for a new era in the ranching community. You at the helm of the Rafter O and me here at the Wild Cow. We might shake this county up a bit."

They both laughed.

"Let's do it. And I have one more question. How's that Lank Torres treating you?"

Carli smiled at the mention of her ranch hand's name. "Oh, he's treating me just fine. Thanks for asking."

Carli didn't offer any more information, just squeezed her legs urging her horse Beau to speed up. He shot towards the red metal-roofed buildings coming into view.

The thought of her and Angie hunting down criminals, righting wrongs, and making a difference in their small community made her sit a little straighter in the saddle. It was going to be an interesting spring at the Wild Cow Ranch. Could they really fix things on their own? "The good Lord willing and the creek don't rise," Carli said under her breath.

Chapter Two

Within the next hour Carli and Angie were headed into the little town of Dixon. Carli pulled to the four-way stop at the intersection of Main Street and Main Avenue. She glanced longingly in the direction of B&R Beanery and Buns, the local coffee shop, but she and Angie were on a mission. They had some meth cookers to apprehend.

Carli went three blocks and parked in front of the sheriff's office. The sign on the dark gray building read, Dixon City Historical Museum, but that had closed long ago due to a lack of volunteers to keep it open. And lack of visitors, if truth be told. It's not like there were droves of people busting to find out about Dixon's forefathers.

Angie and Carli walked through the front lobby area decorated with black and white photos of the town, past an antique dining room table that served as the front reception, and then past one deputy sitting with boots propped on his desk. Deputy Jack Skinner didn't even glance up from his phone. Nothing much exciting happened around here that would warrant his attention.

"Girls." Sheriff Anderson greeted them from another room. Leaded glass double doors stood open so that the man behind the desk had a view of the entrance.

"Where's Thelma?" Angie asked.

Thelma had manned the front of the Dixon County Sheriff's Office since before the town site had a post office, or so it was said. Her husband had been sheriff for over thirty years until he was killed in a domestic dispute. No one had the heart to tell Thelma she'd reached retirement age years ago.

"Visiting her sister. What do you want?" Sheriff Will Anderson didn't smile nor did he rise to come out from behind his desk, instead looked back down at the file on his desk, a frown of deep concentration on his face.

Carli hesitated, but Angie walked in like she owned the place and swung an oversized black garbage bag from her shoulder. It landed with a plop in the middle of his desk.

"What in the name of Pete is this?" His voice boomed within the building causing the deputy to stumble to the doorway of the office.

"Evidence." The girls answered together.

"Of what?"

"We discovered some idiots setting up a meth lab on my ranch this morning." Carli stood square, hands on hips ready for a fight if necessary. Being with Angie instilled bravado.

"You can get prints from this stuff, can't ya?" Angie asked with a sniff. She wiped the dust from her face with her shirtsleeve.

Carli scrunched her nose and said, "That smell was awful. I'll never forget it."

"We put our gloves on. It was really gross," Angie offered.

"Can it make us sick, Sheriff?" Carli's mind still churned with worry over the discovery of the meth camp. She had never before come in contact with drug people or criminals. The idea that they had set up their lab on the Wild Cow, with seemingly no concern for trespassing, made her jaw clench with irritation.

The sheriff just stared at Carli without any answer.

In the next second time seemed to stand still as her mind raced with thoughts and her heart filled with sympathy for the people who depended on these idiot drug dealers. The way any kind of narcotic addiction destroyed individuals and families saddened her. Even if dealers were in it just for the money, what a horrible and illegal business to be involved with. She also thought of how they might not even care about the end user. She'd heard about methamphetamines. Carli had known people in Georgia who had gotten mixed up with drugs. It literally destroyed their lives and everyone who cared about them. Her mind quickly darted to thoughts of her birth mother. Drugs had destroyed her life as well as caused heartache for Carli's grandparents. And propelled Carli on a lifelong path of questioning why her mother left her in exchange for a life of drugs.

Carli recalled her ranch foreman's wife, Lola, mentioning in her Bible lessons for the yoga ladies about Satan. He was known as the thief whose mission was to rob people of their lives. Carli thought that was a perfect way to describe him and the way he pulls some people away from God. It was easy for Carli to remember where to find the verse Lola had taught. "John 10:10," she whispered to herself.

The thief's purpose is to steal and kill and destroy. Jesus's purpose was to give people a rich and satisfying life if only they'd listen.

Why did some people, like Raven, make the choices they did—drugs, stealing, lying, cheating, even murder. She couldn't begin to understand their motives. God would be their judge, but she could still feel tremendous sympathy. Her mind was spinning and she didn't have the full answer or solution to this huge problem, particularly when their bad choices impacted her life and property. She stood still as if in a trance.

After rotating her head from Carli to the sheriff, Angie spoke up. "There's more. You're gonna love this, Sheriff. They drove off in such a hurry after we hollered at them, they forgot to take their camper trailer with them."

They both chuckled. Carli could not get the image out of her mind of the dopers driving away in such a rush and leaving the camper behind. It was like a scene out of a comical movie.

The sheriff raised his eyebrows at that. "You don't say?"

"I'll go check it out," offered Deputy Skinner as he nodded his head towards the women. "Mornin' ladies. Which pasture, Carli?"

"The back one, P6."

"Hang on, Deputy. Think I'll go with you." The sheriff stood and retrieved his Silverbelly Stetson from the top of a coat rack made of horseshoes. He turned towards them with a look in his eyes that caused Carli to cringe. "As for you girls, never, ever get close to a meth camp again. Do you understand me? Those guys will let nothing come between their end game of getting their product out. You could have been seriously injured or worse. What in the world were you thinking?"

Carli swallowed the lump in her throat and hoped that Angie would pick this one time to remain silent. Anything they said at this point would not do them any favors.

"Yes sir," Carli quickly answered.

The sheriff turned squinty eyes to Angie. She opened her mouth as if to speak and then mumbled, "Yes sir."

"Now get that garbage off my desk and stay out of trouble." His voice boomed as they followed him out the door.

On the way to their vehicle, Carli turned to

Angie. "That went well. Why don't you come over and eat dinner with us tonight? Lank's teaching me how to rope and I promised that I'd cook."

"I hate being the third wheel."

"You won't be. Colton will be there too."

"Colton Creacy? I haven't seen him around town in years."

"He's been pushing cows on the north range for an uncle, I think. He and Lank are joined at the hip now that he's back. Please come," Carli pleaded, putting a hand on Angie's shoulder. "I really need a girl to talk to. You have no idea how annoying it is to not be included in the inside stories and never understanding what they're even joking about."

"Okay, I guess so," Angie agreed. "My horse is already at your place anyway. Might as well get some roping practice in myself. But I should run home first and check in with Dad. If you're sure it's okay to leave Magic with you a little while longer, I'll be back."

Carli couldn't help but beam from ear to ear as she climbed into her pickup truck. A part of her felt guilty. It was going to be interesting to see how the spitfire Angie might tangle with that smart aleck Mr. Colton Creacy. They were certain to get along like fire and water, but it would definitely liven up the evening. She chuckled to herself.

"What's so funny?" asked Angie as she snapped her seatbelt in place.

"Nothing." Carli just grinned. "It's been a fun morning. Really glad to have you along."

Chapter Three

Angie Olsen unsaddled her horse and left him in the pen at the Wild Cow Ranch, then drove back to the Rafter O. She walked as if on a mission to the main house, hoping her father was in his study before she lost the nerve. Their visit with Sheriff Anderson had got her thinking. There had to be something they could do to improve ranch security. Set up a watch schedule and send a couple of men out on patrol to look for signs of meth camps, coordinate their efforts. She walked into her father's study, a cool quiet settled her after the hectic morning. Oak bookcases and leather wingback chairs were typical of any rancher's office, the room having remained the same for generations. With the exception of two computer monitors, the Wall Street market scrolling constantly.

Skip Olsen sat behind his leather tooled and carved desk. It had been his father's and grandfather's before that, shipped here by steam train and mule-powered freight wagon all the way from an antique store in Boston. Certified European antiquity.

Angie couldn't help but smile fondly every time she saw it. She used to curl up under the huge desk when she was little and run her fingers along the carved details. While her brothers and sisters squealed, the back door banging as they ran in and out until her mother told them to stay outside, Angie was under the desk. They never knew where she was nor did anyone care. As the middle child she floated between reality and the made-up world in her mind. It was okay though. She felt safe under that massive piece of furniture. It was like her own playhouse when her father was elsewhere.

But today. Today was different. Today she had been the one in the thick of it all. She had been on the front line of an event and it was one that she could report to her father.

Throughout her life her father had always used his oldest boy, Nathan, as a sounding board. But Nathan was gone. Moved to Santa Fe, New Mexico to pursue his dreams of becoming an artist. Now was the time for Angie to step in and take up a leadership role at the Rafter O, or so she hoped. She squared her shoulders and walked into the study, spurs jingling on the mahogany wood floor. She slipped off her cowhide gloves, slapped them on her thigh to shake the dust loose, and then tucked one end in the front of her belt.

"Hey, Dad." He glanced up for a brief second and looked back down at the papers spread out on the desk. Skip Olsen remained stubborn in many ways,

Angie thought. He refused to get a computer although one sat to the left. He was traditional about so many things—one of them being that females do not run cattle ranches. And in other ways, he was the most God-fearing man she knew. His faith was extremely important, which is why she couldn't stay irritated at him for very long.

"How's my angel today? Out riding?"

Angie gritted her teeth at the endearment, but she pushed her annoyance aside. "Yes, and no. I need to talk to you about something. Is this a good time?" She plopped into the leather guest chair.

Without glancing up, he said, "Sure, sweetie."

"Are you aware we have a serious problem with meth cookers in this county? Carli and I came across some guys cooking dope this morning on the Wild Cow."

"Oh yeah?" He looked up this time, a frown creasing his face with a look of concern. "You didn't confront them, did you?"

"Yes, sir. We ran them off. Carli recognized one of the guys."

"You what?" He banged his fists on the desk and blasted out of the cowhide chair. His voice nearly shook the walls. "Don't you ever do anything like that again. Those are dangerous people. What were you girls thinking?"

"I'm a big girl, Dad, a woman. I can take care of myself."

"This has nothing to do with you taking care of yourself, Angelina Christine. This has to do with very dangerous people. Where was it? I need to call Sheriff Anderson. I'll talk to some of our neighbors and the Special Rangers."

"We've already talked to the sheriff. Took him a whole garbage bag of evidence too." She frowned and refused to let her father know that the sheriff had yelled at them too.

"I cannot believe you'd be that reckless. You know better." He stared at her, his eyes hard and narrowed.

Skip Olsen had a way of cutting a person down to size and making them feel like they were still in grade school. He looked at her the exact same way as he did back then. Didn't he realize that she was older and wiser now? That look wouldn't break her down to tears like it used to. She gritted her teeth and met his stare.

"I want to talk to you, Dad, about our own ranch security. Do you think we have a problem? After all, we're twice the size of the Wild Cow."

Surprise reflected in his eyes. "There's no need for you to worry yourself, Angel. I'll handle it." With that, he turned his gaze back to the papers on his desk.

"No. Sir. I want to talk about it now. I want to help you, and to do that I need to know what's going on." Truth be told the set jaw and calmness on her face concealed sheer terror inside. She had never disagreed with her father before in her life. If there was one thing the entire family knew, when Skip Olsen said the last word, it was end of discussion.

No exceptions.

He looked up, in part surprise and part annoyance, crossing his arms calmly in front of him on the desk. "You want to help, do ya? You can start with riding through those last ten heifers that have yet to calve. If any of them need assistance, I expect you to help with the birth. And then you can take the four-wheeler tire to town and get that hole patched. We're out of salt block, so you might call the feed store and order a load, and when you hear from the trucker you can meet him at barn with the skid loader to stack the delivery. Bring the load ticket and invoice back here and write a check."

Angie swallowed hard. "Yes sir."

"Do not get anywhere near a meth camp again. I'm talking within miles. If you can see it, that's too close. Is that clear?"

"Yes sir."

He let out a humph sound and shuffled papers.

Apparently, their discussion was over and she had been dismissed. Despite the fact that her heart nearly beat out of her chest, she couldn't help but be satisfied with the end results.

"Is everything all right, dear?" Her mother stopped and asked as they passed in the entry hall.

"Dad just gave me a list of stuff to do," she said. "He's going to realize one day that I'm a serious rancher." And I'm gonna do every single one of those things, even if it's the last thing I do.

"That's good to know, dear." Her mother had turned her attention to an arrangement of flowers that spilled from a vase.

Without another word, Angie slipped on her work gloves and slammed the front door behind her, just so her father would know that she had gone back outside instead of up to her room. She had to show him what she was made of. Skip Olsen was in for the surprise of his life.

Chapter Four

Lank Torres walked with purpose to the corral. He needed to tune on his new horse, Phoenix, before Carli got back from town. He had promised her that they would have a roping lesson, and she had promised she would cook for him. He had to smile at the thought of them being a couple. There was no doubt in his mind that this girl would be a part of his life forever, but he sensed that she held back.

If he was a betting man, he'd lay money down that someone had really hurt her in Georgia. She hadn't told him about it yet, but when she did, he'd be there to listen and tell her all the things bottled up in his heart. It was too early in their relationship just yet. He had to keep reminding himself to give her space and time.

Although imagined, the dusty smell of burning hay assaulted his throat and made him cough. Every time he walked by the hay barn, he could still smell the charred wood and feed, and hear his horse Blackie's whinnies. The barn had been rebuilt soon after that horrible fire, but he still remembered that night with full clarity. Not all men were animal lovers like Lank.

He had run back in to the barn to get his horse but that effort had only cost him a hospital stay. Buck had been hospitalized too. Tragically, Blackie hadn't made it.

Phoenix, a nice bay colored horse, stood with his head over the pipe rail watching Lank. He scratched the horse between the ears and slid the latch open on the gate. Grabbing the lunge rope from the saddle house, he looped it over the horse's head and led him to the round pen. As he guided the horse in circles around him, he thought about dinner.

Carli could not cook. It wasn't through lack of effort. But by comparison to his mother and Lola, the two best cooks in the entire county, Carli really came up short. He hated to hurt her feelings, but he already dreaded trying to pretend he liked her dishes. By the end of the day, he was usually starved because he'd rather continue working than stop for lunch.

His mother made the best Mexican food. He remembered her standing in that tiny kitchen rolling out the soft dough and frying it in her cast iron skillet. The best tortillas he had ever eaten in his life. She didn't measure out the ingredients having learned the recipe from her grandmother who lived near Mexico City. His mother had talked about taking him back there one day to meet all of her family, but she never got the chance. Next time he sees his sister, he'd ask if he could have that old cast iron skillet.

Lank shook off the sadness. He'd been focusing on the memories of his horse and his mother, now both gone. He had to stop living in the past. He turned his attention instead to Phoenix who had a nice trot and lope, but right now was a little rambunctious.

"He's looking nice."

Lank turned and grinned at the decidedly feminine voice. The sound of his future.

Carli was in the process of climbing over the fence. She perched on the top rail and gave him a smile. The only thing he could think of was that he sure wanted to kiss her. Her eyes were shining and she had a glowing energy about her as though she was busting to tell him something. Tugging the lunge rope and telling Phoenix to "whoa", he led the horse to the fence.

"Where have you been?" He started not to even ask, because he could tell she had big news by the way her eyes sparkled. Instead of making her suffer a bit, he asked anyway.

"You're not going to believe it. Angie and I found a bunch of guys cooking meth in P6 so we ran them off and took a trash bag full of evidence to Sheriff Anderson."

"You did what?" Lank stepped back and pushed his cowboy hat back on his head. "You walked into a meth camp?"

"They were harmless; besides I knew one of

them. Remember that kid Raven? He was one of my riding student's boyfriends. I think he and Lexi broke up soon after I had to pick her up from jail."

"Those people are dangerous, Carli. They're doing a job they take very seriously, and they don't like anybody getting in their way. Particularly girls."

"What does that mean? Girls?" She slid off the fence and landed with a thud on both feet directly in front of him, a glint of anger shining in her eyes.

"Nothing personal, it's just you could have been seriously injured. You shouldn't mess with those people, Carli. It's not a game. They could be armed and most are hardened criminals."

"I know it's not a game. This is about me protecting my property from trespassers."

"Just be careful and use your head is all I'm asking."

Carli gave him a shrug of her shoulders. "Is Colton still coming over?"

Lank blinked at the sudden change of topic. That girl's mind shifted gears quicker than he could inhale a whole pizza if he was starving. Right, food, his stomach reminded him. "Yes. We're going to rope the dummy, and then maybe pick up some pizza."

"No. I'm cooking for you, remember? I need to get started. Angie's coming over too."

Lank let out a heavy sigh. He'd tried with the pizza idea. There's still hope that she'll mess up something so bad that he won't have to eat it, and they would have to go out. All the same, his heart skipped a beat as he watched her walk away before turning back to Phoenix.

Lank stood in the middle of a round pen lunging a young ranch horse. "Settle down, boy. Easy now." He kept the end of the rope quiet so as not to spook the rambunctious colt any further.

"Looks like you've got a tornado on your hands there, Lank."

Colton Creacy. Lank's best friend since they were kids. Like the colt, full of energy, but basically just full of himself most of the time.

Lank yanked sharply on the rope to let the horse know who was in charge. The colt gave Lank a sideways glance and bucked his hind legs straight up to the sky.

"Woo hoo, hold on, Cowboy! Don't let 'im git the best of you."

Colton had jumped out of his pickup and made his way over to hop up on the fence and watch Lank work the horse.

"He's young but he's coming along," Lank said. "What have you been doin'? Haven't seen you in a while."

"Been busy. Working here and there. A man's gotta eat." He flashed Lank a big grin and bugged his eyes out.

"Yeah, and drink too." Lank gave Colton a mock stern glare.

He really couldn't judge Colton too harshly since he'd been right there alongside him in all kinds of bars and honky-tonks for years. They were like a team, picking up girls, consuming too much beer, and looking for trouble wherever they could find it. Nothing serious, just making young fools of themselves, sowing their wild oats, Lank thought. But he didn't want that lifestyle anymore. Looking at Colton and remembering all the wild times they had together, made him finally realize it was a dead end. Now he had Carli. And she meant more to him than all the trouble he and Colton had run into over the years. He hoped one day Colton would come to his senses too and make something of himself. They weren't kids anymore. Time to grow up.

"You're not my father, Lank. I've only got one of those."

"All right. I'm just sayin'. Too much drink and a hard life only makes you grow old before your time."

Lank knew Colton didn't like anyone telling him what to do. But he also knew Colton couldn't be upset with him. Their friendship went back too many years and they had always been plain spoken about things.

"I can sleep when I'm dead. In the meantime, there's life to be livin', man. I'm so ready to hit the rodeo circuit. Aren't you?"

"In my head, yeah, but not sure about my body. Besides I need to talk to Carli about it."

"Why? Is the new lady boss not going to let you off work?"

"It's not my job that I'm worried about, it's all those cowgirls you have tagging along behind you everywhere you go. I'm trying to make this a go with Carli. I don't want anything to screw it up."

"But it's rodeo. It's the open road. Your head is fine. It's time to get back in the saddle."

Lank had to admit that he yearned for the feel of that saddle, that eight seconds where man and beast were the only two things in the universe. He liked pushing his body to the limit, testing his endurance to beat the clock. He had promised his mother after his concussion that he was done with broncs. But his mother was gone now, and the rodeo arena still tugged at him, like a drug. A high he couldn't get from anything else.

Colton began reminding Lank of the fun times, with story after story. The two guys went on and on jabbing at each other, laughing their heads off.

Lank pulled the lunge rope again and said, "whoa" to the young horse, who, by that time, was tired and sweaty. Seemed like all the buck was out of him.

A pickup truck's tires on gravel followed by the sound of a door slamming shut caught Lank's attention.

"Hey, Lank!" The "hey" stretched out into two syllables from a Texas twang dripping with honey. He turned to see Angie, her blonde hair shining in the sun and encircling her head like a halo. Both men watched the female walk.

"Howdy, Angie. How are ya?"

She looked over to Colton, then back to Lank. "Just fine. I'm looking for Carli. Is she out here somewhere or back at her house?"

"I think she's at her house cooking."

"Oh no," said Colton, under his breath.

"Thanks, Lank. Are we roping later? I left my horse here after Carli and I rode fence line this morning."

"Sure, that's what I'm planning." And then to Colton he said, "You remember Angie Olsen, don't you? Nathan's little sister?"

Lank had to laugh at the look of shock on Colton's face who said, "Holy cow! You're an Olsen? I don't remember you."

Angie laughed. "I think I was still in junior high when you were in high school, but I remember you. Still causing trouble wherever you go, I assume?"

Colton walked closer, stared into Angie's blue eyes but she ignored him. Instead turning to Lank, she smiled and said, "Thanks a lot, Lank. I'll go find Carli. I shouldn't be too long."

When she walked towards Carli's house, Colton stared at the back of her, from top to bottom. Lank chuckled as he watched Colton frozen in place, transfixed. He couldn't remember a time his friend had ever been speechless. Pale flaxen hair trailing down her back to her waist, form fitting jeans accentuating every female curve with the cuffs tucked into purple boots. She was still wearing her spurs.

"Are you sure she's an Olsen? I've never seen her before. Maybe she's a cousin?"

"Stop staring and watch your manners. That's

Nathan's little sister, Angie. Don't ya remember her when we were kids?"

"Angie? The middle one? Man, has she grown up! I'd like to take her two-steppin'."

"I doubt she'd give you the time of day. Carli says she's not interested in dating; she's focused on her work at the Rafter O. And her dad surely wouldn't want the likes of you sniffin' around."

"What d'ya mean? I'm a nice, upstanding kind of guy."

Lank smirked. "Uh, yeah, right. Since when?"

"Since this very moment." Colton straightened his collar, lifted his cowboy hat off to set it square on top of his head. He dusted off his jeans.

"Let's get this horse put away and set up the roping dummy for the girls. We could all use some practice."

"Looking forward to it. Is there any possible way we can go for pizza after? I'll even buy." Colton half-smirked.

"Don't get your hopes up." Lank knew what Colton was getting at. "Carli says she's cooking for us, so we've got to let her."

Chapter Five

Sitting in the middle of the shop was a metal frame holding a saddle. Underneath, nestled in the belly was a plastic and metal shaped calf with wheels. At the pull of a lever, a heavy spring came loose and pushed the calf out so that the cow puncher sitting in the saddle could rope the horns, or "head" the calf from atop the structure.

Carli and Angie walked into the shop to find Colton in the hot seat and Lank working the lever. There was a lot of hooting and hollering, which, in Carli's mind, didn't lend anything to the ability to rope.

"I'm next." Angie walked across the cement floor with confidence and stood at the side looking up at Colton.

"My turn's not over yet, he said."

"You threw your rope, missed, that's the end. Move, please."

"How did you get to be so bossy?" Colton didn't budge from his seat, only looked down at her.

She stuck her chin out and crossed arms across her chest. "Somebody has to keep you idiot punchers in line because most of you don't know sic 'em from come here."

Lank and Carli looked at each other and laughed. Score one for Angie. That girl could really shine with the comebacks. Maybe it was because she grew up with so many siblings. Colton didn't have a reply, but Carli thought she saw a hint of admiration on his face rather than anger. He may have met his match for once.

"Let's see what you got then." Colton climbed down from his perch.

Angie made her way up to the hot seat, coiled rope in hand and started swinging it overhead. Snap. Lank pulled the lever and the metal framed calf scooted across the floor in a flash. Angie let her rope sail. It hung in the air for a few brief seconds, then floated over the head and horns pretty as you please.

"Awesome!" Carli clapped her hands. "Way to show 'em how it's done, Angie."

Lank whistled and Colton stood speechless. Carli had never known him to not be spouting off about something, and she kinda liked this silent side of him.

"Climb on up, Carli." Lank pushed the calf back into his spot and latched the spring. Angie handed her the rope and she started swinging it overhead.

"Keep your wrist loose. Not too fast." Lank got ready with the lever.

"That's too slow," said Angie.

"Twirl your wrist and get ready." Lank instructed. "Aim in front so that he runs into it."

"But I don't know which way he'll go." Carli was still twirling and twirling, her arm ached as she focused on keeping her wrist loose. "Lank!"

With a hearty laugh he pulled the lever. Snap! The wheels creaked as they rolled across the floor.

Carli flung her rope and caught one horn. She pulled the slack back, yanking the dummy around to face her.

"Good job." Lank grinned. "You're getting the hang of it."

"Let's go again!" Carli was thrilled she was catching on.

While Lank operated the lever, Carli practiced twirling the rope over her head and releasing the loop, focusing on aiming in front of the calf.

"Did Carli tell you we found a meth camp this morning?" Angie turned towards Lank, completely ignoring Colton and going so far as to turn her back on him. From her perch atop the roping dummy, Carli couldn't help but notice the snub. She thought it was a brilliant move.

"You did what?" Colton came alive.

"That was a stupid thing to do." Lank showed his disapproval by turning a deep frown directly to Carli. She shrugged.

"Those guys are ruthless. I've run across a few of 'em and they're up to no good." Colton showed real concern on his face. He walked closer and stood between Lank and Angie. "They'll kill you as soon as look at ya."

"For the one hundredth time, we know how dangerous they can be." Angie gritted her teeth. "We've heard all of this before, but there they were and there we were, and we dealt with it. Didn't we Carli?"

Carli held back her laugh remembering the scene of those dangerous criminals driving away in a panic. "They left their camper behind." For the second time that day when their eyes met, Carli and Angie were overtaken by a fit of giggles.

"It's a serious problem," Colton offered.

"I heard old man Moore caught a few on his place last month," Lank said. "I think rustling is more of the problem than drug cooking. Particularly this time of year, before the calves are branded."

"Do you think we have a problem?" Carli asked.

"The pasture counts are accurate so far but branding is still four weeks away. We'll know for sure after roundup. Who's to say what we may have to deal with?" Lank pushed his hat back off his forehead. "The grass is greening up, and we probably won't be caking every day so I won't be driving every pasture every day."

"I can start driving through on days you don't cake, if that helps." Carli turned to Angie and asked, "What'd your father say about it?" She immediately regretted the question when she saw the look on Angie's face.

"He wouldn't tell me details. Just that he'd handle

it. The day before I had overheard him tell Travis that we're missing a few replacement heifers and a few momma Red Angus and their calves." Angie took the rope from Carli's hand and stepped back so that Carli could climb down from the roping dummy.

"We need to find out who is doing this. I wonder if Raven is involved," Carli asked as she jumped to the cement floor.

"Raven? You mean Johnny Gibbons? That long-haired hooligan. I know him! How do you know him?" Colton asked.

"He showed up at the riding school with one of my students, Lexi. Arrogant and he's got one smart mouth."

"Your riding school. I keep forgetting to ask how lessons are going," Angie said.

"It's going really well, but I've suspended classes for several months. This is such a busy time. We'll pick back up in July or August. If any of you know of some gentle-natured horses that might be good with children, I'm in need. I'd like for every kid to be able to ride and build their confidence without getting hurt. I need some calm, slow lumbering horses."

"There ain't no such thing as a calm horse if'n they decided not to be." Colton laughed.

"Are you guys hungry?" Lola asked as she appeared from around the corner and stepped inside the shop. "Chicken fried steak."

Angie glanced at Carli. "I think Carli is cooking

for us tonight."

"That's great," said Lola. "What are you making?"

"Pancakes," was her simple reply.

"That does sound good." Lola looked around the group.

"With lots of bacon and coffee. Scrambled eggs maybe?" Lank mumbled.

"No, just pancakes." Carli answered as she focused on recoiling the rope. She had thought she was being nice by offering to cook for them, but she had other things to do besides stand in a kitchen. Pancakes seemed easy enough, less time-consuming, and, besides, they were her favorite.

"How about we give you a break this time, and y'all just come eat with Buck and me? There's plenty."

"We'd hate to impose." Angie smiled.

"After Carli went to all the trouble." Colton grinned.

"We know Carli was counting on cooking," said Lank.

"That's enough." Carli snorted a little. "Y'all can shut up now. I am aware that I'm not the best cook and besides I don't really want to cook pancakes anyway."

Carli couldn't help but notice the sigh of relief from Angie, and the glance that Colton and Lank shared. Her cooking skills needed work, just like her roping skills, but how was she ever going to improve if everybody kept eating at Lola's? Granted, her stomach growled and she was thankful to have steak instead of pancakes and syrup. And besides, not every ranch was lucky enough to have a Lola.

"Thanks, Lola. I really do appreciate your efforts. I'm starving," said Carli.

She couldn't help but stare at Lank as she fell in behind the others and headed towards the cookhouse. His pearl snap western shirt stretched tight across his back, his black hair curling just past the top of the collar. And the way he looked in those tight Wrangler jeans always made her heart skip a beat. She shook her head to snap out of it.

Cooking practice wasn't the only reason she had suggested dinner at her house before she had known Colton would be there and before she had invited Angie too. At some point she needed to get Lank alone to clear the air between them. She had poured her heart and soul out to him at the side of the hospital bed after a rodeo accident, but then they'd returned to the ranch and back to the same awkwardness. Staring at each other and saying nothing.

She had to find out what he was thinking. Did they have a future together? They'd either start kissing or she'd have to fire him. One way or the other, she needed to know where they were headed.

Chapter Six

Sunday afternoon burned bright and warm. The trees showed tiny buds, and the winter brown had been replaced with the signs of summer, green creeping across the pastures. Carli turned her face up to the sunshine and closed her eyes. A time for rest, reflection, and peace. Of course, a breeze blew a strand of hair across her face. Always wind in Texas, but she was getting used to it.

Carli had slept late that morning, enjoyed coffee on her front porch, and then wandered over to help Lola. She now stood in front of the two-story cookhouse with the little canine that was quickly becoming her dog, Lily Jane. Although Lank called the dog L.J. and took her everywhere he could, Lily Jane always ran to Carli's house at the end of the day.

"Stay, Lily Jane. You've got to learn this." Carli held her palm flat in front of the dog's face. "No, sit back down. Stay. Don't move." She turned and took a few steps away from the dog, but Lily followed, tail a'wagging. Frustrated, Carli's voice grew sterner. "No, Lily Jane. Sit. Stay."

Lank walked her way from the corral, followed by his ever-present shadow, Colton. Jingle bobs on their spurs caught the attention of Lily Jane who wagged her tail at the sight of Lank. The guys had just tied their saddled horses to the fence.

Carli had no idea what they had been doing all morning, nor did she want to know. Both laughed about some shared joke which only annoyed her. She had yet been able to talk to Lank alone, what with all the work her foreman Buck had him doing for branding. It also bothered her that Lank hadn't included her. Instead, she'd been helping Lola clean the cookhouse, and make list after list of items they'd need to feed around thirty-five cowboys and cowgirls for a week.

Colton's Australian Shepherd, Drifter, appeared from under the corral fence and trotted along with the guys, tongue hanging out as he swung his head from side to side until he spotted Lily Jane. Both dogs met up and started the sniffing game. Round and round they went like a dance.

"No, Lily Jane. Stay. Come back." Of course, the pup ignored her command and Carli was fast losing her patience.

"That dog ain't gonna listen to you, Carli, unless you have a treat. Food always gets their attention," Colton offered.

She glared at Colton Creacy. Smart aleck. More so than even Lank was, in the beginning when she had first met him. He was doing better now that they were dating, so to speak.

"Want me to show you how it's done, Carli?"

"No, thank you, Mr. Creacy. We're doing just fine." She was not thrilled with him. Neither was she enamored with his male dog bothering her sweet female pup.

Lank smiled and came close to put an arm around her shoulder. "He's just trying to help, Carli."

She glared at him too which caused his lips to stretch into a "Yikes" expression, his eyes bugging out. He backed away playfully and held up his hands in surrender.

"Colton, I guess we should leave Ms. Jameson and her dog to get back to their training session. She is the boss."

Carli tried not to smolder. She couldn't help saying, "And I'd appreciate your keeping your dog away from Lily Jane. She's too young for a boyfriend."

Lank and Colton exchanged glances, their eyes wide. But they suppressed their grins.

Just then Buck and Lola emerged from the cookhouse.

"Hey, guys, we could really use your help," the foreman said.

"Yes sir. Whatcha need?" Lank stepped forward, removed his hat, and wiped his brow with his bandanna.

"Well," Lola started, "looks like we need to host Cowboy Church later today. Pastor is under the weather so they called us. We just need to set up chairs and a few tables, and I'm making some food."

Carli piped up. "I can make Morning Glory muffins! That recipe you shared with me last week, Lola."

Looks were exchanged between Lank, Lola, and Buck. Carli waited and didn't understand the delay. She was excited to cook and she knew everyone was skeptical but she'd show them.

"Well, I, uh, guess so, Carli. I don't want you to go to any trouble, but sure, go ahead and make them. That would be really nice of you." Lola smiled, then looked to Buck.

He cleared his throat and said to the cowboys, "C'mon guys, I'll show you where to line up the chairs."

"I'll be glad to help ya, Buck, but I ain't staying. I don't go to church anymore," Colton said.

"Me neither," Lank chimed in. "I've got work to do."

"Look, you guys. I really need you to stay. After church I need your help to clean up and put all the tables and chairs away. And Lank, it would be really nice if you'd play guitar. Just something short, as a favor for me. Besides, Lola's making a bunch of good food and I know y'all don't want to hurt her feelings, do ya?"

Carli had only heard Lank play his guitar twice before. Once, right after inheriting the Wild Cow Ranch, she had heard music coming from the saddle house and then around the holiday, her first

Christmas here. Lank had played for his nephews. He had a shy presence about him when he played, but he was certainly talented.

"Lola's making dinner? I can stay and help, Buck." Colton smiled and punched Lank's arm and the two shoved each other like they were still in junior high. Carli rolled her eyes. Just the mention of food and these guys suddenly turned into A-plus-number-one help.

In the town of Dixon not too far from the ranch there was a small church that Buck and Lola attended every Sunday, Wednesday nights too. They were very involved. Bible studies, prayer team, sometimes hospital visits when time allowed. Carli had heard Lola's phone buzz many a time with texted prayer requests and Carli knew for sure that Lola prayed for all of them.

Carli sometimes joined Lola and Buck for Sunday services since she had become a Christian, but mornings around the ranch were usually consumed with animal chores, feeding and the like. Animals didn't know the difference between weekdays and weekends. Lank assumed responsibility for Sunday morning chores so that Buck and Lola could take off for church.

Occasionally, the neighboring ranches took turns hosting Cowboy Church. The Rafter O was the most frequent location for the get-togethers and the motto was always, "Come as you are." That meant jeans, boots, spurs, and cowboy hats. Sometimes jeans and boots were a little dirty if the wearers had worked that morning, and that was perfectly acceptable with all in attendance. Most of them believed the main purpose of the meetings was to hear God's Word, sing and praise Him, and spread love to their fellow neighbors.

Carli slapped her thigh. "C'mon, Lily Jane. We've got muffins to make!"

The little dog looked at her and then back to Lank. She took another sniff of Drifter but then complied with the idea that she and her co-owner were on the move. Now it was all scampers.

In the kitchen Carli found the recipe, pulled out the many ingredients and set them on the counter, and double-checked her list. She read them out loud, "Whole wheat flour, brown sugar, cinnamon, baking soda, apple, coconut, raisins, grated carrots, walnuts, wheat germ, eggs, vanilla, orange juice, applesauce. Looks like I have everything." Lily Jane wagged her tail in response.

Piece of cake. Or, piece of muffin. She laughed at her own joke.

Pulling out her phone she pressed Angie's name. "Hey, girl! Did ya hear we're having Cowboy Church tonight? You coming?"

"I wouldn't miss it, Carli. My folks too, maybe my brother Travis, and I don't know who else. Do I need to bring anything?"

"Nah. We've got it covered. Lola's cooking and I'm making 'Morning Glory Muffins'!"

"Really? You're getting into that cooking thing, aren't you?"

"Whattiya mean? Why is everyone so stunned? I see those glances y'all exchange. I can cook." Carli's mouth pouted a bit.

Angie laughed. "Okay, okay, no offense. I'll see you later then."

"All right. See ya!"

Carli was excited to have neighbors coming to the Wild Cow, and this time she'd be able to contribute to the food.

Meanwhile she found the dog in the living room tearing up a magazine.

"Good grief, Lily Jane! What are you doing? Give me that. I'm gonna have to put you in your kennel, you little monster." She had recently decided on a cage for the house after Lily Jane had gotten into too many things she shouldn't have. Carli only put her in it sometimes. Those sharp puppy teeth could destroy everything in sight within a matter of minutes.

With Lily Jane sequestered and out from under her feet, Carli got back to her muffin mixture and also made herself some hot tea. "Toast, peanut butter, and honey, yum," she mumbled to herself. An afternoon snack sounded good.

Being extra careful to follow the recipe, she then diced, chopped, and stirred the muffin conglomeration of ingredients. It took her several minutes to find the beaters that went with the ancient mixer.

Zing went the over-achieving red vintage toaster as it catapulted her piece of toast skyward where it turned into a backflip and dove to land, before she could catch it, on the floor. Lily Jane zoomed over and snatched it up before Carli could apply the five second rule.

"How did you get out, you rascal? Give me that!"

After a chase around the living room, she put another piece of bread into the toaster, stood next to it and waited this time, catching it before it hit the ground. She then placed it on a half sheet of paper towel.

Crazy, possessed toaster. She vowed to one day replace the vintage appliances in her grandparents' kitchen. Maybe even remodel the whole place. But then again, she loved the sunny yellow tile and quirky colors of the 1970s kitchen.

"Okay, what was it?" she mumbled. "Two tablespoons baking soda?" She was trying to read Lola's handwriting on the recipe card. "Or is that teaspoons? What does 'tsp' mean anyway?" She realized she loved baking even if she was just learning. It made her feel so domestic. She wondered at the many meals her grandmother had made in this very kitchen.

Maybe I could add some honey to the muffins. More brown sugar? A little more vanilla? Nice and sweet. Yum.

She beat it all again just to be sure. After she had a smooth batter, she carefully filled the muffin paper cups and had to place them on a cookie sheet. There wasn't a muffin tin anywhere to be found. She opened the oven door while balancing the pan in her other hand.

"Oh, good grief," she said. Lily Jane's ears pricked.

The oven was cold. While it pre-heated she cleaned up the mess. She worried that Cowboy Church would probably be over before she could even get there.

With Lily Jane close at her heels, she changed clothes and made it back to the kitchen just as the buzzer sounded. As she removed the pan, she accidently touched the side of the oven with the back of her hand and tipped the pan. "Ouch!" Three muffins tumbled to the floor, and Lily Jane spied the food. She sniffed the muffins, nudged one with her nose, walked slowly around the baked goods several times, and then sat.

Carli took a deep breath. They smelled delicious, a hint of cinnamon and fruit. "You can have a taste, I guess. I'll have to throw them away."

Maybe they were too hot. She broke one open and gently blew on it until cooled and then laid it on the floor in front of Lily Jane. The dog just looked at her with big, sad eyes, refusing to even sniff the treat.

"You don't think I can cook either, do you?" Carli put her hands on her hips. "That's gratitude for you."

Chapter Seven

Buck stood in front of the stone fireplace and welcomed everyone to the Wild Cow Ranch. He read a note from the pastor to the group apologizing for his absence and explaining how he felt sure the regular church would be open the following Sunday. It was just a touch of laryngitis, maybe an occupational hazard.

"Our pastor has been ordered to rest and stay quiet by his wife, and we know not to argue with our better halves," Buck said. "That's like a direct message from above." The crowd laughed.

Folks sat shoulder to shoulder in the dining hall, the tables having been folded up and rolled into the storage closet. Every seat was full with people spread around the dining room.

Carli was surprised at the turnout when she stepped inside with her pan of muffins. The guys had located every available chair they could find, plus a few from her house that had been stacked in the garage. All heads were bowed, so Carli stood at the back of the room. Buck said, "Amen."

Typical of the Sunday evening meetings when scheduled, the potluck stood as a proud tribute to the skills of the small-town wives, or husbands in some cases. The spread was worthy of any magazine photo shoot.

Carli had found a cake stand and arranged her muffins for display. They looked pretty, but she hadn't tasted one yet and now she wondered if she should have brought them over.

After the prayer Buck put his Stetson back on. "It's good to see everyone. As y'all know, we'll be in the middle of spring roundup and branding in a few weeks. With about a hundred new first year mommas, they'll be nervous for their young and not sure which way to go. There's one old bull that's ornery as heck. Last time it took five cowboys to get him to headquarters.

"We have some good old cows that raise some really good calves, year after year. They know the way too. Lank here rides point and those old cows just fall in line behind him every time. And of course, the rest follow.

"We produce cattle, but some of you raise goats or Quarter Horses. I saw some muddy boots when you walked in. Guess you had chores to do before coming." A few heads nodded. "You don't need a tie to worship here. Have you looked at that spread of food? My wife can make a chocolate pie that melts in your mouth, while others can cook a bowl of pinto beans that makes you want to sit up and sing.

Paul wrote in First Corinthians Twelve that there are different kinds of gifts and different kinds of service, but it's the same God at work in all of us. Just like those cows know their place in the herd, some are natural leaders and some follow but all of them know where they belong. I hope that each of you use whatever gift you've been given in the best possible way for His glory. I hope that His presence in your life energizes you. Let us pray." Buck removed his hat.

Carli glanced around the room at the bowed heads and the sight tugged at her heart. A group of people, her neighbors and friends, all together, all believing that there really was a God that loved them, that looked out for them, and who only wanted the best for their lives. Life wasn't perfect, but if tragedy or bad times struck, they all believed God would be at their side to help them through the dark days.

With all heads bowed and eyes closed, she felt so overwhelmingly grateful to be here. Carli felt a tear slide down her cheek. She wiped it away and peeked around, but no one was looking at her. She did see one person staring without eyes closed. Colton Creacy peered at Angie Olsen intently.

And what was that silly looking grin on that cowboy's face? Carli bowed her head right quick and couldn't help but smile to herself. She knew Angie would never give him the time of day.

After the prayer, Buck said, "We don't have a fancy sound system in our cookhouse, but I did ask

Lank to play us a song." He then nodded to Lank who pulled a chair and microphone set up to the center facing the group. A middle-aged woman joined him with a small keyboard that two men had quickly carried for her.

They started with "Amazing Grace" and the group of neighbors sang along.

The lyrics always pierced Carli's heart. "I once was lost, but now I'm found. Was blind, but now I see. My chains are gone. I've been set free."

The music filled the hall as people joined in singing or swaying to the melody. Lank's strumming was so precise and beautiful. As he played, he closed his eyes and seemed to completely give himself over to the song.

"Y'all know the words, so please sing along," said Lank. After a few bars of music, Lank nodded to the keyboardist and then began to sing.

Still somewhat of a new Christian, Carli was learning how to navigate life, and identified with the song. Most of her years she had felt lost, alone in the world, because of not knowing her birth parents. Always different from other kids who had a mother and father. As she got older and more independent, she masked her feelings, put on a brave face to others. This song conjured an image in her mind's eye—she had been like a prisoner to her previous life's fate. Now her chains were gone, and she could be free, to live, to love, to let people in. It brought a tear to her eye to think of how there really must be a God, how He could help her to change the course of her life. He must love her more than an earthly father.

She sang along and closed her eyes. Angie stood next to her and whispered, "You really have a beautiful voice."

Lank and the keyboard player played a contemporary song next that Carli had heard on a Christian radio station. It really touched her, and she believed God could heal broken hearts. Hopefully, He would patch up hers. And even though she was praying, she couldn't take her eyes off Lank. Just couldn't help herself.

When the service ended Buck invited everyone to hang around and polish off the food; otherwise, he'd have to eat it all next week. Lola served a nice stew full of meat, carrots, potatoes and nearly the kitchen sink. Cornbread. Peach cobbler. Other neighbor ladies had also brought food although Lola had tried telling them earlier that there was no need. It was just the way it was around here. Neighbor helping neighbor, everyone pitching in.

Lank came over to Carli and Angie in line for food and Colton squeezed his way between them to fill his plate to overflowing. "Hey! Let's go outside and all sit together. I'll grab a spot for us," he said.

Carli laughed when Angie gave him a sideways stare and a frown of annoyance. If the way Colton had watched Angie during the service was any indication, she was going to be annoyed many more times.

"Y'all be sure to get some of my 'Morning Glory

Muffins'! It's Lola's recipe but I made them myself." Carli was excited like a kid.

They all chowed down on the salad, stew, cornbread, and mac 'n cheese until their paper plates were almost empty. Except for the muffins.

Carli surveyed her friends' plates. "Oh, did you save my muffins for dessert? Go ahead, let me know what you think. Be honest now. I'm trying to learn."

Colton took a nibble, made a grimace, and spit it into his napkin. "Sorry, I'm allergic to carrots. This muffin has carrots in it."

Carli gave him a hard stare and furrowed her brow. "You just ate a bunch of carrots in Lola's stew."

"Oh, is that what those were?" he sheepishly turned his attention back to his plate but it was empty. "I need cobbler," he said, as he scrambled up from the table and disappeared inside.

Carli turned her attention to Angie who tasted a muffin, swallowed, coughed, and grabbed her iced tea. Her tongue slightly went in and out of her mouth like she was trying to figure out the taste.

"Carli, did you put baking soda in these?" Angie asked, coughed again, and took another long drink of her tea.

"Yes. I followed Lola's recipe."

"How much baking soda?"

"A couple tablespoons."

Angie took another drink. "I think it's supposed to be teaspoons. Maybe less than one. How long did you bake them?"

"Well," Carli hesitated. "I set the timer. I'm not sure."

"This was a good try. But a teaspoon is not the same as a tablespoon and you might have cooked them a little too long."

Colton returned with his plate full of cobbler and ice cream. Lank sat down next to him with a muffin and brought it up to his mouth, but Colton put a hand on his arm and shook his head.

Carli watched their exchange. "What's wrong with them? I know they're a little done on the bottom, but not really burnt." Carli bit into hers. And her eyes squinted. Then she reached for her tea and coughed some. "Well, maybe I do need to try it again. The ones Lola makes are so delicious."

Lola and Buck came walking up behind the seated four.

"Hey y'all. You talking about the muffins, Carli? I thought you made an excellent attempt. They just need a few tweaks. I can help you next time. No worries. That's how any of us learn, by trial and error."

"You know, Carli, there is one thing you really excel at. I mean one of many things." Angie patted Carli's shoulder.

"What's that?"

"Singing. You have a beautiful voice. I heard you in the service."

"Oh, I don't know about that. I was just trying to follow along."

Lank reached over and took her hand. "I've heard you before when you were brushing Beau and thought no one was around. You do have a lovely voice, Carli. Don't hide it."

Lola stood behind Carli and placed her hand on the girl's shoulder. "I didn't know you could sing. It's a gift from God. Lank's right. Don't hide it. Maybe one day soon you can sing for all of us and Lank can accompany you on his guitar."

They all agreed. "That would be really cool," Angie said.

Colton gave her a big smile. "Yeah, really cool, for sure."

Carli felt her cheeks grow warm. "I don't think I could sing in front of people. I just like doing it sometimes, when the mood hits me."

Lank raised his glass of tea and the others joined him. "Well, here's to new things in your life, Carli." He took a bite, looked like he had a lump of mashed potatoes that wouldn't go down, and then grinned but didn't chew.

She handed him a napkin. "Maybe cooking isn't my gift."

Lank leaned closer and squeezed her hand. "I'll always be your taste tester."

He gave her a smile that sent her pulses racing, and he still had crumbs on one side of his mouth. She was behaving ridiculously just because a man had squeezed her hand. That cowboy was beginning to melt the walls that protected her. No doubt about it.

Chapter Eight

"Hey! Where's Lily Jane? She was right near me a few minutes ago." Carli got up from the table on the porch of the cookhouse, her head pivoting right and left. "Has anyone seen her?"

"Over there!" Colton spoke. "Here she comes with Drifter from the other side of the barn. They must've been running around, carrying on."

In a deep voice Carli said slowly and deliberately, "There had better not be any carrying on. I told you to keep your dog away from her." She stared him down.

Angie intervened. "C'mon, Carli. I'll help you get her. Do you want to put her in the house for a bit?"

Carli still glared at Colton, but answered Angie. "I'll keep her with me."

"Come say hi to my folks," Angie said.

As they stepped inside the cookhouse, Carli looked over Lily Jane's fur. "Look at her, Angie. Like she's been licked from head to toe."

"Looks like she's grinning. Knows she was a

naughty dog, don't you, girl?" Angie reached out a hand to pet the dog.

"That Colton kind of gets under my skin. I told him about his dog. Lily Jane had better not get pregnant. She's just a baby herself," Carli whispered.

"What is she?" Angie cupped the sweet face in her hands. "Six or eight months now? It is possible, you know. Just watch her and keep her away from male dogs."

"Let's go visit your folks, then I'll put her in the kennel instead of letting her run underfoot in here." Lily Jane gave a small wiggle, but after Carli tightened her grip, she settled down.

"She looks content in your arms," said Angie.

Church members still milled around visiting while others helped cleared tables and picked up trash. Angie's dad, Skip Olsen's big voice filled the air on top of other smaller conversations. He sat at a table were three other ranchers.

Angie and Carli edged closer to the table to hear the conversation but they knew this was a men's discussion. Buck walked up and sat down at the table.

"We've got to put a stop to this. I've lost at least four cows, and last week another three along with their calves. How about you, Jim?" Olsen asked.

Another gentleman answered, "We've got five total from a trap that was right next to our headquarters. I don't know how they're doing it."

A couple of men chimed in.

"Using dogs more than likely, but you'd think we

could hear 'em."

"All good stock. That's big money right out of our pockets. Should we set up guards? Has anyone reported this to the sheriff?"

"I dunno, Skip," one man started. "It's pretty dangerous stuff. Those guys are criminals. And maybe hopped up on drugs. No telling what they'd do if they felt trapped."

Buck offered his opinion. "We've already reported it to the sheriff and I called the TRA. They should be sending someone out next week. Maybe we just wait to hear from them."

"Wait?" Olsen boomed. "If we sit around and just wait, we might lose even more stock. They say rustlers always work on a full moon. Next full moon is tomorrow, isn't it? I'll have Travis round up a few of his buddies. This is meticulous and planned, and I'd bet it's the same group working all of our ranches."

Heads nodded in agreement.

Carli could feel Angie bristle at the mention of her younger brother's name.

The rancher named Jim nodded his head. "I'm going to send a couple of my ranch hands out tonight to look around. Maybe they'll see or hear something."

Carli held tight to the wiggling Lily Jane and caught Angie's eye. They moved away from the table pretending they hadn't been listening to the men's conversation.

Carli whispered, "Maybe we should scout around tomorrow night."

Angie put a finger on her lips as her mother came up between them. "That is the cutest dog, Carli."

"Thank you. She is very sweet. Lank claims Lily Jane as his, but Lily claims me so I guess it's settled."

"That's how it works." Mrs. Olsen laughed. "What are you girls fixin' to do?"

Carli froze, paranoid about the rustler and stakeout talk. She couldn't think of anything to say.

"Nothing," said Angie. "Can we help you with something, Mom?"

"As a matter of fact, I need you to carry my containers out to the pickup truck. And then we'll help Lola haul trash."

"Sure. Which ones are yours?" Angie followed her mother into the kitchen, and Carli slipped out the front door to wait on the porch.

Lank and Colton were in the middle of a group of boys and girls who were swinging ropes and aiming for a plastic calf's head that was stuck in the end of a square hay bale. Carli didn't dare let Lily Jane down because there were ropes swinging at anything that moved, kids and dogs not excluded. Colton's dog kept circling her legs, wagging his tail, and staring up at Lily.

With arms balancing dishes and sacks hanging from both hands, Angie walked to her mom's SUV, placed it all in the back and then made a beeline straight for Carli with a huge smile on her face. "Your place or mine?" Angie asked, her eyes wide with excitement.

Carli laughed. "Whoa now. Let's think about this. Maybe both, and in between is Vera's place.

We'll just take us a drive around and see what we can find."

"I'm in," said Angie.

"In for what?" asked Colton as he and Lank burst onto the porch. Lank ducked. "Hey now!" as a rope loop sailed over his head followed by kids' laughter.

"In for carrying out the trash," said Carli.

"My mom needs your help." Angie pointed to the front door. "There are several garbage bags waiting in the kitchen."

"Walk with me Angie. I need to put Lily Jane in her kennel."

"Sure."

The girls turned without another word to the guys and hurried across the gravel drive to Carli's house. Once inside Carli gave her aching arms a rest and put Lily Jane on the floor. She pointed to the metal crate in front of the fireplace and said, "Kennel" but the pup ran straight to the front door, whining and scratching.

"Lily's got a boyfriend, I'm afraid." Angie patted Carli on her shoulder.

"No. That is not going to happen. I will not allow it. She's too young." Carli sank into the leather sofa.

"Keep telling yourself that." A wide grin spread across Angie's face as she sat on the cowhide chair next to the fire. "Now, let's talk about the full moon."

"With a full moon I'm thinking we can cruise around without our lights on, don't you think?" Carli asked. "I wish we had some night vision binoculars."

"We might have some. If I can sneak into my dad's office tonight, I'll take a look."

"Don't get in any trouble, Angie. It's not worth making your dad mad at you."

"We are capable young women, just as capable as Travis and his goof off friends." Angie stood up straight and paced the room. She stopped and pointed a finger at Carli. "You're a ranch owner now and I've been in this business all my life. There's no reason we can't do our part to protect what is ours. Bring your flashlights too. A warm jacket, drinks and snacks in case we have to be out all night."

"Do you think they'll come back to that same spot on my place? Where the meth cookers set up camp."

Angie shook her head. "No. I'm guessing your drug issue is solved. They won't take another chance, and since we've seen their faces, they'll lay low for a while. They won't risk it."

"I hope you're right." Lily Jane laid on top of Carli's feet, giving up hope that she'd get to go back outside. "By the way, what is TRA? Buck said he called them."

"It's a group of beef producers who pay dues," Angie explained. "TRA employs Special Rangers who investigate crimes that happen on farms and ranches."

"That's good to know. I'd like to learn more about the organization," Carli said.

"Before your grandparents died the Wild Cow Ranch always hosted the local district meeting. Maybe you could do that again."

"As long as I don't have to sing, I'm good to host

anything." Carli joked.

"Yeah, but remember I told you that you had a gift for singing. And Buck talked about gifts tonight. I'm praying we can find our gifts of being smarter than the criminals in the county. You and I can do this, girlfriend."

"I sure hope we can catch somebody." Carli felt somewhat apprehensive, but Angie's total confidence gave her some hope. Maybe they could stop this rustling.

"Me too." Angie's phone buzzed. "My parents are leaving. Gotta go. I'll see you tomorrow night."

"Count on it." Carli walked Angie to the door.

They had a plan. Now they just needed to find the courage to see it through. Carli took a sharp intake of breath. They had completely forgotten to talk about what to do if they actually caught somebody at the deed. What was their plan then?

Chapter Nine

The next morning Carli was pretty sure Lola had already fed Buck and Lank a hearty breakfast and sent them on their way to work on whatever projects they had planned for the day.

Carli was in her house done with coffee and cereal and pulling on her boots to ride Beau.

She couldn't help but smile as she thought of the stakeout planned for tonight's full moon. What would the guys think? No doubt it would be good to include them for extra protection. But Carli thought about how Angie and Colton probably wouldn't get along since they seemed to grate on each other's nerves.

Were all of them Type A, in-your-face personalities? Not Carli, who was comfortable staying in the background, but the others. Colton got a little loud when he was winning, showing off. Which irked Angie. But then Angie was also boastful and bold. She didn't have a confidence problem, that's for sure. And Lank had to hold his own in front of

Colton; couldn't let his best friend get the better of him.

But then Lank was just a little boy in a grown body. She realized that last night at Cowboy Church. He was the one outside playing with the kids, showing them how to hold the rope and toss it. He was always ready with a joke and a helping hand. Her heart warmed at the thought of him, but he kept his feelings hidden so well. It was so aggravating, but then she did the same thing. She'd been guarded and cautious her whole life. How were they ever going to make a go of anything together if they never communicated?

This morning she just wanted to ride her horse, maybe take him out in the pasture to check on the herd. The meadowlark serenade and the unbroken horizon were so different from the woods of Georgia but this was her home now. She had learned to find comfort in the vastness of it all.

She thought about Lank. One part of her yearned for silence but another part wanted him by her side. After all, she was the boss. She could order him to go with her. She smiled again as she grabbed her ballcap.

But it wasn't like that. Their relationship had settled down without all that push and pull they had gone through for so long. He was really kind of different, she knew he'd be tender and caring. Still had some spunk in him though. And that was one of the things she loved about him. She didn't want a weak, passive guy. What kind of relationship would that be, if he sat back and let her make all the decisions?

Stepping onto her front porch she slipped on her sunglasses. It was a bright, sunshiny day. Sounds like a song. She was so happy lately; it was almost sickening sweet.

Lank was in a corral tossing his rope overhead. Ever so gently he aimed for their puppy, Lily Jane, or L.J. as he insisted on calling her.

"Don't you dare hurt my dog, Mister!" Carli called out in a half-teasing way.

"Your dog? I thought she was mine." He flashed his bright smile at her.

"What's yours is mine, and what's mine is mine." She laughed and he furrowed his brows.

As L.J. wiggled in an excited circle, Carli bent over and scooped her up. "Ugh, this puppy must weigh about thirty pounds now. What is she, six months or more now?"

Lank coiled his rope, sent a perfect loop through the air, which encircled Carli and L.J.

"Got ya. I think I'll keep you both." He smiled that handsome smile, his dark eyes twinkling as he moved in closer. Carli's heart fluttered like mad and then he planted a kiss on her cheek, which caused L.J. to lick the other side of her face.

"Aaagh! I've already washed my face once this morning." Carli turned her head away and the dog squirmed from her hands to the ground. But Lank didn't let go of Carli. He pulled her close to his chest, looking deep into her eyes. "So, what are your plans for today?"

"For one thing, you get a do over. Something better than a kiss on the cheek." She glared at him. It was time they moved this thing along, if this was even going to be a thing.

He looked surprised and then kissed her again. Proper this time.

Her first thought was to put the dog down and lean in for another. Instead, she placed her palms against his chest. "Well, I'm not gonna get a thing done if you keep this up, Cowboy. Don't you have work to do, Mr. Torres?"

"My number one job is keeping the boss lady happy. And I believe that is you, ma'am." Another kiss, this time on her neck.

"Hey now, easy on the PDAs, partner." As much as she loved his attention, Carli didn't feel comfortable with a big display of affection in case Buck or Lola came into view.

"Oh, come on now, Carli. Who's around? L.J.? Beau? No one else is here." Then, leaning down to L.J., he nearly goo-goo-ga-ga'd to her. "Close your eyes, sweet little L.J. You're still an innocent babe. Momma doesn't want you to watch."

Carli made a face and shook her head. "I told you, her name is Lily Jane, and she may not be as innocent as you think."

"Why's that?"

"She ran around with Colton's dog all day." Hands on hips, Carli tried to get serious with him. "Okay, I need to ride and you need to work . . . or whatever it is you do around here."

"Well, actually, Boss, I think it's time you learn a little bit about ropin'. It could come in handy someday, when you least expect it."

"Now, why in the world would I need to rope anything? And what needs roping?"

"Let's see . . . a cow maybe? I mean you do live on a cattle ranch." He laughed that infectious deep, throaty laugh, his mysterious eyes crinkling at the corners.

Her knees actually went weak and she couldn't help but be angry at herself. Any minute now she'd start fluttering her eyelashes. What an absolute silly girl she was becoming. In her aggravation Carli almost took her ballcap off to swat him but her ponytail was all secured. Instead, she decided to beat him at his own game. Leaning close she kissed him. She moved in closer and kissed him on his ear, and then kissed him on his eyelid. He froze.

"Okay, okay, Boss. Stop. We need to do this, get to ropin'." He was still cracking up, but then stopped. "You know, seriously, Carli, there may come a day when having this skill could really get you out of a jam."

"Yeah, like what?" Her eyes narrowed into a glare, although none of this was anything more than play fighting.

"Let's say L.J., excuse me, Lily Jane, fell down into a ditch and was in trouble. You could throw a rope and pull her out. Or if a calf was limping and needed to be doctored, I'd need you to help me rope it and hold it until we could take a look. Or, let's say it was me. I might be stuck and ..."

"Hold on. You sure can spin a story, can't you?" She smiled. "All right, show me a thing or two with your lariat."

"First of all, I don't call it that. Rope will do just fine." He got next to her and coiled the rope to explain the parts. "This knot is called the hondo or some say honda."

"Like the car?" Carli's voice squealed a little. She felt like the class clown so tried to regain some seriousness and give him her full attention.

"No, not like the car." Lank glared for just a second. "Now, listen up. You did all right on the roping dummy the other day, but I want to sharpen your skills. You coil your rope in your left hand, like this. The hondo is a looped knot that lets your rope slide through. Some folks have a metal hondo attached."

"You say hondo, I say honda. Tomato, tomahto." She grinned, just couldn't help herself.

"Look, Miss Smarty Pants, do you want to learn this or not? It could very well save someone's life."

He took his roping seriously and she didn't want to upset him so figured she'd better pay attention.

"All right. I'm listening. The hondo lets your rope slide through."

"Follow me," Lank said.

She followed him through the saddle house to the back lawn where a hay bale sat with plastic cattle horns. Lank stood in front of it, coil in his left hand, and the rest of the rope in his right.

"Always point your fingers in the direction of where you're aiming, like this. Raise your right arm straight up, overhead, not behind you, not off to the side. Let the end of the rope open up in a big circle, swing it round and round till you're ready, then let 'er go."

Snap, contact with the horns. "Like that," he said smiling. "Then pull it taut, back with your left arm."

"Okay, let me try." Carli reached for the rope.

"I dunno, you might need to get your own rope. They have pink, red, or neon orange." There was that smart alecky grin again. He held the rope behind his back away from her.

"Oh, aren't you the funny one? Pink rope. I'll show you. You'll be surprised at how quickly I learn this, Lank."

No matter how exasperating he was at times, she knew she was falling for him. They'd been through so much together. A fire, a Texas winter storm, injuries, hospitals. Now, even cattle rustlers. She knew they could face anything together. And Lank had revealed his heart to Carli. He told her he loved her from the second he saw her, arriving on the Texas ranch from Georgia, almost like little girl lost. An orphan, abandoned as a baby, raised by foster parents, and now her birth mother was dead. Her grandparents were never able to find her until just before Grandpa Ward's death. But now she was a ranch owner. She had changed too. And she could see their future together, but lately things between them seemed awkward. So different from that moment in the hospital when they had opened their hearts to each other. She didn't know exactly how to move forward.

Carli grabbed at his arms hiding the rope behind his back and they both giggled and flirted. She loved the way he teased her, the closeness, knowing they were meant for each other.

"Give me the rope, Lank."

"Come and get it." He was laughing so loud, so open and free, and he doubled over at the waist.

Carli wondered if they would always play together like this. She stopped and said simply, "Are we officially together?"

"I guess," he gave a little shrug.

"That's all you got? After we poured our hearts out to each other while you were in the hospital from that rodeo wreck, and now we've moved on to 'I guess'?" She pushed back the frustration and tears that stung the back of her eyes. What were they doing?

"What do you want, Carli?" His eyes were warm and curious. He walked closer, and she wished he wouldn't do that because she couldn't think of what she wanted to say when his body was near hers.

"I want to know what you do all day."

"Oh, this is a work and boss thing. You planning on replacing me?"

One cause of her breakup in Georgia was that they had rarely communicated. She didn't want to make that mistake again. Pride was usually her downfall, So, she had been asking God to reveal the areas where she needed improvement. She knew now that she wanted this to work out with Lank. She'd never felt this way about anybody.

"No, I don't want to replace you. I want to learn everything you do, and since we're about to brand I'm curious. Would it be so awful to have me around?" She hung her head and whispered the last part.

"It would be the best thing in the world to have you around." He pulled her close.

Carli put her head on his chest and her arms around his neck. This day might be the turning point she needed.

Suddenly the sound of a truck and trailer broke their intimate moment and Carli turned around and looked to the visitor. She and Lank froze still in their playful embrace.

"Angie, what are you doing here?" Carli composed herself and pushed away from Lank.

"I could ask you two lovebirds the same thing." Angie's mouth pulled to the side in a pretend-chastising smirk as she parked her truck and jumped out.

"Lank was teaching me how to rope." Carli was a little embarrassed but also couldn't wipe the grin off her face or lose the feeling of belonging to someone.

"Yep, that's what it looked like to me." Angie rolled her eyes. "Ya know, I can give you some pointers too. On ropin', that is."

Lank adjusted his hat against the sun and ignored her comment. "I've seen you rope. You're a real hand, Angie. Just don't take my job away." They all chuckled.

"No harm in us both giving her some lessons, right? She might pick it up even faster. But that's not why I'm here. I've got some news about those guys who were trespassing. Carli and I have some work to do."

"Now, wait just a minute you two." Lank was stern about this. "You ladies had better not go anywhere near those jerks. Could be dangerous."

Angie looked at Carli who smirked back. "Ladies?"

Chapter Ten

The Texas sky burned pink and orange with the setting sun. Angie Olsen tapped on the front door of Carli's house before walking in.

"Wanna take my truck or yours?" she called out.

"Which is newer? Maybe it would be the quietest," Carli replied. "Do we need jackets?"

"The nights can be chilly if there's a breeze, but I can't imagine we'll be walkin'. Just watchin' out for lowlifes from the safety of our vehicle."

"I'll take one just in case. Also, I have a cooler with snacks." Carli appeared from the kitchen lugging a hot pink cooler and a cowboy hat in her other hand.

"I brought snacks too. Let's do this." Angie's boots sounded on the floor.

They walked outside, Carli shutting the door behind her as they stopped to survey the trucks. Carli was still driving her old truck from Georgia. Angie's wasn't any newer. Angie couldn't help but notice Carli's wide-eyed eagerness and hurried steps. She hoped their efforts paid off.

"You should invest in a new vehicle. You are a ranch heiress now, ya know," Angie said.

"The thought of the Wild Cow funding me a new vehicle has never crossed my mind. I'm just the new caretaker. Everything is on loan from my grandparents."

"That may be true in your mind, but on paper you own it all," Angie said.

"I'm still trying to wrap my brain around the fact that a grandfather I never knew left me his ranch. Maybe after we ship steers in the fall and I can put a pencil to the numbers, then I'll see where we stand and if we can afford a newer truck. What about you? Your vehicle looks like it's on its last leg."

Angie laughed. "That's my dad's used pickup, two pickups ago. He just keeps passing 'em down and he drives the new one. It's got over 200,000 miles on it, but still gets me where I need to go."

"It also has your brand and a big Rafter O logo painted on both doors. Maybe we should take mine. Less obvious."

"We could take Lank's or the ranch feed truck." Angie stopped to look at Carli who shook her head with a no.

"Lank and Colton aren't back from a roping yet. Besides I don't want him to know what we're doing."

"I thought y'all were dating." Angie transferred her cooler and jacket into the back and climbed into the passenger seat.

Carli said, "If that's what you call it, but we've never been out on an official date. I don't really know what we are. You'd think we would be more involved on a day-to-day basis. We're both so busy. It's very irritating."

The last glow of light from the setting sun suddenly winked out as they left the headquarters and made their way over the cattle guard turning onto the caliche county road, Carli at the wheel.

"Are you sure tonight's a full moon?" Carli asked. "With that cloud cover we may not be able to see anything."

"Weather app says tonight's the night," said Angie. "As soon as the clouds break, we'll be able to see."

"Now where do you want to start?" Carli asked.

"Is there an overlook hill or small rise on your place?"

"Actually, we could park by the hay barn," Carli mentioned. "It's on a high hill and from there we can see the county road and vehicles coming in either direction. Is there a spot like that on the Rafter O?"

"Yep. Several."

"How about we rotate between them then? Sit a while on my place, and then we'll mosey over towards yours."

Angie nodded in agreement. "That might work. We can take the long way through Vera Allgood's, keep our eyes peeled there too."

Carli edged her pickup truck as close to the hay-barn as she could, parked, and killed the engine.

The last light faded from the far horizon and the night suddenly grew dark. Angie hopped out to rummage around in the cooler. "Want something to drink?

"Sure. What'a ya got?"

"Seltzer water. Juice. Several kinds of soda or just plain water."

"I'll start with water," Carli said, "and see how the night progresses before I try something stronger." They chuckled.

Angie handed her friend a bottle.

"How long should we stay here?" Carli asked.

"An hour I think." Angie rummaged around in her canvas bag of snacks and held out a plastic baggie. "Take this."

"What is that? I can't see it."

"Something healthy and good," Angie said. "You'll love it. Trust me."

"That makes me suspicious." Carli scrunched up her face. "Lola is always sneaking this healthy stuff into her muffins and then making me try them."

Carli cautiously took a tiny bite from one corner. "Where's my water?" She coughed. "Not bad, but it definitely tastes healthy. What's in it?"

"Pistachio oat bars. No sugar, only local honey from the farmers' market. Yummy, aren't they?" Angie had made them special for their stakeout. True, they were a tad dry because she may have baked them a little too long, but they were full of energy and good things. "They'll keep you regular."

"Definitely something I'm always looking for

in my snacking options." Carli rolled her eyes but took another bite. She coughed again and reached for her water.

"It's an acquired taste but just remember that you're being good to your body." Angie took a bite and put hers back into the baggie. Definitely over-cooked.

Carli suddenly pointed to the road just as the lights blinked off. "Do those look like car lights to you?"

"I don't see anything." Angie squinted.

Carli glanced from side to side, watching the horizon. "The road dips. Keep watching. It was several miles away I think."

Angie spun around sideways in her seat and rested an arm across the back. "I'll keep watch out the rear, if you'll watch the front."

"Can do," said Carli.

"Now, spill about you and Lank. I've got all night." Angie took a swig of water, noting that the clouds were beginning to break. The sky was not as dark, and had taken on an eerie glow.

"Remember when he had that rodeo wreck not that long ago? I visited him in the hospital. He looked so awful and alone."

"His mother turned over in her grave for sure." Angie adjusted her ballcap. "After he got that serious head injury back in high school, he had promised her he wouldn't ride broncs. She let everyone in town know about that promise too. We were all enlisted as her eyes and ears."

"I bet she was sweet. Wish I could have met the woman who raised Lank. I can tell they were very close." Carli placed a hand on her heart.

"Ana Torres was a force, particularly when it came to her baby boy. So, are y'all a thing or not? You keep avoiding the question."

"At the hospital we both confessed our love to each other." Carli slowly shared. "It surprised me. I hadn't meant to say it, and then he said it too. But now in the light of day I can feel him holding back."

"You both said the three words, 'I love you'? Wow! Maybe it's you who's holding back?" Even in the dark, Angie could feel Carli bristle and she did hear a sharp intake of breath. "You have become one of my dearest friends, Carli, but you are very guarded. In Texas, we strive to be inappropriate at all times with too much information. Some people are put off by that, but we just call it being friendly."

"Yeah, I've noticed that." Carli laughed.

"Now where is that car? They should have popped up over the hill by now. They must be driving real slow."

"There it is again," Carli answered. Sure enough, two headlights stared at them, heading in their direction.

"I see it." Angie perked up.

"Should we leave?" Carli asked as she put her hands on the ignition key.

"No." Angie reached to stop Carli from starting the engine. "Stay here, but lie down in the seat just before they pass. Our faces will catch the headlights. They might see us. Otherwise, it'll look like an abandoned vehicle."

Both grew silent and still as they watched, the two headlights disappearing again as they dipped into a low and eased around a curve, until suddenly appearing at the top of the hill, glaring straight at Carli's pickup truck.

At the same time, they took a sharp gulp of breath and slid down into the seat. Angie squinted against the bright light and quickly batted Carli's cowboy hat from her head which stuck up over the dash.

"Sorry," Carli whispered.

The lights eased by, time standing still as the glow moved slowly past them, the beams casting shadows into the cab and shining through the back window. Chug, chug, chug of an engine echoed in the stillness of the night as the vehicle slowed in front of them. Angie also heard the distinct rattle of a livestock trailer.

Carli reached over and grasped Angie's hand. The chugging motor paused for several minutes right next to them, not moving, just sitting. The idea of boots crunching on pasture grass ran through Angie's mind. What would they do if someone walked over to check out their vehicle?

Suddenly the engine revved and moved away.

Out of the side window, Angie watched the back taillights. It looked like a white truck, maybe silver, with wide chrome bumpers, and that's all she could make out in the moonlight. Even though the sounds of the vehicle and trailer had faded, the girls didn't move.

It was Carli who finally broke the silence. "We're going to need something besides healthy bars. This is going to be a long night."

Angie let out the breath she was holding. "No kidding."

Chapter Eleven

"Now what?" asked Carli, as she turned to look at Angie. "Do you think those were the rustlers?"

They sat in silence for a few moments inside Carli's truck. The clouds had moved on and a bright, brilliant moon was now lighting the pasture that stretched out before them. Silhouettes of grazing cattle dotted the landscape.

"Look. There they go." Angie pointed at two dots of red lights on the horizon.

"I don't think that's the county road anymore. I think that's my pasture." Carli sat up straighter in alarm.

"You're right. Let me drive. I'll slide over." Angie was determined to catch them. She knew that had to be the rustlers. Ranchers don't drive around in the middle of the night pulling their trailer.

"All right." Carli hopped out and hurried around to the other side of the truck.

Angie slid into the driver's seat, picking her legs up over their bags of snacks and jackets, and trying not to squash Carli's cowboy hat. Carli climbed in and slammed the passenger door.

Angie snapped her head around at the sound.

"Sorry." Carli gave her friend a sheepish grin.

Angie eased the vehicle onto the county road, keeping the headlights off. "Was it just me or did you hear a dog bark when they passed?"

"I'm not sure. I can't believe how bright the moon is tonight. Even with the shadows' cast from the mesquite and yucca, I can see every cow." Carli pointed. "Look. There goes a rabbit."

"Which is why the rustlers do their evil deeds under the light of a full moon. Also, we don't need headlights."

Angie stepped on the gas and headed in the direction of the last place she had seen the taillights. "I don't know if that's a pickup truck full of rustlers but it sure is strange how slow they were driving."

"And why did they stop in front of us?"

"Obviously your truck parked next to the hay barn was out of place," Angie said. "Which means they've been by here before. They were being cautious, I think. Tell me if you see anything."

After driving several miles in silence, Carli pointed again. "There. I see it. How will they load the stolen cows?"

"They'd need their horses, maybe a dog or two. How far? Can you tell?" Angie asked.

"I still can't determine distance. Remember I'm used to the wooded hills and streams of Georgia. This vast view of nothing seems strange to me.

That direction. It was right up there, but maybe over the next rise?"

They kept driving, but with no luck. The scene around them was peaceful and still, the moonlight illuminating the pasture. Even though shadows clung dark under every tree and bush, it was as if a glowing lamp light hung over the place.

"Maybe we should head over to the Rafter O," Angie suggested.

"Sounds like a plan to me, but can you stop for a minute? I need something to drink."

"You betcha." Angie pulled over to the side of the road and Carli jumped out before the wheels had come to a full stop. After she latched the cooler shut again and jumped back in, she held out a peach sweet tea.

"We need something stronger, I think," Carli said. "Plus, we'll need to make a pit stop before too long."

"Why didn't I think about a thermos of coffee? That would've kept us awake." Angie shook her head.

They eased along the county road, the wheels making a ba-dump-thump sound across the cattle guard into Crazy Vera's place.

"There," Carli shouted. She pointed along the fence line into Vera's pasture. "I know I saw lights. That way."

"There's nothing over there," Angie said.

"I know I saw a flash of something." Carli sighed. "Maybe it was just a reflection. I could be imagining things now."

"Let's keep our eyes peeled and mosey over to the Rafter O. We have a lot of ground to cover in one night."

They glanced from right to left, and every so often Carli looked out the back window.

"I told you about Lank, so now it's time for you to talk about Colton."

Angie scowled. "Colton? There is not one thing I want to say about that arrogant, self-absorbed cowboy."

"Just wondering." Carli didn't want to press. "If you don't want to talk about him, then don't."

"He's such an idiot. Darlin' this and darlin' that. He's always in my space. Why does he do that? Can't he just back off and let me breathe for a minute? He is the most annoying puncher I've ever known. Seriously. He's full of himself. And he cannot keep his mouth shut. Granted he's easy on the eyes, but there's nothing between those two ears of his. Besides, he didn't even know I was alive until a few days ago."

Carli doubled over in laughter which caused Angie to shoot her an annoyed glance.

"Nothing to say about him? How long would it take for you to say something if you actually had something to say about him?"

"I'm not talking about Colton Creacy anymore, so don't ask." Angie huffed.

"Sounds like love to me." Carli's laugh escaped.

Just talking about Colton made Angie clench her jaw and the smallest twinge of a headache was coming on. Just great. She couldn't push the image of him from her mind, but she'd never admit that to Carli. Him laughing at something she'd said. His laser-focused glare when he looked at her. That silly grin that made her heart skip a beat. Colton was a force of personality that was hard to ignore, but she knew the type. Easily bored. Once the battle was won and he had the attention he sought, he would be on to the next giddy girl that crossed his path. There was no commitment in that handsome face. She knew better than to get involved with the likes of him.

Instead of turning off the county road into Vera's place, they cruised by slowly. The gravestone in Vera's front yard bearing the name of her first husband rose like a creepy image in the moonlight. Angie could see Vera's goats grazing at one side of the yard. They continued on with the headlights off.

After several more miles, they bumped across the cattle guard into the Rafter O, passing under the metal header displaying their brand, an O with a rooftop.

"I know the perfect spot to park," Angie said. "We can't see all of the back pastures, but we'll have a good view of the county road which is the only way in or out. If anyone is driving around, we'll see them for sure."

She turned off the caliche and drove on a bumpy, washed out dirt road with clumps of sage and tufts of grass growing up in the middle of the tracks.

Making a sharp turn, Angie gunned the pickup truck up a steep incline to the top of a hill and parked under towering metal utility poles. The wires glistened in the moonlight, the powerlines stretching from pole to pole threaded across the vast expanse of their ranch until disappearing into the shadows of the horizon.

"Now what?" asked Carli.

"We wait." Angie was determined to wait as long as it took until she saw something. In her gut she knew the men were out there. Odds were not in their favor that the target would be the Rafter O, the Wild Cow, or Crazy Vera's, but she had faith. She had to prove to her father that she was more than capable of being trusted with ranch operations, and one way to do that was to catch rustlers in the act.

"What will we do, if we find them?" Carli asked.

"Not sure, but I'll know when the moment comes. We have to be bold."

"That's great but I think we should be bold in our faith too. Just so you know I'm praying that we come out of this unharmed." Carli dug around in her snack bag. "It's really hard for me to sit still. I have to be doing something."

"Keep your eyes peeled," instructed Angie.

"There," Carli said pointing.

"I see 'em." They watched red taillights emerge from the top of a rise, suddenly turning and moving across the horizon.

"Look over there!" Carli pointed again.

In the opposite direction, they saw headlights from a second vehicle as it made its way towards the red taillights of the first.

"Looks like they're heading towards each other. Let's get to the middle spot first." Angie turned on the engine and gunned the truck down the steep incline. The pickup roared onto the pasture road, and then Angie slowed as a small dip descended into a dry creek bed.

"I'm going to use my lights," she said. "Those little black calves are impossible to see in the dark and sometimes they hide out in the plum bushes."

Long, spindly branches from a clump of mesquite trees reached out and scratched the truck on both sides as they eased through the wide washout and then up the steep embankment. Angie gunned it when they got to the top and made good time. They bumped and bounced along the pasture road, which made her wish she hadn't drunk all that tea and water.

"Your lights!" Carli shouted.

"Drat," Angie growled. "How far do you think we've gone?"

"The road has stayed in the lows. We haven't driven over any hills, so we may be okay."

Carli's reasoning made sense to Angie, so she breathed a little sigh of relief. Hopefully no one had noticed their vehicle.

At the top of the next rise, with lights off, Angie stopped the truck. They rolled down their windows to look and listen for any sounds that might not belong. Suddenly, on the same road heading straight for them a pickup truck roared into life. Not only with headlights, but a powerful high-beam spotlight that suddenly clicked on and made both girls squint.

"They found us!" said Carli, her voice tinged with fear.

Angie stared at the light, her heart pounding. She clenched her jaw. Whoever it was, they were trespassing on Olsen property and she had no problem in telling them to get off her land. Angie slowly opened the door of the pickup cab, stepped out and squared her shoulders, ready for confrontation and then anger punched her in the gut.

"That's not rustlers. It's my idiot brother and his friends."

Chapter Twelve

"Is that you, Sis?" Travis Olsen shouted in the still night. Angie could hear his boots hit the ground with a thud as he jumped from the back of his truck and walked towards her on the dirt road.

Behind him, guys started piling out of the cab of the truck and the back. A clump of cowboy hats bulged onto the road, skinny bodies that couldn't stay still. One punched a buddy in the arm. Another stuck out a boot to trip a gangly friend as they walked closer to the girls.

"Y'all out huntin' coyotes?" Colton's voice boomed in the quiet night as he emerged from the driver's seat.

Angie fumed, hands on hips, as she glared at them. Too bad they couldn't see her face that well in the moonlight, because she could usually silence her younger brother with one icy glance.

"Hey, darlin'."

Angie cringed at the greeting. "What are you doing here?" There was no welcome in the stare she directed towards Colton as he walked closer to her. "And can somebody turn off that stupid spotlight?"

"The question is what are you girls doing out here in the middle of the night?" Travis emerged from the shadows and raised one arm in a wave. "Hey, Carli."

"Just girl talk and drivin' around." Angie crossed her arms, trying to look innocent and disinterested in what he had to say.

"That's a lie. It's a full moon and you're trying to catch some cattle rustlers." Travis got in her face and patted both cheeks. "I know you, Sis."

"What exactly is your plan, if you was to happen upon some bad guys?" Colton asked.

"Talk 'em to death maybe," one commented from the bunch. The other dirt clods snickered.

Angie's face flushed, partly because Travis had guessed what they were doing and partly because she didn't have to answer to him. This was her ranch same as his.

"Tell us what you've seen and where you're goin'. Maybe we can work together." Colton slung an arm around her shoulders. "There's no reason we can't be partners." Again, that silly, toothy grin.

Angie was surprised that he actually made sense and might have a good idea, but then his breath was warm against her ear and she forgot what she was going to say. A chill started in her jaw, moved into her neck, and then worked its way all the way down to her toes, making her shiver.

"Do you need my jacket?" Colton asked, squeezing her tighter. "It's in the truck. I'll get it for ya."

Angie wanted to shrug out of his embrace, it made her furious, but then she was frozen in place. She couldn't move, his arm grew heavier across her shoulders. If she turned just a bit they'd be face to face, cheeks touching.

"I like that idea, working together," said Carli. "We've been following the taillights of a white pickup that passed through the Wild Cow over an hour ago."

Angie glared at Carli and shook her head, but Carli refused to look her way. Appears she was going to blab everything she knew.

Carli continued. "We just saw it again at the top of the hill over there. And then we saw beams from another vehicle coming in the opposite direction so we thought we might meet whoever it is when they both reach the middle."

"There are two of us now. No reason we can't work together," said Travis. "How about it, Sis?"

"The question is was it us you saw or another vehicle?" Colton asked.

"We did think that white truck was suspicious. They were pulling a trailer and it stopped right next to where we parked. Maybe we can trap them," Carli suggested.

"You're not going to sneak up on anybody with that big floodlight." Angie wanted to take charge. "All you're doin' is flushing out the coyotes and upsetting the new calves. And we aren't lookin' for any help. We can manage by ourselves just fine."

"I guess then the safest thing is for you gals to head back home. Load up, guys. Let's make another round." Travis whirled his arm around over his head as the punchers scrambled back into the truck, not at a loss for comments.

"Let's ride."

"If we find them lowlifes, we got some buckshot for their behinds." This one garnered a few whoops.

"See you back at the house, Sis. I'll text you if we see anything." Travis swung up into the back of the Rafter O truck. "Hey! Where's my driver?"

"I may as well hitch a ride with the girls. Make sure they make it home all right." Colton followed close behind on Angie's heels. She spun around.

"No. That's not happening." Angie pointed a finger in his face so he'd know she meant business. "This is girls' night. You ain't invited."

Colton's bottom lip came out, pouting like a spoiled toddler. Angie had no sympathy for him.

Carli snickered. "Nice try, lover boy. Catch you on the flip side."

With Colton behind the wheel again, the guys' truck pulled into the grass and passed around them, driving slowly. Carli gave another wave to the bunch and giggled again.

"Did you see that look on his face? You totally broke his heart." Carli grinned.

"What an idiot." Angie gripped the steering wheel so tight it made her fingers ache. "Yeah, I'm all broken up about it. I cannot handle any more 'darlin's' or 'pretty lady'. Does he think that makes him more attractive? It makes him creepy, that's what."

Carli released a deep belly laugh which went on much too long, in Angie's opinion. "You two are destined for each other. It's so obvious."

"The only thing I'm destined for is to stop this gang from draining the county dry of cattle, and then I'm going to run the Rafter O one day. You can count on it."

"I really hope that's the case, Angie. But in the meantime, you have a lot of convincing to do. Your father is not going to be easy. So, what should we do next?" Carli looked at Angie with that wide-eyed eagerness again.

"You said something back there. About setting a trap. Why couldn't we do that? We know when the next full moon is." Angie's mind was churning.

"How are they in and out so quick? With so many pairs missing this season, they have to know the ranches," Carli pondered.

"That's right. I bet they spend a lot of time driving around. They're familiar with the pasture roads and they know how isolated some places can be. They figure out who's at home and who isn't," Angie said.

"That makes sense." Carli nodded in agreement. "We just need to think like they would. Figure out what their next play will be."

"Set a trap and we've got them."

Angie pulled to a stop at the top of the rise, shut off the engine, and rolled the windows down. She looked out over the moonlit grassland that stretched as far as she could see. The sight always took her breath away. The land that had been worked by her family for generations. Countless numbers of cattle, horses, not to mention the wildlife, that had lived their best lives here. She liked to think that the human intervention all had a hand in making it even better with each generation that came along.

The Rafter O meant more than life itself to Angie. It was her reason for being. When she felt sad, at her wits' end, or at times she couldn't face her father's obvious indifference as to what she was capable of, the sounds of the grassland became her solace. The endless sky and the view of another rising sun became her strength. The blessings of this life reminded her to turn to God. She needed to trust Him more. She needed to have faith that this was where she belonged for the rest of her life and that she had the ability to continue the Olsen legacy.

Angie glanced at Carli. Her friend was silent and taking in the scene as well. It made Angie smile to see the look on her face. The heiress to the Wild Cow Ranch was beginning to understand the responsibilities of land ownership, and of having so many families depend on you to keep everything churning. It appeared to Angie that Carli was beginning to appreciate the beauty of this stark land and call it her home.

"Takes your breath away, doesn't it?" Angie broke the silence.

"I had no idea a view could mean so much," Carli said. "There's nothing to look at. No trees, no streams or rock formations. It's just grass, but it means everything."

"I know." Angie took in a contented breath through her nose.

They sat in silence for a few more minutes and then Angie put the wheels in motion and turned on her headlights.

They eased across the Rafter O, winding around, up and down, the pasture roads taking in the nighttime view that was afforded them under a full moon.

"There goes a coyote," said Carli.

Angie grinned. "You're like a kid in the candy store."

"I never knew a full moon could be so bright. It's like God turned on his own spotlight."

As they crossed the cattle guard into Crazy Vera's, a glow from her barn shone like a beacon leading the way.

"Was that light on when we came by here before?" Carli asked.

Angie didn't answer, instead relying on her mind's eye to visualize Vera's place. They hadn't turned in, but she remembered the goats. They were gone now.

"I don't think so. Let's check it out."

Both gasped as they made the sharp turn and crossed another cattle guard into Crazy Vera's headquarters. A white pickup with a livestock trailer hitched to it was parked in front of Vera's barn.

"What do we do?" Carli was literally bouncing up and down on her seat. "Should I call the sheriff?"

"I'm gonna pull up behind them, blocking their way out. You stay in the truck while I go around the barn and flush them out."

"Okay," responded Carli with absolutely no confidence in her voice.

Angie stopped the truck, beams directly on the other vehicle, and gave Carli a pat on her hand. "You'll be all right. Just stay in here."

Ever so quietly she slipped out of the truck and gently pushed the door closed. Angie crept around behind the barn and eased over the fence, immediately crouching on the ground to peek around the corner. She saw three men. And then a stupid cow dog spotted her and gave a loud bark. Busted.

Typical of how Angie handled things, she faced the danger head on. "You boys have no business in here," she said, stepping into the dim barn.

And then not one, not two, but three cow dogs let loose with a frenzy of barking and growling. Angie backed up and hopped on the fence, the pack snarling at her feet. In one fluid motion they turned and ran away from her towards the entrance. A whistle sent the dogs in a spin and out the door.

Angie ran after them. As she got to the barn's exit, she flipped on the outside floodlight. She wanted to see their faces.

Just as she dashed around the end of the trailer,

she saw the brake lights come on as it backed up. With gears grinding, they slammed into forward motion. Turning sharp to miss where Angie had parked, they were on a beeline course for Carli who had stepped from the vehicle.

"Carli! Look out!" yelled Angie.

In her haste Carli backed up but tripped, landing flat on her butt. With a cloud of dust and gravel, the rustlers roared out of Crazy Vera's place, hitting the cattle guard with a loud thud, and then rattled into the night.

Carli was sitting motionless in the gravel, her eyes closed.

"What hurts?" Angie asked, horror clutching her heart. "Did they run over your legs?" She couldn't stop a tear that trickled down her cheek.

"I'm remembering. One dent in the top left of the tailgate. Another dent in the fender. And there was something else. I can't remember. Chrome. Words. Dang it!" Carli bounced to her feet and dusted off her backside. "We almost had them. And that trailer was full of goats."

Angie let out a whoosh of relief to see Carli standing in front of her, unharmed. "I guess we should call it a night. Look on your weather app and see when the next full moon is."

"What are you thinking? What are we going to do?" Carli's eyes were wide.

"I have no idea. But we'll be ready for them next time."

"Yes, we will," whispered Carli.

Chapter Thirteen

Lank Torres walked with determination across Wild Cow Ranch headquarters towards his boss's house. If what he'd been told was true, she had a lot to answer for.

He pounded on the front door. "Carli. Are you awake?" He hit the door again with his fist. Nothing stirred from behind the door. L.J., his dog, had run ahead with excitement but now sat patiently at his feet. Suddenly the dog stood with tail wagging so fast it made her entire body wiggle. The door swung open and Carli appeared out of the shadows. She didn't even offer a greeting or invite him in. He pushed the door open wider.

"Good morning, sunshine," he said. Carli glared at him wearing pink and turquoise pajamas that displayed horses, hay bales, and horseshoes. Slender legs, short-shorts, toes painted pink, and she hadn't bothered to grab a cover-up. The shirt read Crazy Horse Lady, her hair and the look on her face confirmed that phrase. She bent down to give Lily

Jane a rub on the head.

All business, she didn't wear her emotions on her face and giggle every two seconds like some girls he knew. But he could never really tell what was going on in that head of hers. She had depth and understanding about life, which was one of the things he loved about her. For all her tough exterior though, he was always surprised at how vulnerable she seemed at some moments. Even with all that gruffness and resilience, she could totally knock him to his knees with horsey PJs she must have had since grade school and neon toenail polish.

Lank swallowed hard and smiled brightly. "I'll make you some coffee." Still no answer, but she did move out of the way so he could come in.

Carli followed him to the kitchen where she plopped down in a chair and rested her head on folded arms. Although it had been barely audible, he heard a soft moan when her bottom hit the chair. She sat up, rotated her shoulder for a second, and then stopped when she saw him watching.

"So, what's going on?" Lank asked, turning his back to her as he measured coffee beans into the grinder. Let's just see what she has to say for herself after spending all night galivanting around the county. Inside he fumed but he tried not to let it show on his face when he turned around. "I can fix you toast. You look like you don't feel so good. Rough night?"

Carli remained silent. She didn't even look at him.

Lank turned to pour water into the coffee maker. He slammed the lid down a little too hard. That got her attention. She raised her head and rubbed the sleep from her eyes and ran a hand over her head to smooth her hair.

"Couldn't sleep. That's all." Carli stood to find coffee cups in the cabinet and filled the sugar bowl. "You like sugar, don't you?"

"Yeah, sure." He crossed arms over his chest and watched her. Should he ask about last night, or should he wait until she offered up some account. What if she never mentions it? Then what? The one thing they needed as a new couple was trust. They had to be honest with each other above all else.

No matter what she said, he'd never understand why she and Angie went out last night looking for rustlers and didn't think to tell him. A girls' night out he could forgive, but something so dangerous as mixing it up with criminals was unacceptable. They both were old enough to know better. He waited until the coffee was done, then filled two mugs, while Carli rummaged around in the pantry and appeared with a box of multi-colored cereal that small kids usually eat.

Lank sipped his coffee and watched Carli eat. She tipped her bowl up almost covering her eyes and drank the last little bit of milk. He couldn't stay silent any longer.

"Colton called me late last night."

"Oh yeah?"

"Says he ran into you and Angie on the Rafter O."

"Yes."

"And?"

"And what?"

"What were y'all doing?"

"I was with Angie. What's with the inquisition this morning?"

"I need to know what y'all were doing."

"You're not my father, for one. And two, I don't have to check in with you every single second of every day."

"It'd be nice if you would." Lank could see her bristle, her shoulders squared as she glared at him. He cleared his throat. Might as well get it all out in the open. "So, I called Travis to confirm Colton's story because, honestly, he sometimes gets the facts wrong. And sure enough. Travis saw you too."

"Yes, he was there." Carli refilled her mug, her face remaining stoic.

Lank could not read what she was thinking. No anger, no confusion, certainly no love. Just nothing.

She slid into the chair at the table. "Let me get this right. You're questioning your friends to check up on me. Is that it? Has it ever occurred to you to simply ask me?"

"That's what I'm doing now."

"No, you're quizzing me like I'm a teenager who broke curfew. So, just ask."

"Ask what."

"Ask me what Angie and I were doing last night." This reply was definitely not using her inside voice.

Lank blinked and waited for her temper to cool

before answering. "What were you and Angie doing out driving around last night?"

"It's none of your business. I need a shower." Carli shot up from her chair and headed down the hall, Lily Jane close at her heels.

"Wait. No." Lank rushed after her and grabbed her arm. "We're going to settle this. You can't shut me out like that, Carli. We're supposed to be a couple."

That stopped her dead in her tracks. She slowly turned and faced him, at first struggling from his arm, but then softening with a sheepish look on her face. "Sorry, I guess you're right."

They walked into the living room and sank into the leather sofa, side by side. He put his arm around her. Instead of continuing to prod her for information, he decided to be patient. She suddenly sat upright and scooted away from him.

"I'm not very good at this you know," she said.

"Chasing rustlers? Just tell me what happened last night after you drove off. Colton said Angie came back really psyched about something. Said she almost had 'em in a head lock, but they got away. You saw them?"

"No. I mean yes, we saw them at Crazy Vera's, but that's not what I'm talking about." She clasped her hands together and looked down at her lap. "This relationship thing. I'm not very good at it. I'm sorry."

"It's gonna take some time. And I'm sorry too."

"For what?" she asked.

"For the stupid guy who broke your heart back in Georgia and made it hard for you to trust. I'm not going anywhere. I really want this to work out between us, Carli." He leaned closer and kissed her lips, warm with the lingering taste of coffee.

"I need some time to get used to us."

"Take all the time you need. I can wait. This can move as slow or as fast as you want. Are you ready to talk about last night?"

"Yes."

"It would be a whole lot easier on me if you could wear something besides those pjs." He glanced at her, from head to toe, and grinned with a wink.

Carli laughed. "I'll be right back."

While she got dressed Lank rinsed out the coffee pot and washed up their mugs and the cereal bowl. He was drying them when Carli came back into the room wearing jeans and a T-shirt, her hair brushed to a shine, and her lips glossy. Disappointment shaded his thoughts. He'd never forget those horsey pajamas for the rest of his life.

Chapter Fourteen

Carli stared at Lank's handsome face, his eyes reflecting worry. The morning light from her kitchen window made the dark scruff on his jaw appear denser than she remembered. Was he growing a beard? She wanted to memorize every part of that face, every line, even that sexy mouth that was not turned up in a smile at this moment.

She wanted to tell him everything, but something was niggling at her brain. There was a detail she needed to know, or a bit of information she should have remembered in the daylight. She had been so exhausted last night and had fallen into bed with no idea of the time.

"I've heard Colton's version and Travis's version. Now I want to hear yours." Lank gave her a stern look.

He was losing patience, she could tell. And she didn't want to fight again. Part of her, the stubborn part, refused to tell him a darn thing just because he had shown up this morning demanding to know. The other part wanted to make peace and kiss some more. She sighed and slid into a barstool.

"Angie and I went on a stakeout. It was a simple plan really. We would rotate between the Wild Cow, make a pass through to Crazy Vera's on the way to the Rafter O, and look for headlights."

"Did you see any?" Lank didn't sit beside her, instead stood on the other side of the counter with arms folded across his chest.

"A white truck pulling a trailer slowed when we were parked at the top of the hill by the hay barn, and then we saw two sets of headlights in the Rafter O pasture. We thought to intercept them and that's when we ran into Travis."

"I doubt they could catch a flea from the noise his truck makes."

"They had a spotlight too."

She sank back into one end of the couch and stretched her bare feet out between them. She winced from the pain in her hip, but it was too late to conceal. He saw her expression.

"There's more? How did you get hurt?"

Lank Torres didn't miss a detail, that's for sure. It aggravated Carli that he was so observant.

"I just fell back on my rump is all."

He raised his eyebrows and his expression grew serious.

"At Crazy Vera's barn," she offered, but didn't say anything more. Maybe she should skip this part.

"Carli." That came out more like a growl instead of her name on the lips of a boyfriend.

"We saw a white truck pulling a trailer at Vera's barn, and Angie went inside to check it out. When they all jumped in to leave, I had just stepped out of the truck and I fell back."

"Did you see their faces?"

"No. It was too dark, plus they had hats on which concealed their identity. Three of them. Two of them looked older, and I could swear one of them was Raven. But he never wears a cowboy hat. He's more of a punk rocker type, all black, combat boots with rings on every finger. It just doesn't make sense that he'd be rustling cattle."

"You should talk to the sheriff. And I can't believe Vera didn't chase them off."

"We never saw her. Maybe she was out of town. And there was something else I saw, but I can't remember what it was. Maybe I recognized them, or maybe something about the truck." She yawned. "I'm too sleepy to remember."

"You'll think of it, but we need to visit with Sheriff Anderson this afternoon. You need to tell him what you saw. How many vehicles were there again?"

Carli sat bolt upright on the sofa. "That's it. I saw red taillights between the Wild Cow and Vera's place. I'm sure of it, but I can't remember how far along the fence line they were. Angie never could see them so she kept driving."

"Now is as good a time as any to check it out. I'll get the horses up. We need to ride that fence line." Lank turned and left. The slam of the front door vibrated throughout the old house.

A quick search located her boots and a cap, and then she was out the door to hop in her truck. To save time she thought they could trailer the horses across the Wild Cow and unload them at Vera's cattle guard. By the time she had the trailer hitched and walked into the saddle house, Lank had the horses ready to ride.

"Hey pretty boy," she said to Beau. His ears pricked and turned in her direction. They led the horses to the trailer, got them loaded, and were on their way.

Carli rolled the window down, closing her eyes to let the breeze push hair out of her face. It felt good. And it felt really good to be with Lank. They didn't have to talk. She always felt relaxed and content with him nowadays, unlike when she first met him and thought he was a smart aleck.

"Tell me about the guy you left in Georgia."

That was certainly an out of place comment destined to destroy a peaceful morning. Carli didn't want to remember that horrible day, much less try to put the whole incident into words. She hesitated trying to decide where to begin. Okay, if he wants trust between them, she'd have to be honest. She just couldn't do it. Maybe someday, but not now.

"I can't talk about it," she said.

Lank shrugged his shoulders and didn't say anything more. They drove in silence.

"Stop here," Carli said. "I saw the lights in that direction."

They unloaded the horses and took off down the seven-strand barbed wire fence that stretched to separate the Wild Cow from Crazy Vera's. Carli glanced at Lank from under her lashes. Was he mad? She couldn't tell, but she didn't want to talk about the past. How would that help their relationship now? She couldn't make any sense of why he wanted to know about an old boyfriend. If truth be told, she had no interest in hearing about his girlfriends, and no doubt there were many. She could only wonder at the trouble he and Colton had gotten into when they rode the rodeo circuit.

"Look at that," Lank broke her out of her thoughts. He was pointing to the fence and then she saw the huge gap. They reined up and hurried over to inspect the damage.

"These wires have been cut." Lank knelt on the ground holding up a few end pieces. "We need to fix this gap and then get a count in this pasture."

They hurried back to the trailer, returning to headquarters to load fence material in the truck before heading back again. After the fence was repaired, they drove to every corner of the pasture until they had an accurate count. The cows were spread out grazing, and, sure enough, several were missing.

Carli was frustrated with herself. They had been so close to stopping them. She wanted to call Angie and they needed to pay a visit to Sheriff Anderson again.

Chapter Fifteen

Carli and Angie sat in her office waiting for eleven o'clock to roll around for when a Special Ranger from the Texas Ranchers' Association was coming to meet with them. All totaled, after talking with neighbors, the tally for missing livestock did not look good.

"This has to be the work of one group," said Carli.

"I agree. And I think you're right about that Raven kid being involved in some way." Angie leaned back in the oversized leather chair and stretched her legs on the ottoman. "I think they're rotating between ranches. They know the pastures. They know when the ranch hands will be around and when they won't."

"Come fall shipping time, that's a lot of money out of our pockets." Carli pushed a stack of bills aside and propped one boot on the corner of her desk. She cut a curious look at her friend. "So, what do you think about Colton?"

"Colton?" Angie scrunched her face into a sour frown. "That boy is more trouble than he's worth. He's an arrogant know-it-all and does not have one sincere bone in his body. It's all about a good time for him. If there's a party, he'll be there, and he never leaves alone. I have no use for a guy like that."

"Why don't you tell me what you really think? Please, don't hold anything back."

The girls laughed.

"Why do you keep bringin' his name up? I'm too busy for a boyfriend. It's all I can do to stay one step ahead of my father."

Carli studied Angie's face for a minute, doubting her insistence that she wasn't interested in Lank's friend. She had seen the way they kept glancing at one another the evening they'd all roped together. And then at the stakeout she hadn't exactly moved out from under his arm.

"He just kept watching you is all. And I thought maybe there might be a spark there. That's the only reason I'm asking."

A knock at Carli's front door interrupted their conversation, then Buck called out, "Carli, you here? You got company."

"C'mon in, Buck." Carli pushed her desk chair back and walked to the front room with Angie. They both followed Buck outside.

"Special Ranger Derek McKinney, this is the ranch owner, Carli Jameson. Carli, this is Ranger McKinney."

"Call me, Derek, please." A young man, in his

late thirties, stood at attention below the first step and extended his hand. Wearing starched jeans, white shirt, dark aviator sunglasses, and a Silver-belly Stetson hat, he held a large blue binder in his left arm. A dark tie and an intimidating side-arm completed the picture of a no-nonsense lawman.

"Ms. Jameson? Carlotta Jean Jameson?"

"You can call me Carli." The clean-shaven friend-ly face greeted her with a warm smile as he turned the most beautiful blue eyes full on attention to her.

"I'm Investigator Derek McKinney from the Texas Ranchers' Association. You reported some missing cattle?"

"Yes, sir, I did. This is Angie Olsen with the Raf-ter O. They have a problem too."

"Miss Olsen. Good to meet you."

Angie stood open-mouthed as she shook his hand. She didn't reply to the greeting, which made Carli nearly giggle. For once, the girl was speech-less.

"You reported this to Sheriff Anderson in Dix-on, ma'am?"

"Yes, I did."

"And he put you in touch with the TRA?"

"Yes, that's right."

"Actually, I called your boss as well," Buck said to Derek. "He and I go way back. We really appreciate your coming out today."

Carli glanced at Angie again and couldn't help but notice how she kept her eyes locked on the Spe-cial Ranger. He was handsome. And all business.

Carli could tell he was going to go by the book every step of the way.

"Can you show me the pasture where the cows were taken? We can all hop into my vehicle."

"Sure. Thanks." Carli and Angie followed the Ranger to his white pickup truck.

Buck motioned for Carli to take the front. "I'll leave you to it. I have some things I need to tend to, but here comes Lank. "

Angie got into the back and Lank climbed in the other side offering his hand across the backseat to the Ranger. "Lank Torres."

"Glad to meet you." Derek turned in the seat and shook the extended hand.

Carli pointed the direction. "It's one of our back pastures, where we share a fence line with Vera Allgood."

They rode in silence, bumping along the pasture roads after leaving the main caliche road. Two dirt trails now separated by green clumps of weeds and grass. She pointed again when Derek needed to veer onto another road.

Derek rolled his window down. "Is that too much wind back there?"

"No." Lank and Angie both said in unison.

Carli opened her window too, and couldn't help but feel pride at the momma cows that turned to look their way as they drove past. The calves scampered in the opposite direction of the road, sporting new ear jewelry that dangled clean and shiny in the sunlight, their experience with roundup and branding long forgotten. The thought that some-one was stealing these babies and cows, and that they might be suffering, made her blood boil. If anyone had told her a year ago how much a ranch, she never knew existed, would mean to her, she'd have thought they were crazy.

Today the sky was peppered with white puffy clouds against a brilliant blue. There were so many different shades of green littering the landscape, it surprised her every time she looked across the Wild Cow. From the buffalo grass, blue stem, and clumps of yucca to an occasional grove of mesquite or chinaberry reaching upwards toward the nev-er-ending sky. She absolutely missed the streams and dense woods of Georgia, but she now knew this vast emptiness is where she was meant to be.

"We found the fence down over there," Lank said.

Derek steered the vehicle off the road and they bounced across the pasture towards the far fence line. He parked a good ways back and got out, hold-ing a notebook and tape measure.

The others followed him.

"This is where the fence had been cut." Lank showed.

"Are these tracks yours?" Derek asked. He point-ed to the ground. "And whose place is that?"

"Those would be our tracks when we repaired the fence," Lank explained.

"It's Vera Allgood's place across the fence," said Carli.

"And past her place on the other side is where the Rafter O starts," said Angie.

"Is there a gate close?"

"Yes. Top of the hill by that windmill up there or back the other direction is the cattle guard across the road that leads into Crazy Vera's." Lank pointed.

"Let's drive over into Vera's place," said Derek. "Not sure why you call her 'crazy.' Hope she's not." He grinned just a tad.

They piled back into the truck, drove up the small rise, and as he stopped at the wire gate, Carli hopped out to open it. The unwritten duty of the shotgun rider in the front passenger seat, they always open and shut gates. She knew this back in Georgia too. Anyone with a pickup had learned the rule.

"I can get that," offered Lank as he opened his door, but Carli was faster.

"No problem." She hopped out and dashed to the gate, and then stepped back while Derek drove through.

"Thank you, ma'am," Derek said and tipped his hat toward Carli. She flashed him a bright smile and couldn't help but notice the frown on Lank's face. That was interesting.

She glanced at her friend as the truck went by, and when their eyes met Angie fanned her face and mouthed, "Wow." Carli held in a giggle. She could hardly wait to quiz her about not having time for any cowboys in her life. Maybe Angie was reconsidering and would make an exception for a Special

Ranger with the Texas Ranchers' Association.

Carli closed the gate and hopped in the truck.

Derek drove down the fence line on the other side, parked a good bit from the curled wires where the fence had been mended, and got out of his vehicle again. "Be careful where you walk," he said.

Just to be sure, the others stayed back behind him when he kneeled on the ground. "They parked over here." He pulled out his phone and snapped a picture. "This would be the pickup's tracks and over here the livestock trailer. See how it's backed up to where the gap was? I'm guessing Ms. Allgood had a few cows hanging around here with a few of the Wild Cow Ranch herd on the other side, and he got them all in one load."

"The wires have definitely been cut," said Lank.

"How could they do that? This is out in the middle of the pasture," Angie asked as she moved closer to stand next to Derek.

"Dogs," replied Derek. "Here are their footprints. I also see two separate boot tracks, so there were at least two men, maybe three, with trained cow dogs. You'd be surprised how fast they can load a few cows. How many head you got missing from this pasture?"

"By my count from yesterday, right after we fixed the fence, three cows and their calves," Lank said.

"I'm confused," said Carli. "When the trailer was parked at Vera's, I saw goats in the back, no cattle."

"They could have seen you or heard your truck," said Derek. "Maybe they dropped the goats off and came back for the cattle. Let's drive over and visit with Ms. Allgood, but I need to take some pictures first."

Lank, Angie, and Carli leaned against the truck and watched Derek at work. He intently studied the ground, took a few measurements, and wrote in his notebook. Carli had so many questions about what he was doing and what he was learning, but she kept silent as they piled back in the vehicle and drove in the direction of Crazy Vera's place.

what he was doing and what he was learning, but

Chapter Sixteen

Derek McKinney, Special Ranger with the Texas
Ranchers' Association, pulled his truck into Vera
Allgood's place. Past a skull and crossbones on the
fence, past the sign saying a trespasser wouldn't
have time to call 911, they slowly made the circle
around the drive stopping at the front entrance.

"There's a grave marker in her front yard," Derek said.

Carli laughed at the surprised look on his face.
For the entire morning he had not shown any emo-
tion or said much as they drove across the Wild
Cow Ranch. He had spent the entire time mea-
suring tire tracks, making notes, and walking the
fence line looking for clues. He definitely appeared
to take his job very seriously. "That's her soulmate
and first husband," said Carli.

"Crazy Vera and her one true love together forever," Angie said from the back seat. "She can go
outside and talk to him anytime she wants."

"It's kind of romantic, I think." Carli hopped out.

"I bet Vera's at the barn."

Lank, Angie, and Derek followed Carli across the gravel drive towards the towering two-story barn.

"Vera!" Carli called out as she stepped inside. Smells of fresh hay mingled with horse sweat and manure. Carli took a deep breath. She loved barns. It made her heart warm, like she'd stepped into a place of safety. The one childhood memory that she cherished. It also reminded her of the horse arenas in Georgia where she had spent the majority of her time. The peace and quiet, the connection with the horses had always calmed her troubled mind. And lately she had discovered the barn was the perfect place for praying as well.

"Vera! It's Carli," she called out again.

"Over here," came the reply, her voice echoing in the space.

Carli saw her neighbor in the far corner kneeling on the ground outside a pipe railed corral. Inside the pen stood a solid black bull, well over one thousand pounds, pawing the ground, his head lowered and staring with mean, beady eyes. He looked as if he might charge at any moment. No fence could ever hold him back if he got the notion.

"Got a limp but he won't let me look at it," Vera said.

"Poor baby," Carli swung one leg over the pen and climbed slowly into the enclosure.

"Watch it!" Derek's voice boomed throughout the barn.

"It's okay," she answered softly. "This is my baby. Hey, Maverick. What's wrong with you, boy?"

Lank walked closer to the pen and stepped up on the lowest rail. Maverick snorted.

"Get back," Carli said. "He remembers what you tried to do to him."

Lank ignored her warning and Angie and Vera laughed.

"Carli raised Mav from a bottle calf," Angie explained as she leaned her arms on the rail next to Derek, their elbows touching. Carli didn't hide the smile that came over her face when she looked at the two of them.

"He was a handful and ate a ton." Carli beamed like a proud mom.

Angie continued, "When Lank and Buck tried to turn him into a steer, Carli put her foot down and stopped it right away."

Vera added, "Maverick has made a fine herd bull for me, but I think he'll always be Carli's baby."

With that Maverick slung his head towards Carli as she approached. She slowly eased closer, reached out and scratched him between the ears but stayed ever aware in case he got too grumpy. She'd simply take one leap over the rail and be out of his way in a flash.

"Can you get him into that chute so I can take a look at his hoof?"

"Come on, Maverick. This way, sweet boy." Carli walked towards the narrow alley. "We have to see what's wrong with you. I know you're hurting."

Maverick lifted his head with soft, dark eyes and watched her walk away. Just after she stepped inside the curve, she hoisted herself up to the edge as Maverick lumbered past. The bull stopped, keeping his weight off a back leg. Lank stepped in with a long pole, flag on one end, and popped Maverick's backside.

"I've never seen anything like that in my life," said Derek.

The group gathered on one side of the chute, all kneeling to get a better look at the offending hoof.

"A little puss pocket. He must have stepped on something, don't you think?" Vera moved to one side so that Lank could get a good view.

They poked and prodded the hoof for several more seconds.

"Could have been a wire or a sharp rock," Lank said. "A shot of bute and some antibiotic, if you have it, should work. I'll relieve the pressure, if you want me to."

"Sure, thanks. I'll go find a syringe." Vera was up and over the pen before Carli could blink an eye. Despite her size and girth, that woman could move faster than the rest of them who were half her age.

"You might want to turn your head for this," said Angie.

"Why?" Carli rested an arm on her friend's shoulder.

"I know how weak your stomach is. Trust me. You don't want to see this."

But Carli didn't turn her eyes away fast enough.

Lank poked the cyst with his knife and a thick liquid came drooling out. Carli spun her back to the procedure and focused on Vera's beautiful horse, Pinto, part-draft, part quarter horse. The one thing she had not gotten used to yet were the medical issues that revolved around livestock. With show horses, she'd call her vet in Georgia, the problem was fixed, and Carli would pay the bill. There were some things she had learned to do on her own back there like giving a horse mineral oil if it was colicky. Or cleaning cuts and scrapes. But with a cattle ranch it was a little different. The vet was called only as a last resort in dire situations.

Cattle ranch owners were punchers, doctors, building maintenance, nursemaids—whatever the job called for—as Carli learned, they jumped in and just did it. And men's work rarely differed from women's work. Everybody pitched in and did their part. After inheriting the Wild Cow and moving to Texas, Carli was determined to learn as much about the cattle business as she could, but she still lacked a few skills. Her sensitive stomach was going to be her downfall every time.

Vera returned with several bottles. While she filled syringes, Lank administered the meds. With Maverick doctored they turned him out into a smaller fenced run attached to the barn because Vera wanted to keep him close for a few days in case the infection grew worse.

At that point introductions were finally made by Carli.

"Vera Allgood, this is our new TRA man, Derek McKinney."

"Pleased to meet ya, young man." Vera's hand engulfed Derek's as they shook. "I'm missing some goats and cows."

"I'd like to ask you a few questions about your stolen livestock, if I could, ma'am."

"Sure thing. Fire away."

"Your brand is registered with the county, correct?"

"Yes, it is. And I'm missing two cows and their calves."

"We think we found the spot where the rustlers cut the fence. Looks like they made off with cows from your ranch and the Wild Cow. Do you remember hearing anything strange several nights ago, Ms. Allgood?"

"I've been gone," Vera said. "Took my goat cheese and hand creams down to a festival in South Texas. I just got back this morning. Made out all right too. Sold the whole kit and kaboodle and came back with orders to fill."

Carli caught Angie's eye behind Derek. That explained a lot if Vera had been out of town. The rustlers could have driven by her house and into the pasture without anyone knowing. And then finding her cows standing next to Wild Cow Ranch stock, it had been the perfect opportunity. They must have known that Vera was gone.

"Now would be the time to tell them," Lank said, with a hard stare at Carli.

She swallowed the lump in her throat and glanced at her friend who had the silliest look on her face. No doubt they were guilty of something by the look on Angie's face.

Derek turned with a look of curiosity. With all eyes focused on her, Carli coughed. They had been trespassing, truth be told, but where to begin?

"We were on your property last night, Vera," Angie started.

"There were some men in your barn," Carli added.

"And they just about ran clean over Carli when they drove away," Angie blurted.

"Are you okay?" Vera turned a concerned glance to Carli.

"Did you get a look at them or a license plate number?" asked Derek.

"It's a wonder you weren't seriously hurt after being so stupid." This from Lank with that same annoyed glare on his face as before.

"We know it wasn't the smartest thing to do, but Angie jumped out and ran into the barn," Carli said. "We wanted to see what they were doing."

"I hadn't noticed anything missing." Vera spun on her heel and disappeared into the barn. They all followed.

"You might as well start from the beginning." Derek pulled a notebook from his pocket. "What time were you here?"

Between the two of them, Carli and Angie pieced together the events of the night before, as the other three asked question after question. Nothing was missing from Vera's barn that she could tell so they walked outside to show Derek where the truck had been parked and how Angie had tried to hem them in.

"Here is where I fell," said Carli. And then the words flashed in her brain. Heavy Duty. That's it. By the light of the barn and in aluminum letters across the back of the tailgate as they drove away. But there was something else and she couldn't remember no matter how hard she tried to focus on last night. She needed more coffee maybe, or a nap.

Mentioning that detail was on the tip of her tongue and then she stopped herself. Was it necessary that Derek know everything? Why couldn't she and Angie keep a few clues to themselves?

Carli was convinced there had to be a way to set a trap for the rustlers.

And it was up to her and Angie to do it.

Chapter Seventeen

The tin-roofed sale barn in the neighboring town of Spring Lake held a livestock auction every Thursday. Carli and Angie decided to scope out the place and look for any suspicious looking white trucks. Derek had explained how the brands might be altered too, so they were going to keep an eye out for small groups of pairs, cows and their calves, that might have suspicious looking brands.

Coming into the arena the girls were met with a sea of cowboy hats. A cloud of dust hung overhead kicked up by the cattle in the center pen. There was a lot going on. Carli had been to a couple of auctions back in Georgia but they were smaller than this one.

"Let's sit up high so we can get a good view," Angie said as they made their way to the stands.

Sounding a bit like gibberish the auctioneer followed the bids and tried to move the purchase price higher and higher. This was part prime beef and some culls from the smaller ranches. Tack would be viewed around noon and then horses up for sale in the afternoon. No matter the diverse options of stock, people's livelihoods depended on top dollar.

Carli couldn't understand all the auctioneer was saying but it was sure exciting to follow the action. The ring men watched the crowd for any signs of a bid and conveyed that back to the auctioneer.

Angie leaned over to Carli and chuckled. "Don't you dare touch your hair. Or pick your nose. They might think you're bidding."

"I'm gonna sit on my hands."

Six black angus steers were huddled together and moved around a central pen by a man with a flagged pole for the crowd to view. Carli saw that most of their rear ends and other parts were covered with a mixture of manure and dirt from the ground where they had been resting until their turn was called. During her Georgia days she might have found the smells offensive but after working with the cattle on her ranch since coming to Texas, she'd gotten used to it.

Leaning close to Angie she whispered, "How are we going to see brands on the black-haired ones?"

Angie looked at the people around them, and whispered back, "Sometimes they're visible like white on black. It'll be easier on the red Angus."

After forty or so minutes of watching the cattle and not seeing any recognizable brands or cow/calf pairs, they decided to head to the snack bar. Sometimes that was where the social action was at these local events. Instead of date night, or teens hanging out at the bowling alley, some ranchers and their families looked forward to every Thursday at the cattle sale.

Carli felt eyes on them as they walked across the bleachers to the steps leading to the dirt floor. She knew Angie drew attention, partly because of her being an Olsen and partly because of her tight jeans and long blond hair. She wondered if anyone looked at her and knew she was the owner of the Wild Cow, and then she thought that maybe her Grandpa Ward had stood right here in this very spot sometime in the past before she ended up at the Wild Cow. A sadness settled over her heart for one fleeting moment.

They chatted as they walked, ignoring the stares.

"I need a water," Angie said. "None of that snack bar junk."

"Me, I'm gettin' a greasy hot dog, maybe fries too."

Angie rolled her eyes at Carli. "You've got to be kidding. You know that stuff'll kill you, right?"

Just then an older man was in their path, slowly making his way to the snack bar. He turned around at the sound of their voices and said, "Why, Angie Olsen. How are you? Is your dad here?"

"Oh, hey, Mr. Gallagher. Nice to see you. No, my dad's not here."

As the man engaged Angie in conversation and seemingly held her prisoner, Carli soundlessly mouthed to her and pointed in the direction of the snack bar. "I'm going . . ." and made an okay sign.

Angie nodded but looked really perturbed by the man's interruption. The smile on her face was fake but she didn't interrupt him.

After standing in line for her hot dog, fries, and Coke, Carli balanced it all over to a high-top table. She took a giant bite of the hot dog then a big gulp of the soda.

As she was cramming food in her mouth and people-watching, she couldn't believe her eyes. Is that Lexi? The wayward girl from her riding school that Carli had helped. And the guy next to her. Not Raven, was it? She wasn't sure. Old, dirty jeans, black combat boots. He was wearing a pearl snap shirt, worn and ripped on the sleeve and a cowboy hat pulled tight and low to shield his eyes. But then Carli spotted some of his pitch-black hair, long and scraggly, fastened in a ponytail and hanging over his collar, unlike most of the cowboys at the sale who wore their hair neat and trimmed, or buzzed.

When he lifted and placed his arm around Lexi's shoulder, Carli spotted a familiar mark on his inside wrist—the black tattoo she had seen before when he came to her ranch and acted like a fool, of a raven.

Was he pulling Lexi in somewhat of a struggle? Carli could see Lexi's face was not smiling, instead grimacing.

She thought about calling out to Lexi but didn't want to spook Raven. Trashing the food but keeping the soda, Carli followed them mixing herself in between the crowd. A hand on her back scared the wits out of her and caused her to jump and twitch.

"Geesh," Angie said. "What's the matter with you? Kinda skittish, aren't ya?"

"Shhh, not so loud. That's Lexi with Raven. Don't let them see you. I want to follow them, see what he's up to."

"All right. I'm glad I finally got away from that rancher. Hope he doesn't tell my dad that he saw me here. Are you sure it's Raven?"

Leaving the sale barn, the bright sunlight made Carli wish she hadn't left her shades in the pickup truck. With less people outside, Carli and Angie might stick out like a bawling baby calf at weaning time. But they pressed on and hid as they could weaving behind vehicles and livestock trailers that stood every which way in the parking lot. There was no order or marked spaces.

A couple of cowboys who had just parked saw them and wanted to strike up a conversation. "Hey, there. Whatcha doin' tonight?"

In a strong voice, Angie chastised but gave them a pretty smile. "Move along, guys. We're busy."

Turning to Carli, she said, "Normally, I'd give that jerk a piece of my mind. But we've got a mission. Keep going."

Carli was grateful to see the cowboys heading into the sale barn.

Up ahead the brake lights of a white Ford dually glared red and Carli saw Raven helping, or more like pushing, Lexi to climb up into the middle seat. He had a tight grip on the top of her arm.

"Look, Angie, there they are! Someone else must be driving. And it's a white truck."

They crept closer hiding along the side of a vehicle and peeking over the back truck bed.

"Hey, look at the bumper, Carli. Kind of crooked on the right side like it's loose. And a dent the size of a fist, or a boot. Didn't you notice that from the truck the other night? Except this one's a dually. Dang, what should we do? Follow them? Or tell the sheriff we saw Raven and describe the truck?"

"I dunno, Angie. This is kinda scary. I'm not sure what he's capable of."

"If we were closer to my truck, we could do a high-speed chase."

At that moment Lexi paused and looked over her shoulder right at Carli. Their eyes met. Carli saw pain, and anger, but more than that she saw fear in Lexi's face. For a fleeting second the young girl's eyes were wide and panicked, and she looked right at Carli like a plea for help.

Carli suddenly went into high gear and ran towards the truck that was about to take Lexi away. She feared for her young friend's life.

"Carli! Wait! Be careful," Angie called out.

But it was too late. Carli was running towards the dually truck.

It moved slowly, creeping along the gravel edging around a trailer. Carli had time to reach for the passenger door and grab the handle. Without even thinking, she yanked it open.

Lexi's eyes were wide and Raven yelled, "What

the heck do you think you're doing? Get your hand off the door!"

"Raven, you let her out, right now! She doesn't want to go with you!"

Carli stepped up, balancing on the running board, the other foot still on the ground. She pulled on his sleeve, and yelled, "Angie! Call the cops!"

Raven's mouth looked like a wolf growling and he screamed again at her, "Leave us alone and get off the truck, you b----!"

With that he pushed her shoulder and Carli lost her balance. The driver gunned the truck and as they picked up speed, Carli hit the gravel, hard. Her shoulder came into contact with sharp rocks.

As the truck sped away, she rolled over and sat up. Aluminum letters were on the back tailgate, Heavy Duty. Carli pointed and shouted, "Hey!"

That was it. Except the entire words weren't fully there; the letter "e" was missing. This was the same truck they had seen at Vera's. But it was a dually and the truck at Vera's had not been. What are the odds that the same letter would be missing from two vehicles? Carli shook the fuzz from her brain.

Grimacing at the pain in her shoulder, Carli allowed Angie to help her to her feet. She brushed off the back of her jeans.

"That's the truck," she said. "We need to tell Sheriff Anderson, but he'll never believe us."

"How can you be sure?" Angie asked. "That was a dually."

The last thing Carli had heard before she saw stars was Lexi's scream. "Carli!"

She'd never forget that sound of panic and fear in the girl's voice. And she was going to do everything she could to find her.

Chapter Eighteen

"I'm taking you to the hospital," Angie said as she
pulled out of the auction parking lot and turned on
the road towards the clinic.

Carli held her shoulder, moaned, and managed
to mutter, "No."

"Are you sure? Your face is pale. I can tell you're
hurting."

"Just take me home." Carli tried to suppress a
moan again but she couldn't when Angie hit a small
bump in the street.

"Your shoulder needs to be looked at, Carli. I'm
not joking. You kind of bounced and slid. Anything
else hurt?"

"My bottom. But I'm tougher than I look. I've
been bucked off horses, trampled on by calves, and
tripped over my own two feet more times than
I can count. I'll be fine." It took every breath she
could muster to say all that and she didn't want to
argue anymore. She just wanted to get home and
take a hot shower.

"That looked like a similar truck to the one we saw at Vera's, but it wasn't a dually," Angie said.

"It was the same one." Carli was positive.

"You can't be sure, but it's obvious that Raven may be involved in everything. The meth camp, the rustling. That little criminal gets around. What's his story anyway?" Angie drove fast, to match her racing talk.

"I don't know anything about him. But I do know that I have to find Lexi." Carli looked at the palms of her hands and scraped off bits of gravel. "She keeps hanging around that kid. What is it about bad boys that's like a magnet to young girls?"

"I don't get it myself. Dad always kept us too busy for dating. We were always out riding, doing whatever he asked of us. I'd rather be ropin' calves than kissin' on some boy," Angie declared.

"I remember being horse crazy. Winning and competing was my passion. Boys just didn't fit into the equation and then when I finally took notice..." Carli paused and choked back any tears bubbling up. So stupid that she still couldn't say his name aloud.

"What happened?" asked Angie. "Spill it."

"It didn't end well. Let's just leave it at that." Carli shifted the subject away from her Georgia boyfriend back to the problem at hand. "Did I tell you about the words on the tailgate? I knew there was something about that truck I had forgotten. It had the words Heavy Duty in chrome letters on one side of the tailgate, but the letter "e" was missing on the truck at Vera's. I know the truck we saw at the sale barn is a dually but it's the same truck."

Angie glanced at her with a skeptical look. "They could've removed the outside tires when they were on my property that night."

"Is that possible?" asked Carli.

"I suppose. Confuse tire tracks. They'd be different in the pasture with only one set of back tires, but in town driving around it would be four back tires. Just a normal dually pickup truck."

"Except for the dents on the tailgate and bumper. And now with the chrome letters," Carli said. "There is no question that's the truck we saw drive by when we were parked at the hay barn, and at Vera's barn. I just know it. The question is who is helping Raven?"

Lost in their own thoughts, conversation halted until they hit the Dixon city limits.

"Let's get a coffee. You need something to stay awake because I'm not so sure you didn't bang your head too." Angie pulled to a stop in front of B & R Beanery.

"Sounds good." Carli hadn't thought about Belinda. If anybody would know who might be helping Raven, it would be the owner Belinda, the 'B' in B&R. She had the pulse of the entire town, and most of the county. It's not that she was the town gossip or anything like that. She was a good listener and everyone that came in her coffee shop had something to tell. And Belinda was careful not to spread rumors. Belinda and Carli became friends right after Carli moved to the ranch. She hadn't known a soul and the local coffee barista had become one of her trusted confidants. Belinda would tell her anything she wanted to know.

The bell tinkled above the door as they walked in and Belinda gave them a wave. An older couple waited on their order at the counter so Angie and Carli slid in to bar stools at a taller table in the back corner.

Belinda counted out change and smiled as the couple made their way out the door, with a few stories and pleasantries along the way. She followed them to the door, and then turned to the girls. "What are you two doing? Something's up. I can tell."

Carli had to laugh at the look on Angie's face. She did look guilty, all the while trying to keep a straight face. "Nothing much. Just driving back from the sale barn."

"Nothing much?" Angie shouted and gave Carli an incredulous look of surprise. "She almost got run over for the second time this week, and we are hot on the trail of rustlers."

"Run over?" Belinda hurried over to Carli and looked her in the eyes. "What hurts? Did you hit your head? Is anything broken?"

Before Carli could answer, Belinda patted her shoulder, the sore one, and Carli couldn't hold back a moan. "Uh, I'm fine."

"Let me see it." Belinda's mom radar was in overdrive.

"Would you please fix our order first?" Carli asked.

"No ma'am, I will not. Let me see your injuries," Belinda demanded.

Since Carli couldn't convince her to fix their drinks, she removed her overshirt. Underneath she wore a sleeveless tank top. Both of her friends studied the scrapes on her upper arm and elbow. She flat out refused to wash the blood off in the restroom. As soon as she got home, she was going straight to the shower.

The girls placed their order. Belinda insisted on more details so Carli and Angie told her about their stakeout and the incident at the auction. "Raven is one of the rustlers," said Carli.

"Johnny Gibbons? The one that keeps tagging after Lexi?"

"Yep, that's the one." Carli didn't reveal that Lexi had driven off with him.

"Any ideas who he might be hangin' with?" asked Angie.

"It all makes sense now," said Belinda as she brought their coffees. She eased into the barstool at the end of the table, and took her time, looking at Carli and then to Angie. She wanted to say something but hesitated.

"Tell us. What do you know?" Carli sipped her hot latte and felt her neck and jaw relax. She was going to be sore in the morning.

"I heard that his Uncle Melvin is out of prison and has moved in with his brother, Raven's dad,"

Belinda shared. "There's been an uptick in crime lately throughout the county. Car thefts, break-ins, and you say meth cooking and now rustling. Appears Uncle Melvin has set up his own little crime syndicate in Creek County."

"Yep. That's what it sounds like," Angie agreed. "And enlisted his nephew in the process."

"Maybe Raven doesn't have a choice." Carli always believed that people have a bit of good inside. It's just the circumstances sometimes that causes them to make bad choices.

"Nope. That Johnny Gibbons has been bad news since he was a little tyke."

But Carli didn't believe Belinda. What if the uncle had forced Raven to help him? Threaten him in some way? She had to talk to Lexi and then maybe she could get to Raven. If she could talk to him, maybe she could get him to see how wrong he was and that he didn't really want to go down this path. And he certainly didn't need to take Lexi with him. It would destroy both of their lives forever.

The friends chatted for another half hour or so about nothing in particular. Carli tried to keep her eyes open, but she was suddenly so tired.

"Stay awake." Angie snapped her fingers in Carli's face. "Shouldn't she go to the hospital?"

Belinda leaned closer to Carli. "Her eyes look all right. I don't think she has a concussion. I can't feel a bump on her head." Belinda ran her hands over Carli's scalp.

"One thing's for sure, she'd make a lousy criminal. She can't keep from falling down." Angie looked at Belinda and they both laughed.

"I'm sitting right here while you talk about me." Carli sneered at them. "I'm ready to go."

Belinda followed them to the front, gave them both a hug, and opened the door. As they walked out, a group of high school kids barreled in, all laughs and jostling like they were the center of the universe. School was out so the place would stay busy over the next hour or so.

"I still say we can trap them." Carli followed Angie to the truck. "What do rustlers want?"

"They want livestock. And they don't want to work that hard for it."

"Exactly. There has got to be a way to entice them to a certain spot and then we jump up from a hiding place."

"And yell, 'Stop it.' Think about what you're sayin', Carli. What do we do when we catch them?" Angie asked. "I think we need the guys with us. As much as I cringe at the thought of Colton, we may need him."

Carli agreed that Angie had a good point, but if she told Lank then Lank would tell her to stay home and not get involved. And then he would take over, and then the sheriff would get called for some reason, and then he would say there's nothing they can do. Same old song and dance. Carli wanted action. She wanted to make a difference. She wanted to catch the men who were stealing from her. And she wanted to save Raven, and Lexi, in the process.

It's a lot, but is it too much to ask God for?

After a dinner of cereal and bananas, all she had in the pantry, she talked with Angie about every possible scenario they could come up with. They had several more weeks until the next full moon. There had to be something they could do.

Next week was branding and the calves would have a new brand and a new ear tag, but the brands wouldn't be scabbed over. They'd be new and easily altered.

Instead of going home, Angie insisted on staying in the guest room. "I'm not convinced that you didn't hit your head. I want to make darn sure you don't go pukin' up your toenails."

Carli gave in. With Angie cozy and settled in one of the guest rooms, Carli flipped out the lights and went to her bedroom. She surveyed her bruised shoulder before getting in the shower and washed off the blood, but was too tired to put cream on the cuts. On the outside, a few scrapes but on the inside far worse. She did not want to go to the doctor and explain what an idiot she had been. Why would she jump onto a vehicle?

But she couldn't get Lexi's voice out of her head. Screaming "Carli!" It was the panic in Lexi's voice that terrified Carli. Should she call Lexi's mother? Should she drive around and try to find where Raven took her?

Carli half-dried her hair and considered options. She couldn't decide what to do, or even if she wanted to get involved in Lexi's life again. Giving her riding lessons was one thing, but imposing herself into the girl's life was another matter. Carli wanted to scream. She was at the end of her rope. So, she prayed.

She prayed for Lexi to be safe. She prayed for wisdom and guidance. How could she help this girl before her whole life is ruined by some idiot kid? And who was Raven? Where did he live? Why had he turned to a life of crime and why was he dragging Lexi into the pit with him? Carli felt so helpless.

Lola always said to pray and let God take over. That was the most difficult thing for Carli to do. She had been on her own for so long, it seemed almost irresponsible to not be more proactive on some matters.

Chapter Nineteen

The next morning Carli's whole body was stiff and sore. Her hip and bottom were aching and she had to roll to her side to get out of bed, slowly. Was this how it felt to get old?

The aroma of grinding coffee beans gently and gloriously assaulted Carli's nose. Crazy dreams had filled her night, images of Raven as a hungry, drooling wolf terrorizing her. And Lexi screaming like a baby lamb. It was as though she hadn't slept at all. She'd never get the image of Lexi's face out of her mind as the young girl was hurriedly ushered away from the auction, by who knows who, Raven's tight grip on her arm.

Grateful that Angie had spent the night, Carli ambled towards the kitchen surprised at the twinges of pain that shot through her hip and shoulder. Her head pounded like a drum brigade. The smell of coffee brewing was the only reason she decided to get out of bed.

"Well, there you are, Super Hero Ninja Girl. How

ya doin'? Ready to take on a gang of rustlers?" Angie slid a mug of caffeine towards her on the counter.

Carli's pushed her long, tangled hair out of her eyes. Teeth not brushed yet. Still wearing pajamas. "Ugh," was all she could get out, then took a long gulp of coffee that Angie had added a little cream to.

"I think that's how you take it, right?"

"Mmm, perfect, thanks." Carli rubbed her eyes and raked her fingers through her hair. She tilted her head in all directions trying to work the kinks out of her neck, then lifted her shoulders up and down, backwards and forward. She sat up tall on the barstool and arched her back as she rubbed it and then felt the knot on her thigh.

"I feel like that truck ran over me." Carli stared into her mocha-colored drink, then looked up at Angie. "I have bruises on my bottom." She collapsed onto the counter, her head resting on folded arms.

Angie tried to hold back a snicker with her hand, but failed. "Well, I'm sure you do after landing on those rocks like you did. What a jerk that kid Raven is. I'd like to get a hold of him and—"

"I'm sure we'll solve this soon." Carli sighed. "I'm just worried about Lexi. Maybe Raven kept her out all night. I can't even remember if she's turned sixteen yet. Do you think I should call her mother?"

"Well, if Raven took her against her will, that's kidnapping a minor," Angie said. "He could get into real trouble."

Carli's cell phone buzzed and after looking at

the screen she frowned to Angie. "It's Sheriff Anderson."

"Answer it."

Rolling her eyes, then clearing her throat, Carli pressed the speaker button. "Good morning, Sheriff."

"It's closer to afternoon, Carli. I need to talk to you. And Angie. Is she there? I see her Rafter O truck. I'm out front and I'm coming in."

Carli scrambled and stood. Instead of answering she choked, coughed, and then managed to say, "Could you give me a few minutes? I'll be right out." She clicked the phone off.

Angie held her hands up and shrugged. "I'll let him in."

Carli squeaked an almost inaudible "Wait." But it was too late since Angie was already at the front door. Carli made a mad dash to her room to find jeans and threw a jacket on over the baggy T-shirt she had worn to bed.

She couldn't imagine why the sheriff was here. They had talked about reporting the truck they'd seen at the auction, but then decided no one would believe them. Carli and Angie were still determined to stop this rustling ring on their own. Did they really need a man to take over and do everything?

"Come on in, Sheriff," Angie's bright and sunny greeting echoed throughout the house and made Carli's head hurt even more.

The sheriff's voice boomed in the entry hall. "Good morning, young lady. And here comes Lank.

I'll talk to him too."

Carli appeared from around the corner, skidding to a stop in her socks. "No, wait, wait, Sheriff Anderson, don't talk to Lank! He has work to do. What can I do for you?"

The sheriff said, "Why don't you want me to talk to Lank?"

Carli walked around the sheriff and stood at the entry. "Lank, I know you have lots to do today. We're just visiting with Sheriff Anderson for a minute."

The two men looked from Carli to each other and back again. Carli knew she must look like a mess, long hair whipping in the breeze that rushed through the front door, and her crazy mismatched outfit with bright purple socks. She hadn't had time to change out of her pajama top, just slung a red sweater on instead—as opposed to Angie who stood next to her, bright and shiny, not one blonde hair out of place, falling instead in a neat braid down the middle of her back. She still wore the same jeans, now dusty, but had on a black tee with fringe around the collar.

"Is that my shirt?" Carli asked when she took a double take at Angie.

"Yeah. Found it in your closet this morning. Thanks, by the way."

The sheriff moved his hat back a bit and rubbed his chin. Quiet and low he said to Lank at the doorway, "I always said the female species was hard to figure out. Wish me luck." The men stifled grins.

"What'd you guys say?" Angie asked sternly.

"Oh, nothing important," Lank said as he backed away from the door.

The sheriff glanced at Carli from head to toe again, and asked, "You sure you're ready for company, Carli?"

"Sure, sure, Sheriff. Come right in."

She sent Angie a frightfully serious look. Maybe she should change into a real shirt? Angie took over, offering the sheriff a cup of coffee.

As fast as she could, Carli ran to her bathroom, brushed her teeth, washed her face, dabbed on a little lip gloss, dashed a brush through her hair, then twisted it up into a ponytail. Pulling out a clean T-shirt, she was ready to go. Two minutes flat.

"Sorry about that, Sheriff. Thanks for waiting. What can we help you with this morning?"

The sheriff was perched on the edge of a bar stool, hand on his mug but not drinking. "Someone reported that you girls had some trouble at the auction yesterday."

Leaning against the cabinet on the other side of the bar from the sheriff, Carli and Angie exchanged quick glances. There appeared to be a few dirty rats in the county.

"That's two towns over. How did you hear about it?" Leave it to Angie to not mince words. She always got straight to the point. The question hung in the air with no response.

Carli was all fake smiles as she tried to mask her emotions and act as though she had everything under control, big ranch owner that she was. Things couldn't be further from the truth. Her stomach clenched.

The sheriff's brow furrowed as he watched her smile performance, then cleared his throat.

"Not talking? Let me go over what I heard and maybe you can elaborate," the sheriff said. "So, you and Angie were at the sale. And you saw John Gibbons, also known as Raven, and you chased him resulting in you, Carli, falling off his truck." The sheriff flipped open a small notebook and removed a pen from his front shirt pocket.

Carli barely heard the knock when suddenly Lank walked into the kitchen, spurs jingling on the wood floor. He removed his hat and sat on the stool next to Sheriff Anderson. She had hoped to keep the incident under wraps until she had time to tell Lank in her own way. He'd be furious no doubt.

"You fell? You chased someone?" He had heard part of the sheriff's conversation as he came through the door. She'd never seen Lank's eyes so menacing, almost like the wolf in her dreams.

She gingerly walked around the bar, trying not to limp much, to stand by Lank, holding her breath as pain stabbed her back and leg. She rubbed her thigh.

"Now, Lank—"

He looked at the way she was grimacing and moving in slow motion. "What's the matter with you, Carli? Why are you all stoved up? Are you hurt?"

Again, the sheriff cleared his throat and flipped a

few pages of his notebook. "According to witnesses, might have something to do with her falling from a white dually pickup truck onto the gravel road."

Carli whipped her head around and glared at the sheriff.

"Are you hurt bad? What were you thinking, Carli?" And then Lank turned to Angie. "Were you with her?"

Angie didn't have much chance to answer. She pursed her lips, tilted her head, and shrugged, when suddenly another knock sounded at the door. This time Lola called out. "Carli? It's me."

Carli exhaled, putting her hands on her hips. "Great. Party at Carli's."

"I'm sorry to interrupt, Carli. But that TRA Ranger Derek McKinney is outside. Said he heard about you and Angie having some trouble at the auction yesterday."

Sheriff Anderson spoke up. "I called him. He asked to be kept informed on any new developments."

"Great, show him in," Carli said, defeated. Then mumbled to herself, "Just let everyone in."

Derek McKinney walked into an already crowded kitchen, tipped his hat and removed it. "Ms. Jameson. Sheriff. Lank." He lingered on Angie. "Ms. Olsen. Nice to see you."

"You, too, Derek. And call me Angie."

"Okay, Angie."

Carli couldn't help but raise her eyebrows as Derek walked farther into the kitchen to stand next to Angie.

"You can call me Carli. I guess you heard about the auction incident last night. You might as well join us too." She motioned to Lola who pulled up a stool on the other side of the sheriff. As they all squeezed into her kitchen, Carli raised her hand. "It appears that Angie and I have been ratted out. Let's go back to her earlier question, Sheriff. Where did you hear about this?"

Derek cleared his throat. "I wanted to let you know what we found about John Gibbons, aka, Raven. I sent my report over to your office this morning, Sheriff."

"Yes, I got it, thanks."

"It seems that Raven's uncle has a long record," Derek said. "Burglaries, auto theft, prior rustling in Oklahoma. He was just released from Crabtree Correctional Center after three years. His brother, Raven's father, works as a mechanic, tends to like his whiskey, and allows Raven to do whatever he wants."

Sheriff Anderson nodded. "We agree on one thing. Uncle Melvin is leading things and may have pulled Raven into their ring. Raven's dad as well."

Carli was losing patience. "Who told you that I fell?"

Sheriff Anderson kept a bland look on his face and flipped through his notebook again. "The eyewitness said the 'crazier one' jumped in the truck and attacked the passengers. There was a scuffle, and she fell."

"That's ridiculous!" Carli shouted in the over-crowded room.

"Why were you two harassing people at the auction?" The sheriff gave them a stern look.

"It's the same pickup truck that drove through the Wild Cow," said Angie.

"I remembered the chrome lettering and Angie remembered the dent. We know it's the same truck that we saw at Vera's too," said Carli.

"The tracks on Tuesday near the fence line gap were made by single back tires, not a dually pickup truck," said Derek. He too conveniently pulled a notebook from his pocket and began flipping through his notes.

"You can keep reading from your notes all you want, but we know what we saw," said Angie.

Carli glanced at the circle of disbelieving faces. Even Lola was looking at her like she'd gone mad. For some reason she and Angie had suddenly turned into the bad guys. The whole time Lank was listening in silence, shaking his head, and staring straight at Carli. She didn't miss the disappointed look on his face.

"I have one question for you," Lank said, slow and low, his gaze never leaving her face. "Did you fall or did someone push you?"

Carli swallowed the lump in her throat. It had happened so fast. She saw Lexi's face, so pale and scared. She balanced on the running board, the door was open. The driver put the truck in gear, although she never really got a look at his face. She was focused on Lexi. But then a sneer turned up one corner of Raven's mouth and dark eyes full of hatred, a fist reaching out and a punch to her shoulder. Carli gasped.

"Carli." Lank closed in and put his hands on her arms. "Tell me."

She winced when he touched her. The same side that had taken a punch had broken her fall.

"I was pushed." Her answer came out barely audible, in a soft whisper just as Carli realized the truth. She had been telling herself it had been because of her clumsiness.

"That's what I thought." Lank's eyes were full of fire as he leaned closer, his breath soft and warm in her ear. He whispered, "Don't worry. I'm going to handle this."

Fear gripped Carli's heart at the thought of what he might do to Raven. Or what Raven's uncle, straight out of prison, might do to Lank.

Another knock at the door.

Carli mumbled, "Good grief." Lank stepped back away from her.

Buck poked his head in. "Someone opened all the gates! We've got cows wandering all over the place."

Lank shot to his feet and ran out the door with Buck.

Sheriff Anderson turned to Carli. "What's this about Vera's house?"

Carli looked at Angie who was staring at Derek and not paying any attention to the pickle they were in. Unblinking with a face set in stone, the sheriff kept his pen in hand poised over that stupid notebook. She might as well make another pot of coffee. This was going to be a long interrogation.

Chapter Twenty

The feeling of relief when she pulled to a stop at Rafter O headquarters surprised Angie. Couldn't be homesickness. She had only been away one night, just at the neighboring ranch, the Wild Cow. But she felt it—glad to be home. After stepping out of her truck and following the path around the house, she opened the back door and entered the Olsen homestead. Using the bootjack, she then walked in her socks to the kitchen.

The family didn't usually come in through the front door, company did on special occasions. An enclosed porch partially served as a mud room where they could take their boots off and leave the dirt out where it belonged. Angie still got a chuckle when a lot of family members left their boots in a line and all sizes and colors were on display.

As much as Angie Olsen loved her home, it had been good to be away from the Rafter O for a few days—doing things with Carli, both of them being truly independent, and using their God-given brains to solve the crimes taking place on their ranches. But good grief, the events of this crazy week swirled in Angie's head. A lot had been going on—the stakeout, and even though she had no time for dating, meeting that notable Ranger Derek McKinney, then the auction and running into Raven, all culminating with Carli falling from his truck. Or was she pushed? It seemed impossible to consider that Raven had shoved Carli from a moving vehicle.

It was becoming too much for her mind to take it all in. And she was exhausted. Still tired, maybe more emotionally than physically, from the late-night stakeout illuminated by the full moon Monday night. And drained from all the stress and drama. But her young body also told her it had been exciting, charged with the electrifying jolt of being fully alive, taking the bull by the horns and being in the middle of making a difference.

She felt her cheeks grow warm. That Ranger Derek was someone who might make her reconsider the no dating rule. Handsome in a lot of ways. Those blue eyes had fixed their laser beam right on her and through her. Tall, athletic. Sharp dresser, all starched and pressed. And all business, that guy. Sure takes his work seriously. She wondered if he ever smiled.

But Angie saw the way he looked at her. That wasn't all business. She might be able to bring a smile or two to that handsome face. Looks like he'd take his fun seriously too. Not in a Colton Creacy kind of way. That yahoo was just a wild 'n crazy, fun loving, trouble causing, life of the party cow puncher. Always lookin' for a good time. She could find his type everywhere if she wanted one, and she didn't want one.

Why was she thinking so much about those guys? She rubbed her eyes and loosened her long blond ponytail. It was giving her a headache. And since she had stayed to help round up some of Carli's herd this morning after gates were mysteriously opened all over the Wild Cow Ranch, she was now in need of a shower, clean clothes, and maybe even a short nap.

It seemed unusually quiet around the Rafter O and Angie hadn't seen anyone when she came in. Maybe her mom and dad were napping before supper. Good. She decided to get a little snack in the kitchen before heading to her room for that shower.

"Is that you, Angelina? Come in here right now!" Her father's voice boomed from his study down the hall.

That doesn't sound good. What in the world was he so upset about? Before answering him, she rummaged in the pantry for crackers and found cheese in the fridge. She wiped off her hands on a towel and headed his way still chewing on her snack.

"What's up, Dad?" She stood in the doorway of his office.

"Where have you been? And what, in God's name, have you been doing?" His voice was at a very loud decibel. She wasn't sure why.

Transfixed, she stared at him for maybe a second too long and was hit by his bellowing voice again.

"Answer me, Angelina! What have you done?"

She drew a big breath in through her nose and willed herself to be calm although she felt as though smoke was escaping from her ears.

Slowly, she said, "What are you talking about, Dad? You knew I was at Carli's. This morning they discovered someone had left all their gates open. I stayed a while to see if they needed my help."

Straightening tall and placing a hand on her hip, she promised herself she would not let him bulldoze her down into a little girl. She'd been out of high school five years, for gosh sakes.

Skip Olsen took in a few short breaths, but with his face as red as the setting sun she knew he was only revving up for another blast.

"What were you doing at the auction Thursday? We don't buy our registered livestock from the local sale barn. You know that."

"I was helping Carli. How do you even know I was there?"

"I need to know why you were there. Are you trying to hide something?"

She didn't like it when he got like this. He really was a good man. But "pigheaded" came to her mind. He always had his thumb on everything they did, and even though his children were grown that hadn't changed.

"Dad, I am not trying to hide anything. I told you, I was helping Carli."

"Well, Ray Gallagher phoned me. Said he saw the two of you. He wondered why I wasn't there with you if we had business at the sale."

"Oh, good grief, Dad. So, you're all upset because old man Gallagher is being nosy and spying on me? I bet he called the sheriff too."

"Don't be disrespectful, Angelina. He's been a friend to this family for years, since before you were born."

Angie shifted from one foot to the other. She was physically tired and just wanted to get to her own room, but she was also tired of her father's cross-examination. Why did he have to be this way? Why couldn't he see her as an equal partner in the Rafter O? Didn't he trust her judgment and abilities?

She breathed fully in and let out a big sigh. "Can I go now? I've got to get cleaned up and I'm pretty tired."

He frowned but seemed to have given up on the questions, and she was darn sure going to stick to her guns and not give him any answers.

The sound of boots and spurs jingling came from the kitchen, and suddenly her little brother Travis appeared from around the corner. Angie noticed he hadn't removed his boots out back like she had. A smile lit up his face. "Hey, Sis. Did you and Carli survive your crime spree?"

"What crime spree?" Instead of a booming voice filled with aggravation, this question came out of her father deep and low and mean.

Angie's brows furrowed and she looked directly into his raging eyes. "I'm not sure what you're asking."

"Where were you?"

"You know I was at Carli's. Why the second degree, Dad?"

He stared at her, took a sip of his coffee, and appeared to be making her wait.

"It was the funniest thing ever, Dad. Angie and Carli were in hiding on the ranch looking for rustlers. You should have seen the looks on their faces when we spotted them with the light." With that, Travis doubled over in laughter before plopping in the leather loveseat and stretching his legs out over the arm.

"Is that true, Angelina, after I strictly forbade you to get anywhere near those dangerous criminals?"

Unbelievable.

"Travis and his band of rowdy jerks were there too. Why aren't you getting on to him?" Her face was reddening.

"Do not speak to me in that tone. Just answer my question. Is that what you were doing?"

Her insides were fuming. I'm gonna beat that boy. She was not going to let her father, Mr. Gallagher, and baby brother Travis all gang up on her. She was not going to kowtow to them, be the sweet shrinking violet who always apologized first. Did they think she had plans to only cook and clean? Be some simpering airhead who only cared about clothes and makeup and keeping a man happy.

Dadgummit, didn't they see her doing as much work as any man on the ranch? Didn't they think she had a brain in her head?

Remaining straight and tall as a soldier, one hand hooked on her belt, she was the epitome of unwavering strength. She didn't want to be defiant. But she wouldn't buckle under such prejudice. She looked a little above her father's head at all the books lining his study's shelves, trying to get her thoughts together and not give in and beg for forgiveness. Like she always did. Then she squinted some and stared right through his eyes.

"Yes, Dad, Carli and I were lying in wait for the people who have been stealing cows from the Wild Cow and the Rafter O. Both Carli and I feel obligations to protect our ranches. No one else is doing anything but us. We were the ones who found the meth cookers' camp and gave that information to the sheriff."

"You're not the only one trying to save the day, big sister. What do you think we were doing?" Travis stood like a rooster surveying his hens. "They're just going to make a mess of things, Dad. Girls shouldn't be allowed out after midnight."

Angie refrained from arguing with her brother, because they could go at it for hours, and instead chose to ignore his stupid comment. "Monday night we were hoping to spot illegal activity, again to inform the sheriff. And Thursday at the sale we actually did come across the same vehicle. We know who they are, Dad. I'd say that's a lot more than any of the other ranchers in this area have done."

She intentionally left out the part about Vera's barn. She and Carli had just explained that to the sheriff before she came home, which meant if he happened to mention it to her father, she'd be standing in front of him again. Why add more fuel to this heaping pile of—well, it wouldn't be nice to say what kind of pile this had become.

Her father was about to sputter out some words, but she beat him to it. This time her voice was a little melancholy.

"Why can't you give me any credit, Dad? I work just as hard as my brothers on this ranch. But you always held Nathan and Travis in higher esteem. I guess you just wanted me to get married and have babies. Is that it?"

She stared at the books again. Darned if she was going to cry. But she had one more thing to get off her chest.

"You always said God had a plan for our lives. Well, wonder if His plan isn't your plan? Did you ever consider He might want me to be a rancher? He designed me with all the right qualities. And He had you teach me everything. Why would He let all that go to waste?"

Angie half-turned and was about to leave when one more sentence came out of her mouth. "If I can't do real ranching at the Rafter O and be a trusted and appreciated part of this family, maybe I should use my skills somewhere else."

With that she turned to leave and no matter how bad she wanted to, she didn't look back and she didn't apologize this time.

No tears, Angie. You can do this.

Chapter Twenty-One

Angie could hardly believe she had exploded at her dad like that. But it felt good. Must've been sort of like what her brother Nathan had felt before he left town to follow his dream. He stood up to his dad. Why couldn't she? Did they not expect it because she was a girl? Hogwash. She marched in a huff to her bedroom and slammed the door behind.

Yanking her socks and dirty clothes off she stepped into the shower and let the water comfort and massage her achy body and exasperated mind. Would her dad ever understand her, think of her as more than his "little girl"? How would he react to her outburst?

She turned the water off, and wrapped her long, blond hair in a towel. Slipping into clothes, Angie emerged from her bathroom to find her mother, Grace Olsen, sitting on her bed.

"Mom, what are you doin'?"

Mrs. Olsen smiled. "I brought you a sandwich." She pointed to Angie's dresser. "I don't think you got to finish your snack downstairs what with all that hollering." Her mother's eyebrows raised some but not in a judgmental way, more like a humorous, loving badge of camaraderie.

"Thanks, Mom."

"So, you want to talk about it?"

Angie felt the volcano still brewing inside. But she didn't want to yell anymore. Especially at her mother.

With a big sigh she said, "What's there to talk about? He thinks I'm still a little girl and doesn't give me any credit for my intelligence or ranching know-how. I'm never gonna get through to him. Not in a million years."

Angie took the towel off her head, sat on her bed near her mom, and began the task of combing through her long, wet hair as she looked in the dresser mirror.

"Now, Angie." Her mother bestowed grace, just like her name, to the whole family and created an atmosphere of love and peace. She was like a gentle sprinkle of sunshiny rain, a mist. "You know your father is traditional. He was raised by very strict parents and grandparents. Gender lines were clear cut. Back then it was almost unheard of for women to herd cows, brand, or do some ranch work. Although many did. For the most part though, females took care of the house. They cooked, raised the children, and filled their homes with love and peace for the whole family. It's really hard for your father to accept a different way."

Angie had to interject. "Then why did he teach me the same things as my brothers learned? Why did he instill in us that everyone helps on the ranch?"

"Because it's true, everyone does pitch in. We're a ranching family and we have a big ranch to manage. There's a lot to do to keep it running."

Angie stayed quiet. She didn't want to explode again but frustration mounted up in her mind after the discussion with her father. His words still made her blood boil.

Her mother continued. "Sweetheart, listen. I don't always understand your father and I'm been married to him for thirty-one years. But I hope you know he loves you. He loves all of us and wants the best for us. He's one of the hardest working men I've ever seen. It might be that he's okay with you helping with all the ranching duties, but he draws the line at your trying to apprehend the rustlers. He worries about you and doesn't want to see you get hurt. And plus, I think his pride was bruised when you disobeyed him. He asked you not to go near the rustlers. And you defied him. Does that make any sense?"

"Yes, except that Nathan got a free pass when he defied Dad and took off for Santa Fe. I think it's because he's male." Angie stood with a hand on her hip.

Grace Olsen rubbed her hands and brushed an invisible crumb from her lap. "That's a hard one, Angie. We miss Nathan terribly. Your dad had dreams all his life of his firstborn son taking over the ranch someday. For Nathan to turn it down was hard to take. But after a while your father realized he couldn't force Nathan to stay. Just like, I think, one day he'll realize that you have your own dreams. It's a new world for your dad. Give him time. Patience. I love you, Angie. You know I'm always praying for you and for him, and for every single member of this family."

"I've never wanted to be anywhere else, Mom. That's why I'm not in college. This ranch is my life. There's nothin' else I'd rather be doin'. I don't think he understands how much the Rafter O means to me."

Angie could feel the volcano inside subsiding, just a bit. Her mother always had that effect on her. When Mrs. Olsen stood and placed her arm around Angie's shoulders, Angie couldn't help but relax and bask in her mother's love. She leaned her head against the older woman and relaxed as tears slid out of her eyes and down her face.

Her mother tightened the grip on her daughter. "It's gonna be okay. After you eat and take a little rest if you need to, why don't we both go talk with your dad? We can't let this sore between the two of you fester into something bigger. God tells us to forgive and respect each other. Do you believe that?"

"Sure, Mom. It's just hard sometimes when the other person is so . . . uh, so rigid." She didn't want to say "pigheaded."

Her mother smiled. "I understand. Remember, God told us we would have trouble in this world but that He overcame it. Do you know what that means?"

How could she forget? The Olsens had always gone to church and the kids all were raised with the Bible stories.

Angie looked at her mom and smiled. "It means God will always be with us. He'll walk through any trouble with us."

"Right. So, you pray and I'll pray that God will soften your father's heart. Let God fight your battles."

It did make sense. "Thanks, Mom. I love you."

"I love you too. Now get a little rest, sweetheart."

When her eyes opened, she wondered if she had slept for most of the afternoon. But checking her phone revealed her power nap had only been about thirty minutes. She stretched her arms and yawned. Seemed like every tension had drained from her body. Her hair still felt a little damp. She rarely used the blow-dryer.

Time to face the music. She really didn't want to look at her father, let alone speak to him again. But she could do this. And, like her mother had advised, better to patch things up instead of letting the prior outburst turn into a range war in their own home.

She found her mother in the kitchen chopping vegetables for dinner. Whenever Angie thought of her mom, this was the prominent image that appeared—in the kitchen. It was comforting some-how. Reminded her of her childhood and she hoped it would always be this way. She couldn't imagine life without her parents in this world.

"C'mon," her mother said and held out an arm to embrace Angie. "Let's go talk to him."

Angie's bravado has shrunk a little but not all the way. She and her mother stepped into the father's study. He was hunkered over his desk, bifocal glasses lowered on his nose, papers cluttered before him. His face still had a red tint to it and his eyes never made contact with them.

"Hon, Angie and I would like to talk to you."

He grumbled, at first inaudibly, and then, "I'm really busy. This ranch ain't gonna run itself."

Angie had heard him say that her whole life. Sometimes she thought she heard it in her sleep.

Grace Olsen gingerly tweaked Angie's shoulder to prod her on, then nodded to her.

Angie stepped forward. She wasn't exactly sure what she would say.

"Dad. I'm sorry. I don't want us to fight."

He stared at the papers and moved a couple of them back and forth. He didn't look at either woman.

"Dad? Did you hear me?"

"I heard you, Angelina. What do you want me to say?" His voice was strong like a bulldozer digging a deep hole.

His wife moved towards his desk. "Hon, Angie just apologized. You both need to forgive and find a way to work this out. Can you do that? For Angie. For yourself. And for God and our family."

He seemed to soften a little. That was a tall order Grace had laid out.

Looking to Angie, he asked, "Will you do it again? Go near those rustlers?"

Angie paced herself and chose her words very carefully. "Carli and I are working with Sheriff Anderson and Special Ranger Derek McKinney. We're trying to protect our ranches. We won't do anything dangerous."

"Will you let me know any new information you find out? As soon as possible. And you'll ask for help from me or your brother Travis, if you need it?"

"Yes, Dad."

Skip Olsen adjusted his glasses and went back to his paperwork.

She wondered if that was it. She half-turned to leave his study.

He called out, his voice softer. "Angie, I love you. I'm sorry."

His wife kissed his forehead.

Angie's heart warmed at the way her mother could always handle her father. If the opportunity came up to trap the rustlers, she wouldn't hesitate. As she walked away, she noticed that her father's face still had a worried expression, his brow coming together in a scowl. Angie frowned too, but her mother was absolutely beaming. A truce had been negotiated. At least for now.

Chapter Twenty-Two

After tossing another set of sheets in the cookhouse washer, Carli loaded wet sheets into the dryer. She had volunteered to help Lola with the chores needed to be done in order to get the bunkhouse ready for the cowpunchers who would be arriving next week. They were expecting a full house of hired dayworkers as well as a few fence line neighbors who wanted to pitch in. Even though this would be Carli's first roundup at the Wild Cow, it didn't take her long to realize how important the week was. Branding week was a social event, too. A time to see friends, work together, eat together, and catch up on everyone's news.

"Carli, how's it goin'?" Lola Wallace called from the doorway of the cookhouse laundry room.

"Good. I've already got a couple sets washed and folded and the last load is in the dryer." She pushed the door shut and turned the knob. "I'm ready to make up some beds if you want to."

A buzzing bundle of energy at least one foot shorter than Carli, Lola was the grease that kept the wheels running around headquarters. Not only did she keep everybody and everything in forward motion, she was one of the best cooks Carli had ever known. Her homemade fried sopapillas, an art she had learned from her Mexican grandmother, were unbelievable. Carli never imagined that flour, water, and a dash of salt could taste so good.

Lola opened the storage closet. "After we finish the laundry, we can make a grocery list and head to town. I've already started one. Looks like we're good on detergent, but we do need dryer sheets. And while we're out, let's pick up the meds at the vet clinic, too."

"Sounds good. Do you decide the menu ahead of time?"

"Yes, especially the desserts. I can make some of them this weekend before the boys get here Sunday night."

Lola meant a lot of things to Carli and the Wild Cow Ranch—chief cook, her foreman Buck's wife, ranch peacekeeper, yoga teacher, Bible study leader for a growing group of ladies, and helper with Carli's riding school for the at-risk kids, which she planned to start up again. But Lola was more than all of that. She was always there for Carli. During the barn fire that claimed one horse and nearly killed Lank and Buck. When Carli was lost in a winter snowstorm, Lola had prayed and welcomed her home after she was rescued. Along with Buck, they had explained to Carli how much God loved her, which changed Carli's life forever. Lola was almost like the mother she never had. She could tell her anything.

Carli had considered talking to Lola about Lank. Was it appropriate for her to be dating the ranch hand? Probably not. If things went bad between them, she'd have to fire him. And even more worrisome should their relationship get serious, was he the right man for her? The one to take as her husband? Or would that be a big mistake? They weren't that far along yet, hadn't even discussed any kind of future. But she felt in her gut that the topic was on his mind. She saw how he looked at her and she definitely recognized what that look did to her insides.

Lola interrupted her thoughts. "Let's go make up a couple beds."

"Sure."

On one end of the upstairs were four extra bedrooms that shared one bath and opened onto a balcony which looked over into the dining area. Lola and Buck's small apartment took up the other end of the top floor with a master bedroom, large bath, and sitting area. The commercial kitchen, a second bathroom, and pool table room were downstairs located under the second floor.

The dining hall stretched on the other side of the building with twenty-foot ceilings. Oversized windmill fans circulated the air, and in between were reproduction lantern chandeliers. The ceiling tiles were also reproduction, stamped tin in silver, which reflected the light casting a bright glow over the rows of tables and chairs.

In the first bedroom, decorated with Navajo red blankets and rough-hewn log headboards, Carli and Lola unfolded sheets and helped each other stretch them onto beds.

"Something on your mind? You seem to be thinking mighty hard and it's not about bed sheets." Lola laughed.

Carli paused before she answered. In some ways it didn't seem right to talk about her personal life with her employee. "How did you know Buck was the one?"

"Gosh, Carli, that's complicated. It would be easy to say it was love at first sight as some people might tell you. But for me it wasn't. It would be easy to say 'I just knew' or that I felt a special something in my heart. All those things are almost true. Well, maybe not the 'love at first sight' thing." She laughed. "He was covered with dirt, grease, and sweat as he was working on a tractor."

"So how did you finally know?"

Lola bent down to tuck the sheet under the mattress, tight like a drill sergeant.

"Well, it was a process. We spent time together and got to know one another. People around here knew him and his family and said he wasn't a criminal or anything." She chuckled. "It does help to know someone's background and where they came from. Oh, and there was The List."

"List? What do you mean?"

"Well, I had been a Christian before Buck came

to faith. I don't exactly remember where I first heard about it, but different mentors and friends of mine at church told me to pray and ask God for specific qualities in a husband. I think I came up with something like thirty."

"Thirty!" Carli gasped. "That's a tall order for any guy to meet."

"I carried that list in my wallet. And you know what? Buck ended up fulfilling every single quality I wanted in a husband. And then some."

"You're kidding. What did you put on the list?"

"Oh, things like he must be a man of God, which he became early in our relationship. Have a sense of humor. Faithful. Love me unconditionally." Lola counted off the traits with her fingers. "I can't remember them all. Hard worker and not a loafer, helps others, kindness, honesty. Lots of things. And, oh yes, be attractive, at least to me." They both grinned.

Carli pondered for a few seconds, then said, "I guess what we want isn't always what God wants for us. Say you think you're falling for a Georgia horseman but God has somebody entirely different in mind for you."

"Sounds like you're speaking from experience. I firmly believe God wants to give us the desires of our hearts, Carli. I believe He would have changed me so that I would accept and embrace His plan. And love the man."

"Yeah, I guess. You know that Lank and I are officially dating, although we haven't gone out anywhere. We're too busy. There was a time when I thought he was the most annoying guy ever. But we've been through a lot together—the fire, the snowstorm. And just working the Wild Cow. The guy is growing on me." Carli didn't add that she had spilled her soul when Lank was laid up in the hospital after his rodeo accident. At the time, she had meant it with all her heart, but now in the light of day it seemed so foolish to rush this.

"I've noticed." Lola grinned. "It makes me really happy for you both. Lank needs someone. I've been worried about him since his mother died. He seems to be a bit lost and lonely. I hope you know that Buck and I have been praying for you and your decisions and we will continue to pray. So, what's troubling you?"

"Lank seems so certain about things. It's not really anything he's said, just a feeling I get when we're together. He is moving too fast for me."

At that Lola took on the persona of a mama bear ready to fight for Carli's reputation and protect her. "No means no, Carli. I hope you'll love with all your heart but make decisions with your head. You both have to set boundaries."

Carli was shocked that Lola might think their relationship had moved to the physical level. "We're not sleeping together if that's what you're thinking. But the way he talks, I think he's planning a future for us."

"What do you want, Carli? Can you see a future with Lank? Would he make a good husband?"

"Sometimes I really can. We're just so comfortable together. We fit. Almost like we were made for each other. The things we talk about, the way we love the land, the animals. He's the first thing I think about in the morning and the last person on my mind at night. Is that true love?"

"That's how God intended life partners to be, I think."

"Then there are times when he's with Colton and they both act like teenage boys. Making stupid remarks. It reminds me of when I first came to the Wild Cow. Lank seemed so full of himself then."

Lola said, "When he's with Colton he reverts back to grade school, I think. They've been friends that long. Inside every grown man is a little boy waiting to burst out. They never grow up. You just gotta love them as is."

Carli could hardly believe how their conversation made the work go by so quickly. To her surprise they had finished washing and changing all the sheets. Carli followed Lola downstairs where they folded towels.

"Men are complicated, Carli. Just like women are. It's amazing to me that God created two really different beings and melded them together in such a beautiful way. Not just physically. But in a caring, complementary way. We're like two halves meant to be one."

"I don't know if I'll ever understand men." Carli sighed, then added, "Another thing I wonder about is if I decide to marry, how can I be sure that it's forever? And how would I know that my real soul-mate isn't out there, around the corner? If I decide on one guy, I might miss out on someone even better, someone truly meant for me." As usual, Carli created more problems in her own mind as compared with reality. It was a self-destructive habit that seemed impossible for her to break.

"You can't be looking for a guarantee. There's no such thing in this life." Lola's voice was gentle, compassionate. "Don't be looking for perfection—a perfect life, a perfect man. If you really pray, God will give you His supernatural peace about your decision. You'll know for certain if Lank is the man you can't live without, the one you want to be with forever. Now, let's grab a sandwich in the kitchen and go over our grocery list. We can talk more if you want on the way. We won't be able to find everything in Dixon."

Lola handed Carli the list.

"You're all about making lists, aren't you?"

"I don't want to forget anything. We feed about thirty to forty cowboys before the week's work is done. Read me the list."

Carli read out loud as Lola checked the cabinets and fridge.

"I'll make some desserts," Lola said. "Cobbler, chocolate cake, pies. Oh, let's get some ice cream."

"This is a ton, Lola. Will it all fit in my truck?"

"Let's take Buck's. It's bigger."

Feeling confident they were ready to head to Amarillo. Carli and Lola hopped in Buck's truck,

Carli at the wheel. "You don't mind driving, do you?" Lola asked. "I want to doublecheck and make out a menu."

"No worries. I like driving Buck's truck."

They waved out the windows at the guys as they passed the corral Lank and Buck were working in, hammering fence boards.

"I guess it's kind of like a grocery list."

"What is?" Carli asked.

"The List. For husbands." Lola replied with a smile.

"Oh, that. How so?"

"Well, you put in your requests to God. Include everything you think would make you happy, everything that's important to you. Like a grocery list. You need the foundation—meat, potatoes, veggies. But you also want the dessert. The sugar. Or, if you're from Georgia, I guess it's 'Shugah'. Don't forget the honey, Honey." Lola gave Carli a mischievous grin, tilt of her head, and raised eyebrow.

"You are something else, Mrs. Wallace. Better behave yourself or I might have to tattle on you."

"Who would you tattle to? Buck? He would probably love my interpretation of this Bible teaching."

The two of them laughed like young girls as the warm breeze filled the truck and their hair flew freely. It was at times like this that Carli really felt like she belonged with Lola and Buck at the Wild Cow Ranch. She sometimes imagined what her life might have been if she had stayed in Georgia and had never met them. The picture in her mind didn't look as great as her reality was now.

Carli hit the button to close the windows as they got off the gravel road and onto the asphalt.

Lola's phone buzzed. "Buck is reminding me to stop at the vet's office for the black leg vaccine. We'll do that before getting all the groceries. That way, when we're loaded up, we can just hit the road."

"Sounds good to me. Shugah." Carli gave Lola her best Georgia Southern drawl. Maybe one day she'd figure out how to add a Texas twang too.

Chapter Twenty-Three

Smoke billowed from the pile of kindling as Buck added more twigs to the middle of the stone circle. Carli watched with interest and then had to walk to the other side as the wind shifted. Her eyes watered.

"Patience is the key," he said. "You have to let the fire breathe before you start piling on more fuel."

Flames popped up through the smaller pieces and Buck slowly added more twigs, and then larger branches until the flame burned bright and strong. He balanced a metal grate on the ring of rocks.

"Fire's almost ready. Where are the burgers?" he called out.

From across the grass in the shade of the cookhouse porch, Lola raised an arm to signal that she heard and continued to salt and pepper a huge platter of hamburger patties.

Carli turned her attention to a bright red rig, pickup truck and livestock trailer to match, as it rolled past her and pulled to a stop behind the saddle house. She could hardly contain her excitement. Spring roundup started in the morning. This would be her first branding at the Wild Cow Ranch. She'd be able to see every cow and every new calf in the Wild Cow Ranch herd. Her ranch, her herd. It was almost mind-boggling when she thought of where she had come from in Georgia, alone and struggling to make ends meet.

Another rig pulled in, and then another. Lank met the cowboys at the corral. He pointed and led them to their pen assignments where each man's mounts would live for the week. Gates were closed and some secured with extra rope, and hay feeders and water tubs were provided for each section. The human dayworkers would sleep in the top floor of the cookhouse. Lank had a spare bedroom in his house, and Carli had cleaned up her spare bedroom in case someone needed to stay there. By morning all beds would be filled. The remainder of the crew lived nearby and would drive in every day.

Carli's eyes lingered on her ranch hand for longer than was probably proper as ranch owner, but he just looked so Texan and so handsome she couldn't help herself. Her heart fluttered, darn that cowboy. He wore a bright red paisley pearl snap, his jeans tucked into black boots that went to his knees. The silver engraved belt buckle he had won for bronc riding glinted in the sun.

The ranch also relied on several local cowboys and cowgirls. The fence line neighbors were invited to ride, and even if they weren't mounting up at sunrise in the morning, they would join the crew for hamburgers tonight.

Carli walked over to Lola. "Are you ready for vegetables?"

"Sure. You can start setting up the serving line. Buck will toss these on the fire as soon as everybody gets unloaded. They'll cook fast."

"I can do that." Carli couldn't help but notice the excitement fluttering in everyone's eyes and the wide smiles on their faces. Buck and Lola were running around like jumping beans.

In the walk-in fridge Carli balanced a platter of lettuce and sliced tomatoes as she maneuvered it out the door to put on the long table. She had just set it down when she heard the jingle of spurs seconds before two arms went around her middle. She turned her head just as a kiss landed on her cheek. He had shaved his beard but left a triangle of a goatee under his lower lip. It scratched her face.

"Welcome to your first roundup, boss lady." Lank gave her waist another squeeze.

"Is this appropriate in front of the dayworking crew?" She laughed.

"Sure is. I'm making us official. No more gossip. They're seeing with their own eyes that this thing between us is for certain. I'm dating the owner of the Wild Cow Ranch and she's crazy about me. See ya later."

As fast as he was there, he was gone again. She instantly missed the warmth of his arms and he had left her with a wide grin that matched the other faces.

An SUV parked at the hitching post in front of the cookhouse. Carli glanced in that direction and was delighted to see Belinda and Russell.

"Surprise." Belinda set a platter of cookies on the serving table. "I usually help Lola during roundup and Russell gets to cowboy. It's become our annual vacation. Hard work but it gets us away from the coffee shop for something different."

"You didn't tell me." Carli hugged her friend and then waved at Russell as he stood next to Buck at the fire.

"I thought about it often enough, but then we're never sure if the timing is right or if I can get someone to work for me. But everything fell into place. I am so thrilled to be a part of your first branding. This is exciting." Belinda had become one of Carli's closest friends.

On the inside Carli was so happy to see how this week was shaping up, but she tried to maintain a calm on the outside. She didn't want others to think of her as a giddy girl. Instead, she wanted them to see her as capable and worthy of the legacy her grandparents had left.

Carli smiled, shook many hands, and forgot to eat. After supper was over, when she walked into the kitchen the dishes were already done. Everyone else had turned in, but Lola was busy cracking eggs for the next morning. Carli found a lid for the bowl which was placed in the fridge. She then wandered over to her house too excited to sleep. Lying on her back she stared at the ceiling waiting for the day to break on the first branding as owner of the Wild Cow Ranch.

Chapter Twenty-Four

In the pre-dawn dark guided by the single bulb that shone over the corral, Carli made her way across ranch headquarters. The saddle house was hopping with cowboys grabbing their tack. She could feel the buzz of excitement in the air from both horses and riders. Branding week was here.

As she saddled Beau, Lank appeared at her side to give her a quick peck on the cheek. His eyes were bright, a silly grin on his face.

"Morning," she said, taking in his manly scent of soap and dust drifting from his old cowboy hat. He gave her a tight squeeze before rushing over to open the gate for a puncher carrying his blanket and saddle.

Conversation was minimal as everyone concentrated on the business at hand. Carli noticed that Texas cowboys didn't spend much time fawning over their mounts. Not anything like she did with Beau. She got close to his ear and whispered encouragement, giving his muscled neck more than one pat.

To the dayworking cowboys, their horse was a tool needed to get a job done. Just like ropes, saddles, boots, and spurs, the working ranch horse was an integral part of the lifestyle. However, despite their tough exterior, she had seen Lank or Buck reach down to scratch behind an ear or pat a rump. She figured they had a soft spot for their favorites whether they wanted to admit it or not. She knew for a fact the sense of loss Lank had felt when his horse Blackie died in the barn fire, but he never talked about it.

After saddles were secured and breakfasts of hay distributed, the crew wandered in small groups towards the cookhouse. Lank ran up to Carli and rested an arm around her shoulders. She smiled to herself thinking how it hadn't been that long ago when she had been mortified to even consider dating an employee. Now it felt right, his arm and his attention, despite her doubts. Maybe she should just let things happen as they may. But that was totally outside her nature. She seemed compelled to worry and contemplate and run the issues over and over in her mind. Sometimes prayers eased her anxieties, but not always. She was definitely a work in progress.

"Mornin'!" Lola called out as they entered the dining hall. A blinding light made Carli blink. She couldn't help but focus on the sound of her spurs with each step across the hardwood floor. She loved that sound. It wasn't that long ago that her world had revolved around show barns and getting her clients ready for their own competitions. She had never imagined that one day she would be involved in a spring roundup on a Texas cattle ranch.

Carli followed Lank to the coffee urn. He filled a cup and handed it to her. She smiled at Lola just before taking a sip.

"Are you ready for this?" Lola asked. "Your first branding on the Wild Cow. Your grandparents would be so proud. I made blueberry pancakes this morning to celebrate."

"In that case I feel obligated to eat two," Carli said.

Buck put an arm around her shoulder. "We're glad to have you here this year. Welcome home, Little Jean."

Carli's heart swelled at his comment. He had used the term of endearment right after they had met because he said she looked so much like her grandmother Jean.

Carli turned just as Angie Olsen walked up and bumped her with a hip. "'Scuse me, ma'am. You're blockin' the coffee."

"Hey neighbor. Glad you're here." Carli gave her a bright smile.

Travis Olsen wandered in behind his sister and slumped into a chair at one of the tables with a fixed, blank stare on his face.

"Can I get you some coffee?" Carli laid a hand on his shoulder.

"He doesn't do coffee." Angie rolled her eyes.

"I never imagined there'd be a time when Travis

Olsen was quiet." Carli sat down at the table across from him.

"He doesn't do mornin's either." Angie walked to the table.

"Ladies! Are you ready to ride?" Colton slung an arm around Angie and then grimaced when she slid out from under him and sat down.

The room buzzed with energy, low talking as the men sipped coffee and swapped horse stories. Carli looked around the room and realized how fortunate they were to have such a skilled workforce. Some were locals, while others would stay the week sleeping in the bunkhouse.

"It's ready," Lola called out as she carried a pan with several stacks of golden-brown pancakes. The aroma as she walked past made Carli's stomach grumble.

Buck moved to the front of the room. "Let's pray." With all heads bowed, prayers were offered up for a safe week, for both man and beast, and thanks with grateful hearts for a life of caring for His livestock and land. "Bless the hands that prepared it." Buck ended the prayer. "It's tradition that the owner goes through the chow line first."

"Go on, Carli," Lola encouraged.

She felt awkward getting her plate first with a room full of punchers who'd be doing most of the hard work, but she didn't argue with Buck. An array of fluffy eggs, bacon, and a short stack of blueberry pancakes was probably more than she'd eat but it all looked so good. She couldn't help but try everything.

By the time Carli got back to the table, Colton had Travis arguing about the best rope brands. She scanned the room but didn't see Lank. With the slam of the door, she found herself looking up and realized she'd been thinking about Nathan Olsen, Angie's older brother. He had been a true friend when she first moved here. She shoveled in food and passed on a second cup of coffee when Lola offered because she wasn't sure about bathroom breaks on the trail in the middle of nowhere with cowboys all around. Better be safe than sorry.

Angie leaned closer. "Ya got that right. Only one cup of coffee. No trees, no bushes, just miles and miles of grass."

With plates scraped into the trash and stacked on the cart, and silverware in the soapy wreck pan, they all began to file back out into the darkness.

At the corral, Carli led Beau to the line of live-stock trailers. Buck nodded at her and pointed to his ranch truck. She smooched to urge Beau to step up in the trailer and just as she started to step up in behind him, Lank tugged on her arm. "Don't go in the trailer. It's too dangerous with this many horses that don't know each other. Stick your reins through the slats and then walk along the ground pulling the reins and tying them. That way you'll be out of the way and I'll put my horse in right after yours, and so forth. It takes up too much time if we have to wait for each person to come back out of the trailer. Plus, it spooks the horses."

With horses and men loaded, Carli squeezed in the double cab between Lank and Colton. A few guys jumped into the back of the truck and they were off, Buck's headlights leading the way out of the headquarters.

It took four vehicles and livestock trailers to carry the crew. They had about eleven miles to drive to the back pasture. Carli thought about her great-grandpa and how he and his crew probably rode their horses first to get to the spot where the work began. Man and mount must have been hardy back then.

At the cattle guard that led into Crazy Vera's place, Buck turned into the pasture and parked. Everyone unloaded and mounted their horses, forming a circle around Buck.

"What are we doing?" Carli whispered to Lank.

"Waiting on instruction."

The sky was full of light and before Buck spoke, the sun finally made an appearance on the horizon blasting its arrival with deep orange reflected on a few clouds and then fading into a bright blue sky.

Buck looked around the group until everyone had gathered close, and then pointed to his right. "Lank, you take a group with you that way. Travis and the Olsen bunch can go east. Carli, you're with me, up the middle."

"What does that mean?" she asked but Lank had already loped away in the center of a clump of riders.

"That means, boss, that we're riding up the middle," Buck explained. "Lank will drop off a man along this back-fence line and space them out, waiting until everyone is in place. The same thing will happen on the other side. You keep your eye on me. I'll be on one side of you and, that looks like Travis, he'll be on the other side of you. We move slowly forward pushing the herd as we go. Don't lose sight of Travis or me, and don't cross over behind or in front. Stay in your lane. And don't get ahead either."

"Got it," said Carli as she urged Beau forward.

"We'll drive everything to the windmill, let them settle, and then up the hill to the working pens. Welcome to your first roundup on the Wild Cow, boss."

Carli surveyed the clumps of yucca, sage, and green buffalo grass that stretched out before her. Meadowlarks called to each other. In only a few seconds, the colors of the sunrise had changed again fading from brilliant orange to golden. The morning took her breath away. What total strangers had given her could never be repaid. Her grandparents Jean and Ward had left to a granddaughter they never knew a piece of their world. A family legacy that Carli might never fully understand but that didn't mean she couldn't work as hard as they had to create this empire.

Lank's face passed through her mind. She couldn't help but worry what his role might be, if this truly was the path God had set down for her. How did Lank fit in? If she were honest with herself, she just didn't have the energy it took for a relationship right now. She was still overwhelmed with the inheritance of the ranch and everything that might entail. One thing was for certain—she would do everything in her power to continue the Jameson family work.

Chapter Twenty-Five

Carli and Beau made slow progress around clumps of spiky yucca and sagebrush. The pasture of the Wild Cow Ranch stretched out in front of her like a velvet carpet, in more shades of green than she ever knew existed. Tufts of buffalo grass, blue stem, side oats, and many other varieties she couldn't name although she'd been reading up on plants of the Texas Panhandle and trying to identify them. Short grass country is what the old timers used to call it.

Now there was little water, with deeply gouged creek beds that stayed dry most of the year except for when the rainy season brought the occasional torrents of water. From what she'd heard, rainy seasons were few and far between. On the flatter plains, wide shallow playa lakes sometimes held water. These indentions had been made even deeper by the buffalo that once wallowed in the mud centuries before. Spinning windmills dotted the unbroken horizon line. She scanned the area in both directions. There wasn't a cow to be seen.

On her far right, she saw Buck and to her far left was Travis Olsen. Riders fanned out across the back of this pasture which covered four sections and would drive the herd to a common place. In this case Buck had said it was the water tank and windmill on the west side of the pasture.

She steered Beau down into a valley.

Cows are sometimes smarter than humans give them credit for. The ever vigilant, protective momma cows had probably seen horseback riders on the far hill and now the herd was staying ahead of them. Buck had told Carli to check the dry creek beds where cows sometimes hid among the wild sand creek plum bushes. She rode Beau into the sandy bottom but made sure she kept traveling in the same direction. She didn't want to get turned around. It was hard to keep her bearings in the middle of nowhere without trees, major landmarks, or buildings as a guide. The grass all looked the same to her for miles and miles.

The creek bed narrowed, rising up above her head on both sides. The water had etched a sandy trail that wove around an outcropping of rocks and tightly bunched plum bushes. They came out on the other side and she jogged Beau to the top of a point which gave her a view of the wide sloping grassy plains that stretched in all directions. On one side, she noticed Buck pushing four cows and their calves towards her. She loped over to help, easing Beau in the back of the little bunch.

The momma cows continued a non-ceasing bawl as they ambled along. From the distance, behind a small rise, the sound of the herd bellowed as they got closer. A constant symphony of moans and moos that drowned out the meadowlarks. She could now see the windmill in the distance where they would all meet up, as each cowboy pushed the herd together, bringing them in from all corners of the pasture.

Suddenly, one of the momma cows broke and ran right between her and Buck. He pulled off and went after her while Carli worked to keep the bunch together and moving towards the windmill. It wasn't easy. She worked back and forth behind them. Beau didn't have the same instincts as a cowy ranch horse, but he was learning. He knew what he needed to do, but there seemed to be a split-second hesitation. Cows weren't really his life. Carli had to chuckle. This was all new to her too.

"You're doing fine, boy." She reached down and patted him on the neck.

At that moment a hefty bull calf spun and made a dash for the opposite direction. Carli steered Beau to go after him and cut him off before he hit the wide-open pasture. The horse got ahead of the calf that calmed as if giving up, then trotted back to his momma and the herd. Carli squeezed Beau with her legs to keep up.

Suddenly he went to his knees causing her to pitch forward, the saddle horn punching her in the belly. The air left her lungs with a low grunt. She squeezed her legs tight to stay in the saddle. Beau quickly recovered but favored his front leg, so Carli hopped out of the saddle. Bending over to catch her breath, her hands trembled.

Beau never stumbled in the past. She couldn't imagine what had happened. As she bent down to examine his leg, she noticed the ground dotted with soft mounds of freshly dug dirt. One mound had a print where Beau had stepped.

Buck reined up next to her. "Everything okay?"

"Beau nearly fell."

"Gopher holes. Looks like he hit this one square and it caved in. Can you still ride?"

"He's favoring it, but not too bad. Maybe we can make it to the working pens."

"You take it slow and easy and then tie him to the fence. He can rest while we work the cattle."

Carli remounted and kept Beau moving slow and easy at the back of the bunch. As she surveyed how the cowboys worked together to gather the herd, she realized that the entire year culminated in this moment. This is why her ranch produced. Hauling hay and running the feed truck during those bitter cold winter days and counting your blessings at the first sign of spring rains. She was a caretaker of this land, and, through that means, it provided everything they needed.

The outfit pushed the cows up a hill towards the pens and squeezed them through a gate. The noise was deafening as mommas called to their babies and calves answered. The flies were intense this year, as Buck explained, due to the wet spring they'd enjoyed.

Crowded into a pen together the crew began stripping the mother cows from their calves. Carli tied Beau to the top rail, dismounted, and climbed up on the fence to watch.

One man on horseback worked the gate as the others pushed small groups of pairs towards him. His horse was quick. Carli was amazed at its instinct to let the big cows pass and then shuffle to stop the calves which were turned into another pen.

After the bunch was sorted, the real work began. In the middle of the pen a propane tank and steel rack heated the branding irons. Two men on horseback rode into the bunch of calves, twirling a rope overhead. They roped hind feet and dragged the calf as close to the branding fire as possible, where Lank and Travis waited. One tugged on the rope and one pushed the calf to his side, where they held him. Buck motioned to Carli. She jumped from the fence and hurried over.

"You should have the honors," he said. "The first brand at your first branding."

She slipped her working gloves from under her belt and tugged them on, then took the branding iron from Buck. It glowed red hot. She couldn't help but think about the ranch people who had come before. Cattle had been sporting this mark on their left hip for generations. And now she was here. Alone. The last generation to carry on the

Wild Cow legacy. It was a bittersweet moment.

Angie walked over with an injection needle and gave shots against black leg, a horrible, infectious disease caused by bacterial spores. Another cowboy clipped in the ear tag.

"Okay Carli," Buck said. "Go ahead. Make your mark. I'll help you."

Buck wrapped his gloved hands around hers and guided the iron to the spot high on the hip. The smoke of burning hair filled her nose, but it was done in a second leaving a tall and narrow letter "W".

"That's how you do it," Buck said. "That brand is called a long W. That's one down and 699 more to go."

The others cheered and whistled. The riders spun their mounts around, recoiled their ropes, and rode back into the huddled bunch of calves.

Carli's heart pounded in her chest. It all seemed so surreal, like a dream. It hadn't been that long ago that this kind of life would have never crossed her mind.

Lank draped an arm around her shoulders. "Good job, babe." He kissed her ear, quick and sweet which made a chill zap down her jaw. "Your grandparents would be proud."

Yes, she believed they would.

Chapter Twenty-Six

Lank led his horse Phoenix through the gate and into the third morning of branding at the Wild Cow Ranch. Cowboys and horses milled about everywhere in between the parked pickup trucks and trailers. He chose one of four livestock trailers that stood ready with back gates swung wide open. It would be another day of the same as the previous two. Bawling cows, stubborn horses, Texas wind, and the smell of burning hair. He loved every minute of it.

Just as Lank stepped up in the trailer his phone buzzed. He had forgotten to silence it, which resulted in the young horse balking and coming back out of the trailer with a jerk of his head.

"Quit that," Lank muttered. He'd have to answer his phone later. He needed to get his horse settled quick since there was a line of cowboys waiting.

With Phoenix calmed down and loaded, Lank dug his phone out of his pocket and glanced at the text. Kelly, his sister. Call me, it read.

Carli emerged from the cookhouse, her boots crunching on the gravel as she walked towards him.

"Mornin'." She smiled.

He lingered on that smile a moment before he answered, allowing the look that she sent his way to embrace him like warm sunshine on his skin. He broke through her spell and asked, "How's Beau doing?"

"I checked him earlier and he's still favoring that leg. I probably shouldn't ride him."

Lank held up one finger. "Hold on. I need to call my sister."

His phone buzzed again. He'd gotten a few messages from her last night but by the time he had filled water troughs in all the pens, he'd forgotten to call her back. Truth be known, as much as he loved his sister, and as much as they'd been a team visiting their mother in the hospital before she passed, sometimes Lank felt he needed to focus on other things. It was too painful to think about his mom. And sometimes talking with Kelly only reminded him of those heartbreaking memories.

But he couldn't ignore his sis. So, he pressed her number and put the call on speaker.

"You know this is branding week," he said first thing.

"Good morning, Kelly," Carli leaned closer to his phone.

"Hey, Carli. I know y'all are busy this week. Sorry, Lank. But this is urgent. That's why I called last night."

"What d'ya need?" He could hear something in her voice, hesitation, maybe even near tears.

"Can I leave the boys with you? The bosses want Matt in Houston this afternoon and I thought I'd ride with him. You know I'd never ask if it weren't important. It would really mean a lot to me."

"I'm working, Kelly. I can't babysit. Not today. Not this week." Lank pushed his aggravation aside. Horses were almost loaded. He needed to get in the pickup truck. They'd be pulling out soon.

"It's just for a few hours. Matt's mother will pick them up this afternoon, but she has a doctor's appointment earlier."

Carli placed her hand on Lank's arm. "I'll watch the boys."

"Oh, Carli. I can't thank you enough. We're almost there." Kelly ended the call before Lank could respond.

He looked at Carli like she'd grown another head. "Are you sure?"

"It's fine. I'm stuck here without a horse. Please don't make me wash dishes another day. Besides I'll put the boys to work. I could have used their help yesterday. We've got a dining hall to mop. Did you notice that floor this morning? Trash to haul. I'll give them jobs until their grandmother gets here."

"Tomorrow we could saddle another ranch horse for you if Beau is still out of commission. But are you sure you can handle my nephews?"

"Of course. They're just little boys. What could go wrong?"

Kelly was older by a couple of years, but Lank always felt like her protector. Even though each had gotten busy with their own lives, especially now that she was married with kids, he felt a responsibility towards her. With both of their parents gone, she was the only family he had.

An SUV stopped at the cookhouse and the door opened. Lank's nephews were little dynamos and sprang out of Kelly's car at full speed. Racing to grip their uncle's legs, they nearly knocked him down.

"Whoa, little dudes. Take it easy."

Kelly followed them and hugged Lank, a little too much he thought, then hurriedly looked away and headed towards her vehicle, not before instructing the boys to mind their uncle. She hugged Carli too.

"This may mean a work promotion for Matt," Kelly said as she nodded towards the car just as the driver's side door opened and her husband stepped out. "I really want to go with him. We owe you both. Thanks so much," she said with tears in her eyes.

"Hey, man." Matt Reynolds, Kelly's husband, walked towards Lank with his hand outstretched. "We really appreciate this."

Lank shook it. "Y'all have a safe trip." Lank had come to really admire his brother-in-law, realizing how smart he was. As a computer programmer, he had moved up in the company fast and it was no surprise that he might be looking at another promotion. He grew up in inner city Houston, a big city boy through and through, and how he and

Kelly had crossed paths was still unexplainable, but the minute they met they were inseparable. Kelly left the little town of Dixon and moved to the bigger city of Amarillo for Matt, although he would have probably lived wherever she was. The fact that he was black had never been a factor for the Torres family. Lank's mother's side was made up of home-grown Texas Panhandle rednecks and his father's family was from Mexico City, so mixing skin color and tradition never was an issue. Family was family as far as Lank was concerned and he admired his brother-in-law's ambition greatly, something he felt he lacked, content to do what he was doing as a cow puncher.

"Can we ride a horse?" asked Zane, the youngest.

Lank glanced at the buzz of activity. There were only a few horses left to load. He watched Carli and his nephews.

Carli pushed him towards the truck that pulled the trailer with his horse. The passenger door stood open. "Go," she urged.

With a last wave to his brother-in-law and sister, Lank jumped in the waiting truck and thanked his lucky stars for Carli. When it came to his older sister, he could never say no. Whatever she wanted of him, he always complied. But of all days to ask him to babysit. That just beat all. She knew how important this week was to the operation of the ranch. Good grief. And then he remembered how emotional she'd seemed. Whatever was going on with his sister would have to wait.

He chuckled. Carli and his nephews. Wish he

could stick around to watch that. He didn't know if she even liked kids since they'd never talked about it. Why had they never talked about it?

He knew she'd been hurt before by romance and had trust issues. That was understandable after hearing about her childhood—a mother who had abandoned her, no birth father in the picture, raised by foster parents, a Georgia boyfriend who cheated on her. Who could blame her? Maybe she didn't even want to have children. He didn't know if he could go through life without starting his own family.

Lank knew Carli was the girl he wanted to spend the rest of his life with. He'd known it the minute he saw her when the lawyers had brought her to the Wild Cow right after the hearing where the judge had ruled her to be the only surviving heir. And he had always wanted to be a dad, but if Carli didn't want kids would that be a problem between them? He knew he was getting ahead of himself. They were in the beginning stages of officially dating and he sure didn't want to chase her away.

Up ahead, the line of vehicles strung out along the winding pasture road. As they topped a hill, the sun burst through the haze of an unbroken horizon, the sky blending from a bright blue to shades of golden yellow. A few low hanging, dark clouds turned purple. Sunrise was Lank's favorite part of the day. The colors were so bright and bold, and all the racket from the day before was wiped away. He liked the promise and possibilities of starting over each day.

The vehicles pulled into the grass and parked where the punchers unloaded their mounts, saddled up, and encircled Buck as they waited for instruction. Groups were formed and they rode off in their assigned directions. As Lank watched the sky brighten with more sun, he took in the scene around him. The Wild Cow Ranch had been his home for almost all of his life. The Jameson family heir hadn't been anything like he'd expected. He'd gotten lost in her eyes the first time they'd met and he couldn't see past her since.

Would she ever settle for a broke cow puncher who wanted to spend his days in the saddle and his nights lying beside her? The honest truth was that he had no ambition. He would never amount to much, or so he'd been told more than once in his life. It was somewhat true, and this moment in time was where he wanted to stay forever. This was it for him. Riding, roping, and punchin' cows was all he ever wanted to do from the first moment he stepped foot on the Wild Cow Ranch at the age of sixteen. It was supposed to be a part-time job after school, but the lifestyle got under his skin and never let him go.

But he did have his own dreams. Maybe taking on more responsibility around the ranch. Starting his own family. Watching kids grow and teaching them all the things he knew about cows and horses. To have a new generation to pass down the knowledge to was important to him.

The question now was would he have Carli at his side or would he spend his life alone?

Chapter Twenty-Seven

Carli waved at Lank as the pickup drove away and couldn't help but feel a pang of depression as she watched them pass. She wanted to be on Beau in the middle of the pasture too. A light fog of dust from the motorcade of trucks and livestock trailers sifted over their heads. She then noticed the forlorn looks on both of the nephews' faces. They were all stuck with each other until the boys' grandmother got there.

"Well, what are we gonna do with ourselves today, fellas?"

Bright eyes turned to look at her and wide grins covered their sad expressions. "Ride! Ride horses!"

"Can we please, Miss Carli?" This from the youngest Zane. How could she deny that face?

"All right, cowpokes. Great idea. How about we get two of the riding school horses? I need to first tell Lola where we're gonna be. You just got me out of washing breakfast dishes, guys. Thank you."

She held up her hands for a high five. Only Zane

responded, with Zach following behind as they walked into the cookhouse. Carli couldn't help but notice they had the same walk as their Uncle Lank, kind of a swagger.

"We've got visitors," she said to Lola.

"Hey boys. I haven't seen you in a while and I probably need a hug." Lola bent down. "Have you eaten this morning?"

After hugs all around, wide eyes and shakes of their head, she had them lined up at the bar with a breakfast burrito and glasses of milk in front of each. In between bites, Lola kept up a steady stream of conversation asking them their favorite subject in school, their plans for the summer, and if they had girlfriends. The last question was answered with a resounding "no" and "yuck" from Zane.

Carli ended up washing a few dishes after all, drying plates, and restacking them on the serving bar. She wiped the tables down and before she finished, both boys were standing next to her.

"Let's go, if you're done then." She smiled as she realized how much they resembled Lank.

They followed her into the back trap where the riding school horses were being kept out of the way for the week. She called and they all came to her. With bridles in hand, she picked out two of the calmest horses they had — Sally and Mouse.

The older boy puffed up a little, his voice sounding as serious and deep as he could make it. "I can saddle my own horse. Uncle Lank showed me."

"That would be a big help," Carli said. "Like real

cowboys."

The little one was all grins and blushes. "We are real cowboys!" Zane spoke up. "We've rode before."

"Okay, okay, Mister Smart Britches. Let's get you dudes in the saddle."

"We're not dudes." Again, the smaller one. Kind of feisty. She'd keep her eye on him.

"You guys sit there a minute while I get my horse," Carli said.

With horses saddled, they were ready. The oldest, Zach, acted overeager and sent his horse into a trot before Carli could get mounted. Beau seemed all right this morning. He didn't act like he was in any pain, almost recovered. She probably wouldn't work cattle with him the rest of the week, but a nice, easy ride around headquarters should be okay.

"Now listen, Zachary, Junior, er . . . Zach? What do you like to be called?" Carli asked.

"Zachary Matthew Reynolds is my real name, but nobody at school uses my middle name. It's just Matthew after my dad. Dad calls me Zach, my mom calls me Junior, and Uncle Lank sometimes calls me Little Matt." He sighed as if taking a serious pause to consider the question. "You can call me Junior, like my mom."

"Okay then, Junior it is." Carli laughed. That was almost as complicated as all of her names. He won her over right then by suggesting she use the same name his mom used. That boy was a charmer. "You settle down and keep your legs quiet. A real cowboy doesn't act like a clown and spook his horse.

Riding is serious business."

Junior lowered his eyes. "Sorry, Miss Carli."

Zane was quiet as he settled in the saddle and focused on his horse. Both boys had dark hair and as the older brother had aged, he really looked a lot like a miniature Lank with a darker complexion.

Carli let them ride around the corral for a bit. She showed them how to use the pressure from their legs to stop, back up, turn their horse in one direction and then the other.

"Let's work on opening a gate from the back of your horse," she said. Eager faces turned in her direction.

"Are you gonna marry our Uncle Lank?" This from the youngest. The quiet, silent type but obviously the thinker of the two.

Carli gasped in surprise and then giggled. She decided to ignore the question.

"You're doing great, Zane. Now tell Sally to walk. Don't let her trot too fast. And Junior, look at you. You're a natural."

Carli rode her horse near to the boys keeping a close watch, but the question lingered in her mind. Marry Lank. Her heart fluttered. Just hearing the words aloud made her panic and excited all at once.

"Let's unsaddle the horses, put the tack back where it goes. And you guys are welcome here anytime." Both boys gave Carli quick hugs.

After a couple hours of riding, Carli had them help her clean stalls, and soon the boys were tuckered out. And still, the question never went away.

Apparently, the topic hadn't left the minds of the boys either.

"My momma says you're gonna marry Uncle Lank because you kissed him."

"Kissing means people get married?" asked Carli.

"Momma says so," Zane answered with a matter-of-fact knowledge of a six-year-old, wise beyond his years.

"I don't know that Lank or anyone else has asked me to get married."

"Guys ask girls?" Suddenly Junior seemed interested in the conversation.

"That's usually how it works," said Carli.

Carli had the boys fill the water troughs for the cowboys' horses that were scattered around the corral in separate pens. Dayworking cowboys brought their own remudas with them. One day's work might smoke a horse, and they'd need fresh mounts for other days.

Just as they finished, they could hear the herd bawling. Carli pointed to the approaching horses and cattle. "Here they come. Let's get out of the way." She and the boys scrambled onto the fence.

The rest of the morning was spent watching the cowboys separate mommas from their calves, and then two working crews formed on either side of the branding fire. Ropers dragged calves to the pot, flankers laid the animal on its side, and then more punchers stepped up to put in an ear tag, administer vaccines, with Lank and Buck operating the syringes. The Olsens had not made it today, but Angie and Travis planned to be back tomorrow.

By the time the morning was done, Carli was exhausted, mostly from answering questions about everything that popped into the boys' heads. From an explanation about what was going on in the branding pen to what kind of bug was crawling on the ground. They had her mind buzzing. She glanced at her watch. Their grandmother should be here any minute.

At an early age, Carli had decided she didn't want to be a mom. She didn't want the responsibility of managing every single second of someone else's life. What if she made a wrong decision? The kid could end up paying for her mistakes all of his or her life, exactly how her mother Michelle's decisions had affected her.

Spending an entire morning with Lank's nephews had made her realize how inquisitive and energizing kids can be. Despite the constant questions, she had really enjoyed their company. She missed her riding students back in Georgia more than ever, which only reinforced her resolve to work harder on making the riding school here in Texas successful. But kids of her own had always been out of the question, which is why she liked teaching and then sending them home to their parents.

But then a tug on her heart and the idea passed through her mind. Maybe someday I'll have a pair like that. Little Lanks running around. Maybe it wouldn't be so bad. Who knows? Maybe I'd make a good mom.

Chapter Twenty-Eight

As Carli sat on the fence watching the branding crews work, she was amazed at how fast they could process one calf. Everyone worked in sync. The calves were on the ground literally for only a few seconds. The two boys sat on the top rail next to her.

It seemed that the pen was controlled chaos, with double crews working both sides. Two ropers on horseback, traveling back and forth, flankers, vaccinators, an ear tagger, and the hot branding iron. There was also a guy on each side to turn bulls to steers. Not a pleasant task, but necessary.

Over the hustle in the pen rose constant bawls from the mommas calling to their calves who huddled at one end of the branding pen. The hissing propane tank added more noise. In a few hours, the calves would sport a new earpiece and a brand making them officially belong to the Wild Cow Ranch. They'd be back with their mommas before noon, happily suckling with the morning long forgotten.

"What are you thinking?" asked Lank, as he rested an arm on the pipe rail fence next to Carli and laid a hand on her leg.

"It looks as though everybody is within a split second of getting injured. It's so busy in there, makes my mind swirl."

"You gotta trust that we all know what we're doing," he said. "These guys do this for a living. They can anticipate any wrecks that are about to happen. The guys with the knives stand ready and can cut the rope to release the calf in a second. Everybody is watching for a wreck."

That made her feel better, but it still made her nervous with livestock and people moving at such a fast pace. There wasn't much visiting. Everybody focused and worked.

Buck motioned to her.

"You guys stay on the fence. Your grandmother should be here soon," she told Lank's nephews, but suddenly noticed that Junior was the only one sitting next to her. Zane was gone. "Buck, I'll be just a minute," she hollered as she slid off into the grass.

Carli found Zane at the opposite end of the working pen standing by the loading chute at the back of a line of ranch horses that stood patiently at the fence where their cowboys had tethered them.

"Zane," she called out and walked slowly so as not to spook a horse. "Don't get behind those horses. Come sit by your brother."

He glanced up, reluctantly stood when he noticed that she wasn't going away without him, and took his time to follow. Carli climbed back over the fence and hurried over to Buck who stood behind the branding pot.

"Would you like to run the vaccine needles?" he asked.

"Sure. Teach me what to do." Buck showed her where to apply the black leg vaccine in the neck and how to fill the syringe. The cowboy whose place she took went to get his horse so that he could rope and drag.

They processed about thirty more calves and time flew by. In no time someone turned off the propane tank that heated the branding irons; the hissing ceased, and the ringing in her ears quieted. The men remounted, turned the calves back with their mommas, and silence descended over the scene. Carli breathed a sigh of relief. They'd let them settle for a bit before driving the entire group back to their home pasture. Another day done and no injuries. Only thing left for today was lunch.

Carli helped put things back in the medicine cooler, unscrewed the needles, and grabbed a water. As she raised the bottle to her lips, she turned to see Junior sitting on the fence, but Zane was nowhere in sight.

"Where's Zane?" Lank stood at her side. She cringed. Where was Zane? She knew that kid was a handful just from the questions he'd asked her all morning.

"Uncle Lank!" Junior jumped to the ground and

hurried to him.

"Where's your brother?" Lank asked.

"Can I ride your horse?"

"Not now. He's had a busy morning. Maybe later."

"They've already been riding once today," said Carli. "I'll go look for Zane if you can get this one some lunch."

"I can do that. Are you hungry?" he asked his nephew. "Let's go then."

Carli watched them walk towards the cookhouse with the others. Please God, let me find Zane. The sooner the better.

She started by circling the corral and looking in every pen, in and around the loading chute again, and checking both saddle houses. That took over thirty minutes. As she walked by the chain-link dog pen, she noticed that their dog Lily Jane was gone. Lank had penned her first of the week because he didn't want her to get trampled with so many horses and cows moving around. She normally never left Lank's or Carli's side. It would have been too dangerous for her while they were working.

So, wherever Lily Jane had gotten off to, chances were that Zane was there. Or vice versa. Good grief. Carli had been awake since five o'clock and she had hoped for a nap this afternoon. Looks like that wasn't happening.

Now where would a dog and a boy slip off to? The creek that bordered one side of headquarters, with towering cottonwood trees and interesting sights to see. That was the likely answer.

Carli hesitated at the cookhouse. Should she tell Lank that she had lost his nephew? What if the grandmother showed up about this time? What in the world would she tell her? In the next second Carli decided speed was of the essence. She'd hurry down to the creek. How far could one little boy and small dog get in a few minutes? It had not been that long ago when she'd seen him sitting on the fence. She sighed, checked to make sure her phone still had power, and trudged towards the trees hollering "Zane" the entire way. Passing the saddle house, she grabbed two waters from the cooler. She was parched.

As she walked, she drank one in several long gulps, crushed the plastic bottle and stuck it in her pocket. Carrying the other, she bypassed gates, cut across the grass, and climbed several fences. The coolness and quiet of the trees surprised her after the hectic morning. She stopped and took several breaths allowing the peaceful shade to settle around her before calling the boy's name again.

A dove's coo broke the silence, and then she heard the sharp rat-a-tat-tat of a woodpecker. "Zane," she shouted, then listened. Nothing. Maybe she should call the dog instead of the boy. At least one of them was reliable. "Lily!"

She walked the half-mile from the back of the corral to the fishpond and didn't see hide nor hair of either dog or boy. She wrestled with guilt. How in the world could she lose one little boy? She had been the one to volunteer to watch them, and now she had to tell Lank that she had lost his nephew. What would Lank tell his sister? She'd be furious at them both. Carli didn't know what to do other than keep walking and calling. She wished she had checked to see if there was a fishing pole missing. Maybe she'd find them on the other side. Her stomach growled.

"Zane. You answer me right this minute." She raised her voice and put as much authority behind her words as she could muster. Because he's going to start minding her now. Right. Way to go, Carli. Good grief, but her feet hurt.

By the time she walked around the entire fishing pond, she knew she needed help. Zane and Lily Jane were nowhere to be found. And then she had an idea. Instead of causing Lank worry, she'd call in the big guns. Somebody with talent for this sort of thing.

She had to walk to a higher rise to get a signal and then clicked on the number. "Vera. Can you bring Snot over? It's an emergency. I'm at our fishing pond."

Snot, the bloodhound was on his way.

Chapter Twenty-Nine

Carli heard Vera Allgood's truck before she saw it. Gears grinding as Vera shifted down to follow the dirt road up over the dam and then the roar of an engine. The brakes squealed when she stopped and then welcomed silence when she turned the motor off.

Carli scrambled up the bank. "Vera. Thanks for coming so quick. I can't find Lank's nephew."

Crazy Vera stepped out of a faded green Chevrolet that was probably as old as she was and behind her out jumped Snot, her bloodhound. He sported a red bandana around his neck that was sure to be soggy from drool before the hunt was over. Crazy Vera shared a fence with Carli. They called her crazy for many reasons, the main one being her front yard was a mini cemetery and shrine dedicated to her first husband.

Snot stood at the top of the dam watching Carli, seemingly eager, and wagging his tail as if knowing he had been called to do a job. She walked to him and hugged his giant head.

"I found tracks right at the water but I couldn't pick up their trail again. Our dog Lily Jane is with him." Her breath caught for a minute. She had said "our" dog.

"Show me. Snot can get a good sniff." Vera and Snot followed Carli around one end of the pond. Vera grabbed her dog's collar to hold him back while she studied the prints. "Definitely a young boy and dog prints circling his shoe prints here. They headed that way." Vera pointed the way.

Part of her fear had subsided with the arrival of Vera, but still Carli couldn't help herself and yelled again. "Zane! Lily Jane! Come here, girl!"

The wind had died and the pond water shimmered like glass. A small group of ducks circled overhead, their wings beating the wind as they waited for the people to leave their sanctuary. A large crane suddenly took flight. Carli hadn't even noticed him standing at the water's edge. A few turtles bobbed and floated, their heads just breaking the surface to watch the action.

"Let's get Snot on the trail. He'll find them in no time." Vera allowed the dog to edge closer to the water. "Sniff here. Wish we had something of Zane's for him to smell, but maybe he'll pick up the other dog's scent too." She pointed at the tracks.

Snot took longer than Carli would have allowed, but Vera seemed calm and in no rush. On the other hand, Carli's stomach was churning and she felt like screaming. How would she ever explain this to

Lank and his sister?

"Find Zane. Where's Zane?" Vera instructed.

The bloodhound sat down on his rump and let out a blood curdling howl that echoed through the cottonwoods and bounced off the water. A chill ran down Carli's back.

"What's wrong with him?" she asked.

"He's got the scent but he doesn't go to work until he's ready." Vera did not prod or encourage him. She just waited.

Suddenly he took off like a rocket. Up and over the dam and out of sight, that yowl sounding every step of the way.

"Let's try to keep up," said Vera. She moved almost as fast and Carli followed close behind, jogging up one side and down the back side of the dam. Snot was nowhere in sight but she could hear long rooooos in between deep, throaty barks.

"He found them," said Vera.

They walked for about a half a mile where they found Lily Jane circling around Zane who sat on the ground under a tree. Tears streaked his face. Terror etched her heart as the word "rattlesnake" flashed in her brain. Snot had laid down in the shade, calmly watching them all.

"He's sitting on the ground." Vera rushed forward. "Lord, I hope he's not hurt bad."

"What happened?" Carli kneeled beside Zane. She pushed Lily Jane away.

"I jumped out of that tree," the little boy said.

Relief washed over Carli and she almost cried. A

sprain. He had a sprained ankle was all. "Let's get you home and take a better look. I'm betting an ice pack would be just the thing."

"Okay," he said with a shaky voice as he held out his arms. Carli pulled him to one good foot. "Vera, can you help him climb on my back?"

"Lord, girl, you ain't much over a hundred pounds. I can carry him. I'm a bit stouter than you."

"Are you sure?" Carli felt such a strong obligation to see this through. She hated to hand this problem over to someone else, but then again, she really didn't know if she could carry Zane for half a mile. She had already been walking for over two hours. She realized that Lank hadn't called or texted. Maybe it was a good thing they were down on the creek with no signal.

Vera kneeled a bit and Carli lifted Zane onto her back. He put his arms around her neck and she grabbed his legs with her arms. She whistled. "Let's go, Snot."

Carli called, "Lily Jane. Come on, girl." She spun around looking in all directions. "Where did those dogs go?"

And then she spotted them in a patch of grass under some chinaberry trees. "Oh no." She quickly reached up and covered Zane's eyes. "We may have to wait a bit."

Vera let loose a deep cackle. "That's my Snot. He's got a reputation with the ladies. They'll be along shortly." With that Vera trudged along the cow trail towards the pond.

By the time they reached the pickup truck, both Snot and Lily Jane had caught up to them. Vera sat Zane down inside the cab and then opened the tailgate. "In here, boy."

Carli walked around to the back and leaned close to Vera. "I cannot believe Snot did that to my dog. She's still a puppy and I've been good about protecting her. Now this. Do you think Zane saw anything?"

"Saw what?" Vera used the flat of her hand to pat the tailgate. Snot bounded in one smooth motion into the back and Lily Jane followed.

"The dogs. You know." Carli whispered and then felt her cheeks warm.

"The boy was too focused on his hurt leg. I bet he didn't even notice." Vera didn't hold back another throaty laugh.

"How am I ever going to explain this to his mother?"

Carli helped Zane turn sideways in the seat and rest his hurt leg on her lap. Vera eased the truck into motion, and they headed back to headquarters.

As they pulled up to the cookhouse, Lank was the first to meet them, minus a smile. He swung open Carli's door. "Where have y'all been? I've called and texted. Their grandmother left with Junior. She got tired of waiting on y'all. Why didn't you answer my calls?"

The irritation in his voice made Carli's stomach clench. She hated to make him mad, but that wasn't the half of it.

"We had a little adventure," Carli said as she climbed out and turned to help Zane scoot across the seat.

"Lily Jane has a boyfriend," Zane said as he climbed into his uncle's arms.

"What's that mean?" Lank glanced from Carli to Vera. "Carli? What happened?"

Carli took in a deep breath. Might as well confess it all now. Since there was so much to tell, maybe Lank could be mad at her all at once and then they could move on until she had to tell Zane's mother.

"The truth is I lost Zane and went looking for him. Failed miserably and called in reinforcements." Carli rattled on as she followed Lank into the cookhouse. "Snot and Vera came to the rescue. Snot found Zane in no time, and also met your dog. They hit it off right away."

Lank shot her an annoyed glance.

"Do dogs get married?" Zane asked.

"No buddy. Dogs don't get married. Let me take off your boot and sock, okay? I need to take a look at that ankle."

Carli stood transfixed, acutely aware of the gentleness Lank used with his nephew. His face so stern and strong, yet a look of concern in his eyes as he tenderly prodded Zane's swollen ankle. Her heart jumped up in her throat and all she could think about was she wished it were her ankle instead.

"They kissed," said Zane.

"Who kissed?" Lank asked absentmindedly as he continued his exam. "Wiggle your toes. Can you?"

"It's definitely swollen," observed Vera.

"I think you're right, but I don't think it's broken. Just a bad sprain," Lank agreed.

"If you kiss, then you have a wedding. Mommy told us so," said Zane.

"What wedding? What are you talking about?" Lank scooted a chair closer to Zane and gently laid his leg on it. "I need to make an ice pack and then we'll take you to your grandma's."

"I want to go to the wedding," whined Zane as his face scrunched up and his chin jutted out in a stubborn pout. "I'm not leaving."

"It's all right. Don't cry," said Carli. "Where are the dogs?" Suddenly Carli realized their error in leaving the dogs alone again in the back of the pickup truck. She looked at Vera.

"What is he talking about, Carli?" Lank asked. "What is going on and why is he tearing up?"

"The truth is Lank, I think you're going to be a dad," Carli said. "Well, a dog grandpa, I guess is more like it."

Vera threw back her head and howled with laughter. Snot came running and joined her in a baritone bellow.

Carli just shook her head but was thankful to see the anger gone from Lank's eyes when he looked at her.

Chapter Thirty

Thursday branding had been more of the same. A crisp, beautiful morning with meadowlarks singing their greeting. Gray and white clouds dotted a faded blue sky. Carli rode one of her riding school horses that wasn't that tuned in with what the cows were doing, but she enjoyed riding drag and watching the others work. Her horse Beau was still favoring his foot after stepping in a gopher hole a few days before, so she'd have to call the vet next week.

The morning went by in a flash. Lank was focused on his work, but she caught him checking on his dog Lily Jane more than once with a worried frown on his face. She couldn't help but grin. As it turned out his sister Kelly was more than gracious about Zane's adventure and said that he wanders off all the time. That would have been more than useful information for Carli to know before everyone left her to babysit. As far as snakes go, both boys had been well schooled about rattlers and they knew to wear their boots during the summer. The thought of what might have happened still kept Carli awake part of the night. She had no idea what she would have done if things had gotten dangerous or if Zane had gotten hurt. Thank goodness for Crazy Vera and Snot.

On Friday, the last day of branding, Carli decided to ride out with the crew again. It had been a great week. By lunch today, the hired cowpunchers and her helpful neighbors would process this year's calf crop. Carli reflected on the week and what she had learned at her first branding.

The work they had accomplished was the way it had been done for a hundred years or more. Some city folk didn't understand it but ranchers did and that's all that mattered. Taking care of the land, the livestock, and family. The blood that had flowed in the generations before had been ranchers dedicating themselves to the Wild Cow Ranch, and their blood flowed in Carli. The life she had left behind in Georgia after finding out she had inherited this ranch, seemed like a million years ago. She barely remembered the girl she had been back then.

Lank stood up from the table, carried his dishes to the wreck pan, and came back to give her a peck on the cheek. "I'll be at the corral helping everyone get loaded."

Carli was tired, but in a good way. She was so grateful for the professional cowboys and her kind neighbors, all pitching in to help the Wild Cow

Ranch. As they filled their bellies with the hearty breakfast that Lola had prepared, Carli surveyed the crowd seated in the cookhouse dining room and was humbled. To think of where she had come from, the independent life where she only had to answer to herself. Some might think that was great, but at times she was almost consumed by loneliness. Here, she had a sea of people welcoming her to Texas, wanting to know her, offering any help within their power. Thank goodness Lola interrupted her thoughts or else Carli might have started to cry to release the overwhelming feelings filling her heart.

"Hey, Carli, there's Lexi and her mom and brother," Lola said.

Carli had been lost in her thoughts and hadn't noticed the newcomers. She looked to the doorway and saw Lexi sheepishly scanning the crowd. Carli hoped she wouldn't bolt.

"Oh, good. Yeah, told you I'd invited them."

"Hope they're hungry." Lola smiled.

Carli met them at the door. "I didn't think y'all would get up this early, but I'm glad you're here. Hey, Emily, so glad you could come. Brandon, you're taller than the last time I saw you." She smiled at the younger brother who grinned and stood even straighter with shoulders back like a soldier.

Focusing on Lexi, she was glad to see the absence of Emo girl heavy eye makeup, and the neon pink fading from her hair. The young girl had on cowgirl boots and jeans. "I'm glad to see you Lexi. I've missed you. After this busy month is done, we'll get back to riding school lessons, I hope. Looks to me like you're ready to ride. Brandon, are you riding too?" Carli placed a hand on the girl's shoulder.

The boy shyly looked to his mom first who nodded her head, and he answered with a soft, "Yes ma'am."

Lexi frowned and rolled her eyes.

"Emily, do you need a horse?" Carli asked.

"Oh no, I'll help Lola. My horseback riding days are long over, but thanks anyway."

Carli texted Lank. *Saddle up two more horses. Lexi and Brandon are here. Thanks.* She added a kissing emoji at the last minute, and then felt like an idiot but it was too late to delete.

"I hope y'all are hungry. Let's get something to eat, okay?" Carli led the family towards the food.

Brandon's eyes lit up as he glanced at the bar and was the first to speak up. "Yeah, I'm starving."

The mom looked at Carli and shook her head. "Boys. He eats nonstop."

"Let's get in line." Carli let Brandon and Emily go first, with Lexi filling a coffee mug and ignoring the food. "What grade will you be in next year, Brandon?"

As he doused two flapjacks with syrup, he mumbled. "Eighth."

Emily dished out eggs and bacon onto her plate and leaned a little towards Carli. "Thanks so much for inviting us. The kids needed to get out." Then in a whisper, she added, "Lexi's been grounded since I learned she was hanging out with that Raven kid again."

Carli whispered to Emily, "I was hoping I could talk to her today. Privately."

"That would be good. I heard about your incident at the auction. Are you okay?"

Carli was taken back a bit. "Who told you?"

"Lexi actually, but I have heard several different versions around town. You're quite the celebrity." Emily smiled and Carli frowned. "Lexi was all abuzz about it when she got home. We're just glad you're okay."

Carli wondered if she knew the half of it, because it didn't look like Lexi had gone with Raven that night willingly. There was more to the story. Carli held her tongue since she didn't know for sure but had every intention of finding out the truth.

They all sat together. Brandon polished off those flapjacks in record time and went back to the serving line to return with a plate of eggs and bacon. As much as his mother pleaded with him to not take so much and not inhale so fast, there was no stopping this boy. "Slow down, son."

The two women glanced at each other and shook their heads.

Lola slid into the empty chair. "That's what I like. A hearty eater."

"I'm not sure all that food is good just before getting on a horse," said Emily.

"He's a growing boy. He'll do fine." Lola beamed at him.

"Brandon and Lexi," Carli said, "I'm sure that

Lank has your horses ready. Are you ready to ride?"

As soon as she had said it, she was sorry because it only put the boy into hyper-drive and he inhaled the rest of his food as though alien monsters were attacking and he'd never eat again for a long time. "Cool," was his muffled answer in between the gob of food spilling out of his mouth.

"Brandon, don't eat like a hog. I did teach you some manners." His mother looked at Carli with more head shaking. Carli thought that mothering must be one of the toughest jobs on the planet and wasn't sure she'd ever be able to fill that role. In fact, she knew she wouldn't. She had made that promise to herself when her mother, Michelle, had chosen to never be a part of her life. Carli figured she didn't have the mothering instinct. Maybe it wasn't part of her DNA.

The dining hall had emptied, and Carli hustled everyone outside. She led Lexi and Brandon to the corral where their horses were saddled.

"Lank," she called out. "Which trailer do you want us on?"

Most of the cowboys had already loaded their horses and were climbing into the trucks.

At the barn they were greeted with horse nickers. Lexi walked to the side of Sally, the bay mare she had ridden when Carli's riding school was in session.

"Hey, girl," Lexi said real quiet as she buried her face in the horse's neck. More nickers sounded as the horse's topline trembled.

"Told you she missed you." Carli was filled with contentment for this scene, but also serious concern for the teenager. What did her future hold? How would her life turn out? Especially if she chased after Raven who had his own issues to deal with. No doubt that uncle of his was leading the boy down the wrong path. Carli had to bring the subject up.

"Come this way, Brandon." Lank handed him the reins and showed him where to lead the horse which jumped up easily into the back of the trailer. Lank slammed the trailer door with a clank. "Looks like the pickup cab's full, but you can hop into the back with those other guys and I'll help you unload."

Carli paused a moment to watch Lank. He seemed to be everywhere all at once. Laughing with someone in one spot, then helping someone else over there. Her head got dizzy as she watched him. He escorted Lexi out of the corral leading Sally, pointed them to their assigned trailer, and then in one fluid motion landed in the back of the truck bed with Brandon.

Lexi and Carli loaded their horses and then hopped into the back of another truck. Carli did not want to squeeze into the cab with the other punchers and she was thankful for a moment alone with Lexi.

The caravan of pickup trucks and livestock trailers slowly left headquarters leaving a dust cloud hanging heavy in the air. Carli was thankful that branding week had gone well but then she was suddenly sad that this was the last day.

Chapter Thirty-One

The convoy of pickup trucks and trailers passed through Wild Cow Ranch headquarters and turned at the top of the hill. They had one more pasture to work on the last day of branding week but it was one of the larger ones with lots of mesquite, river breaks, and steep cliffs located at the north end of the ranch. It was one of the more scenic pastures and would take several hours to sweep but they had a full crew to help.

From the back of the pickup, Carli was stunned to silence as she watched the sun peek over the clouds washing the sky in pink and orange above the endless stretch of green dotted with spiky yucca. As the sun grew brighter the colors of the sky faded and, in their place the brightest blue she had ever seen in her life. The wind was still for once and the day promised to be hot which was why they had started so early. The work would be done before the noon day heat beat down on their heads. Easier on the new calves and easier on the cowboys too. She glanced at Lexi, noticing that the young girl was soaking in the scenery as well. Carli hated to break the moment but she might not get another chance to talk to Lexi once they get on horseback.

"You know Lexi, I was so worried for you at the auction when Raven was forcing you into that truck. Did you know that I got hurt when I fell off? I'm not positive if he shoved me, but I was really scared for you."

Lexi's wide eyes filled with tears. "I'm sorry, Carli. I never wanted you to get hurt. I was worried about you too."

"Who was driving the truck? Looked like an older man."

Lexi avoided her gaze and Carli could tell she was struggling with how much to say or keep secret.

Finally, the girl answered. "That was Raven's uncle, Melvin."

"Do you know anything about him?" Carli asked.

"He just got out of prison and he's mean."

"He hasn't been mean to you, has he?" Carli was heated and had to suppress any anger that bubbled up in her gut. To be honest, she was furious. There was plenty more on her mind to say, but she wanted this conversation to continue and didn't want to scare Lexi off.

"No, he wasn't mean to me. But he did say bad things about you. Told Raven to make sure you got off his truck or he'd . . . run you over. He called you the b-word." More tears filled her eyes. "I'm sorry,

Carli."

"It's okay, Lexi. But I want you to listen to me. Really listen. This is all very serious. I don't know how much Raven is involved, but these men, whoever they are, are stealing cattle belonging to me and our neighboring ranches."

"It's not Raven. He'd never do anything like that." Lexi was quick to defend the boy which made Carli realize that she'd never be able to reason with her. The girl was smitten. Teenaged first love and angst; there was nothing in this world to overcome it.

"I saw Raven one morning on my ranch with two men and it appears they were cooking meth," Carli said. "And then I'm almost certain I saw Raven at Vera's barn one night. All of these activities are crimes, punishable by jail time. And if you're with them . . . well, you could end up in jail also. Just one moment. That's all it takes. Wrong place, wrong time and your life will be changed forever. You realize that, don't you? You really have to stay away from Raven. I care about you, Lexi. Can you promise me you'll stop seeing him?"

Lexi pursed her lips together and frowned. She looked down at her boots and grew silent. Carli decided to not press her any longer. The conversation was obviously over. And then Lexi broke the silence.

"It's not his fault. He's a good person. If I leave him, he has no one. His dad is mean, hits Raven and his mother. She left. His uncle makes Raven the lookout for him. Raven doesn't want to do it but they push him around. I'm scared for him, Carli. They might really hurt him."

It was as if a dam broke. Carli didn't interrupt the girl and had no idea how to handle the situation. Lexi and Raven were in way over their heads. They'd be no match for an ex-con with something to prove, and now he had his attention focused on Carli too.

"Lexi, we've got to tell this to the sheriff. Do you know the uncle's name?"

"Melvin something. Gibbons, I guess. I'm not sure."

"Does your mom know any of this?"

"No, but she did ground me for going with Raven. One night I didn't come home till real late, almost morning actually. That day we saw you at the auction. The uncle was all upset after you chased us, he wouldn't take me home and kept asking me about you. Later Raven drove me home."

"Lexi, if you say that Raven is being forced to do things against his will, I'll believe you. But we're going to have to talk to the sheriff. Maybe I should talk to Raven first. Will he talk to me?"

"I don't know. He's really mixed up. Scared. Angry. Trying to be tough, stand up to his father and uncle. He's not acting the same as when I first knew him."

Carli realized that Lexi had become more mature than her years in a short time. She did seem to know a lot about Raven and obviously they had spent a good bit of time together. "You don't want him to go to jail, do you? He's eighteen now, right? He could go away for a long time. Let me help him. Set up a meeting, Lexi. I know you can do it. Bring him somewhere on the ranch if he doesn't want to be seen in town. We could meet at the windmill in pasture four. Remember we rode the horses over there during the riding school?"

"Is that the one with the tank that has those orange and black birds?"

"Yes. That's the one. You take the pasture road just before you turn into headquarters. I'll mark the mesquite tree so you'll know where to turn."

"Yeah. I'll try, Carli. If he agrees, I'll text you with a day and time."

"Good, Lexi. Remember, I want to help both of you. I don't want to have to visit you in jail."

They unloaded and joined the circle of punchers waiting on Buck's instruction.

"Brandon, you're with Lank," Buck said. "Lexi, you stay with Carli. Have a good ride everybody."

With that they were off fanning out across the back side of the pasture and waiting for the signal to move. Carli glanced at Lexi and then thought better of continuing their conversation. What more could she say? She'd warned her several times but the girl seemed in awe of Raven. Carli didn't want to be her mother. She wanted to be her friend. She wanted Lexi to feel comfortable confiding in her.

Obviously, Lexi was scared and had felt a need to warn Carli. She wondered how far Uncle Melvin was prepared to go to carry out his threats. Carli wasn't worried. She'd survived Atlanta on her own. Some redneck ex-con didn't scare her, but the fact that innocent Lexi was involved in the situation terrified her to the core.

They had a pleasant ride that morning and got everything pushed to headquarters. Carli admired the shiny black hair on the Angus herd. The calves were stocky and spirited. Buck had mentioned that they'd bring a good price in the fall.

The branding went fast with two teams again working the calves. Lexi hung back on the fence, snapping an occasional picture with her cell phone. Buck had Brandon work on ear tagging. And then they were done. Carli helped them put the equipment up until next year. The meds went back into the refrigerator and the branding irons to their place in a dark corner of the tractor barn. Bridles and saddles were returned to the tack room or loaded onto trailers.

The cookhouse bell rang out over the scene causing everyone to hurry with whatever they were doing and start heading towards lunch.

Lola served barbequed brisket on the last day of branding every year, so she had told Carli, along with pinto beans and coleslaw. The smells that greeted Carli when she walked through the door made her mouth water. Spurs jangled as the men washed up and filed back into the dining hall. They filled their tea glasses and sat down, waiting on the blessing before getting in the serving line.

Buck stood at the front of the room. "On behalf

of Carli who has joined us for her first branding, and the rest of us at the Wild Cow, thanks again for everyone's hard work this week. I know that Jean and Ward are looking down on us with big smiles knowing their only granddaughter has returned to the fold. I'll have your checks before you leave and I guess we'll see you again this fall. Let's bless the food."

Carli blinked back tears. She hadn't expected Buck to mention her grandparents. She went through the line first and invited her guests to follow. She noticed that Lexi must have worked up an appetite, because she filled a plate this time. Brandon kept them entertained with tales of his ride. Lexi rolled her eyes more than once, but actually had to bury a grin at one point.

As Carli followed the Brown family to the door, several of the cowboys said nice things to her, thanks for the food, greetings about the good work accomplished. After she said goodbye to Lexi and her family, she made a pass through the kitchen to thank Lola and her helpers which included some of her friends from church. She was surprised to see Crazy Vera scrubbing the stove.

"Vera. I didn't know you were here today."

"I never miss Friday and brisket," the big woman said. "I hope you can join Lank and Buck next week at my place. I don't have near as many cows as you do."

By the time Carli shook hands with everyone and said goodbye and thanks a hundred times, her face hurt from smiling so much. It had been a good week, but despite the overwhelming sense of knowing she was where she should be, a cloud of stress hung over her. Uncle Melvin would be a problem.

Chapter Thirty-Two

A text from Lexi came through on Carli's phone late Saturday night: MEET P-4 WINDMILL, 10 AM, COME ALONE.

She was up and dressed by half past eight on Sunday. At least the meeting wasn't ten o'clock at night, Carli thought. She was glad she didn't have to sneak out, riding Beau in the dark. Talk about suspicious. A morning ride would make it easier to conceal what she was up to because Buck and Lola would already have left for church. But as she stepped out of her house, she saw their car was still at their apartment.

Entering the barn, she hoped Lank was busy somewhere else on the ranch and not around to butt into her business. No such luck.

"Whatcha up to, Carli?"

Startled by Buck's voice, she stared at him in his starched white shirt and clean straw hat. She tried to act nonchalant and proceeded to lead Beau to the crossties where she hooked his halter. "Oh, just taking a ride, Buck. Aren't you going to church?"

"Fixin' to head that way. Have a nice ride."

Lank stepped out of the tack room, obviously having overheard the exchange. "Sounds like a good idea. Let me saddle Phoenix and I'll join you."

Good grief. Just smile. Act natural.

"If you don't mind, I'd like to clear my head, you know, commune with nature and focus on Beau's foot. Make sure he's okay." She grinned at the two men trying to deflect whatever they might be thinking. Their deadpan faces told her they were suspicious already.

"Carli, you know it's not smart to go off riding alone." Lank gave her one of his sterner looks and then sadness crossed his eyes for one second before he looked away.

With a big sigh and roll of her eyes, she said, "I'm a big girl. I've got my cell phone, and I'm not going far. Be back in a jiffy. Can't I have a little alone time? I'm worn out after branding week. I'm looking forward to a nice, quiet ride." She pushed the guilt from her mind. Truth was she wanted to tell Lank everything. Having someone else there who had her back when she confronted Raven made sense, but when had she ever used any common sense? She usually forged ahead and dang the consequences. With a heavy sigh she placed the blanket on Beau and heaved the saddle on next.

She could tell Lank was exasperated. He let out a push of air and stared at her. "Fine. Go ahead, boss lady. You ain't gonna listen to us anyways."

Buck remained silent. He looked from Lank to Carli. She knew he wouldn't get in the middle of them.

Finished with saddling Beau, she led him out of the barn and hopped on. "I'll be back soon. No worries," she called back to Buck who tipped his hat and headed to his car. Lola had just come out of the cookhouse carrying her purse and Bible. Lank was nowhere to be seen.

As Carli trotted then loped away, she breathed a sigh of relief. Maybe the guys had wondered if she was up to something, but she couldn't think about that now. She had to do this, had to meet Lexi and Raven. She hoped it was only the two of them and that none of Raven's criminal relatives would be there to surprise her.

Beau seemed to be loving the ride and even got a little strong, which he normally didn't do. She tightened her fingers on the reins and slowed him down. "Easy boy, you listen to me. Don't make me nervous. Besides, I gotta pray right now."

She was used to talking to Beau when she rode, even carried on long conversations with him sometimes. His only reply was a twitch of his ears, backwards and forward.

"Lord, please keep us safe. Let it just be Lexi and Raven and not the rustlers. And Lord, please give me the right words to say and let Raven be cooperative and not a jerk. I only want to help them. Thank you. Amen."

A meadowlark trilled loud enough to startle her

from right in front of Beau, and then scurried away. Carli laughed. "Thank you, God."

As Carli loped across the pasture, she had a sudden thought. Or was it a voice from above? An inner feeling kind of voice. Call him John.

"Okay, got it. I'll use his real name, won't call him Raven," she mumbled to herself.

As she emerged from a thicket of mesquite, she saw Raven's car already parked at the windmill and felt relief that they were alone. Lexi and Raven were sitting on the ground, their backs against the windmill tank. She halted Beau and dismounted.

Lexi leaned against the boy, her arm linked through his. She spoke first, her voice soft and tentative. "Hi Carli. This is Raven." She had returned to all black attire and combat boots. A silver chain sparkled in the sun etching a line across her cheek, linking one side of her nose to an ear. Carli raised her eyes in surprise, wondering if her mom knew about this piercing.

The teenage boy looked at her with dark eyes, burning with anger, and then he stared down at his boots. Carli smiled a little. "Yeah, we've met before. You came with Lexi to a riding lesson one time. Hi John."

His head snapped up, surprise in his eyes. Maybe at her using his real name? Couldn't be sure. Black hair hung straight and stiff past his shoulders, and just like before, Carli was struck by how good looking he was with that strong jaw and piercing eyes. The boy really could be a model. The first time they'd met, he had a certain arrogance and self-assuredness but the attitude was gone now. He seemed deflated and spent. The intelligence that she had remembered before was absent from his gaze.

"Yeah, whatever," he said.

"I'll get right to it." Carli looped Beau's reins around a rung on the windmill tower and sat down on the ground across from them. "No use in dancing around what we need to talk about. It's simple. I want to help you both."

"I don't need no help. Just came because of Lexi. She says you wanted to talk to her."

So that's how Lexi had got him here. Carli took a breath to steady her nerves. Help me, Lord.

"John, I'm trying to get some answers about the situation we all find ourselves in. I hope you'll listen for a few minutes. Maybe you can help me. It's really important." Carli looked him square in the eyes.

The boy shrugged a shoulder, pursed his lips, and rolled his eyes halfway. But he remained silent as he cleaned his fingernails with a little stick he had picked up off the ground.

Carli continued. "Someone's been rustling my cows and that of my neighbors too. You've been identified, John, as being with the rustlers. The sheriff and the special agent know who you are. It's just a matter of time before they bring you in. And you're eighteen now. A high school dropout. You know what that means, right? Charges will be filed against you as an adult. You're looking at some serious jail time."

Raven just let out a big sigh like he was perturbed.

Carli looked at Lexi. "The other part of this scenario is Lexi. She could be in trouble just by associating with you. She's only sixteen but they could send her to juvenile hall, take her out of school, away from her family. Is that what you want for her, John? Ruin her life before it's even begun?"

He looked at Carli and didn't sigh this time. He stroked Lexi's hand.

"You love her, don't you? You want to be with her? Protect her?"

Finally, with a whisper, he said, "Yeah."

Lexi smiled and squeezed his hand. Their shoulders touched.

"John, I understand that some things are beyond your control. But you've made some poor choices too and I'm guessing you may have been forced into some of this. The authorities may not see any of that when they place charges on you. They're real tough on cattle rustlers, not to mention the meth cooking part. But if I spoke on your behalf and you cooperate with them by telling the truth, they might show some mercy, get you a lesser sentence. Maybe even some kind of deal if you help them." Carli waited a moment.

"What do ya mean, 'help them'?"

"We need to know for certain who is rustling the cattle. I understand your uncle has served time and just got out. It appears he and your father are involved in many crimes. Looks like they forced you into doing a lot of their dirty work. Is that right?"

"I can't turn them in. They're family," Raven said.

"I understand that. But do you think if they had to choose between their life or yours, would they stick up for you? Or would they throw you under the bus, blame a lot of this on you?" Carli was praying on the inside.

Raven's face turned dark, his nonblinking eyes staring at the ground.

"I need to ask, John. Besides selling it, do you do meth? Do your father and uncle do meth?"

He looked at her warily. "Why?"

"I want to know what we're up against. Drugs can really cloud people's minds. Turn them into completely different beings. Sometimes evil."

"I've smoked some pot." Raven kicked a few pebbles in the dusty sand. "They mostly just sell the crank. Said they'd rather make money than get stoned."

"I'm glad you're not an addict. But you still need help. You don't have to live like this. Please let me help you, John."

"Why?"

"Why what?"

"Why do you want to help me? What's in it for you?"

Tell him. Love him. Tell him I love him.

What would the boy think of her? A stupid woman, religious fanatic? But she had to do it. She'd come this far. And that inner voice was prodding her on, giving her the courage she didn't know she had.

"John, this life is hard for a lot of us." Carli's heart was nudging her on. "You've had a father who's been rough on you. And on your mother. So much so she had to leave."

Raven's eyes almost glistened as he peeked up at Carli.

"I know what it's like. I grew up without a mother or father. On my own. I had guardians who gave me food and shelter, but I was lonely and bitter for a lot of years. I didn't want anyone's help. I was determined to do everything myself. You know where that got me? Nowhere. But then, through various circumstances, God found me. Or should I say, I found Him? He was always there but I ignored Him. Until one day when I took a leap of faith and wanted to change my life. I needed to change. And I've never looked back. It's not always easy. I still make mistakes. But you know what? Now I finally have a Heavenly Father. And I know every day that He loves me like no earthly father ever could. He loves me with all my flaws, all my insecurities."

She took a breath, then felt so much compassion for Raven as though he was a wounded bird who had fallen from a nest above onto the hard ground. Was he dead or would he fly again?

She looked deeply into his eyes that were glistening even more. Lexi held on tight as tears slid from her eyes.

"John, God loves you too. He created you. He's

given us free will. But look what we've done with that. We mess up all the time. I know without a doubt that if you reach out to Him, He'll grab hold and never let you go. He'll walk with you through any trial or hardship. It doesn't mean life will be easy and rosy. It means He'll always help you through the rough times."

Carli reached over and touched his hand. She was surprised when he opened his and held hers.

"My dad has a temper and it's getting worse since my uncle moved in with us. And then mom just left one day. She never told me goodbye. Never said a word to me. How can someone do that to their own kid?" He choked back a sob.

"We can get you out of this mess, John. But you have to be honest. When are they planning to steal more cattle? Do you know?"

He looked at Lexi and she put her arm around his shoulder. He hesitated for several minutes, as if a battle raged inside of him.

"Next full moon," he murmured.

Carli let out the breath she was holding. "Thank you. That's a start. I'm gonna say a little prayer."

She inhaled through her nose and closed her eyes. This was kind of new for her. She wasn't experienced like Lola or Buck at praying out loud in front of others. But she couldn't ignore the overwhelming urge brewing inside. And she couldn't turn her back on God. She had to do this. She had to share what she had learned and what she had received.

"Dear Lord, thank You for being here, for giving us every good blessing, for watching out for us. I ask You now to please be with John and Lexi, protect them from the Evil One, make them strong to get through the days ahead. John wants to turn his life around, but he's gonna need Your help. We're asking You for a miracle here, Lord. Please soften the hearts of the lawmen and help them to show mercy to John. We thank you God and ask all of these things in Jesus's name. Amen."

Lexi and Raven both said "Amen."

"Never had no one pray for me before," Raven said as he leaned in closer to the hug Carli offered.

Chapter Thirty-Three

Lank Torres pushed the lawnmower out of the shed and changed the filter. After filling the tank with gas, he cranked it up and proceeded to the closest piece of grass with no direction or plan in mind. Just mow. Mowing the Wild Cow Ranch headquarters until Carli got back from her morning ride might help him collect his thoughts, and then he'd confront her.

They were going to have it out and clear the air. It hadn't been that long ago she had professed her love while he was confined to a hospital bed after getting bucked off a bronc. The wreck wasn't new to him, but the intense headache afterwards was something he thought he'd shake in a day or two. Now many weeks later he still didn't feel totally fine.

Years ago, in high school, his rodeo career had been shut down after lying unconscious for several days. When he came to, his mother was hovering and she'd made him promise no more broncs. Of course, he had to swear because of the tear tracks on her cheeks and the look of utter sorrow on her face that he had caused. What kid wouldn't promise his mother anything at that point?

Since that day he obsessed about the sport. His mother was gone now, so he had climbed back on a bronc only to face the reality of the situation. His brain couldn't take much more rattling. His bronc busting days should be over, but nobody really cared what he did, so what did it matter? Until he met Carli, that is. He'd give up everything he held dear for her, and he thought she felt the same way.

He glanced over his shoulder and realized he might have just mowed the same spot twice.

Several hours later, he spotted Carli riding through headquarters straight to the barn without waving or acknowledging him. Soon after she made a beeline towards her house and disappeared inside. She was up to something and he had a mind to find out what it was. It had to do with that dark-haired kid, Raven. He was sure of it. His mind blanked with agitation that she refused to take him into her confidence. She was hiding something. They were supposed to be dating. If he had his way, they'd spend every minute of every day together. That's what she'd done to him. He'd become an obsessed stalker.

Moments later, Buck and Lola pulled into their carport back from church. Lank thought he might talk to Buck. He ought to know a thing or two about women. As the couple emerged from their vehicle,

Buck called to Lank. "Working on a Sunday? That should make an impression on the boss. How's it going?"

Lank flinched at the mention of Carli. He wished that something as simple as mowing would get her attention. "Well, let's just say a few blades of grass got done twice."

The two men grinned. Lank added, "Hey, Buck, can I talk to you for a few minutes?"

"Sure, let's go to the barn."

Lola waved to Lank before disappearing inside their apartment.

In the barn Buck sorted items on the metal shelf. He never stayed still for a minute.

Lank fingered a headstall, settled on a stool at the work bench, and used a leather punch to make another hole.

"Something on your mind?" Buck broke the silence.

"Maybe. How did you know?"

"You're not that dedicated of a lawn man. The mower is a good place to think."

"It's Carli." Lank didn't look up.

"What's wrong with Carli?"

"Nothing's wrong with her. She's perfect. You know we're dating."

"How's that working out? Dating the boss?"

"It's not really working. We never see each other because we're both so busy."

"I know you, Lank. Known ya since you was a skinny kid scooping out the horse stalls. And as I recall you've always had a string of girls tagging along." Buck gave him a smirk and cleared his throat.

Lank felt his face warm. He couldn't argue with that. Girlfriends had been scattered in several towns around. Even more so after he began following the rodeo circuit before his head injury. He couldn't deny Buck's comment and he'd never cared which one knew about the other. Silly girls were one of life's distractions, albeit a pleasant one at times.

Buck continued. "In my observation Carli's different. She's not going to tag along and beg for your attention. She's very independent. Been on her own most of her life and that makes her cautious about everybody. I feel it too, but she'll warm up to us. Just give her time." Buck had arranged the curry combs and brushes on one shelf. The bottom shelf was a lost and found of sorts with a jacket, pair of spurs, a purple wild rag, and a cap with a longhorn steer logo.

Lank had never felt this way about anybody. Truth was he wondered if she'd walk away and be out of his life before they'd even given it a try. She was the one that made him think of forever. Deep down she terrified him, but he'd never say that out loud.

"Buck, I don't want to lose Carli."

The minute those words left his lips he wanted to take them back. He hadn't meant to share so much with Buck so fast. The notion was crazy. He could count the times they'd kissed on one hand.

Buck tried to hide the surprise in his eyes but Lank saw it. He and Buck had never been like close friends, not only because of the age difference but things were always work-related between them. Lank had been closer to Carli's Grandpa Ward, who had been like kin to him.

Buck reshuffled the items on the shelf again. "So, what's the problem? Is this getting serious?"

"No." Lank frowned at Buck like he had two heads. He had said too much already.

Buck was quiet and just stared at him.

Lank cleared his throat.

"She said she loved me, but that was back when I was laid up in the hospital. Maybe she was just scared. You're right about her holding back like she doesn't trust me. Or anyone for that matter."

Buck leaned against the shelf and looked over at Lank.

"Women are like a different species from men. Remember we talked about that before?"

"Yeah."

"God designed men and women to be different, that's for sure. But we complement each other. To fit together as one, not just physically, spiritually too. To help each other. If you and Carli keep God in the center of your relationship, your bond will be strong. Remember that verse I told you about? How one person can be overpowered, two can defend themselves, but a cord of three strands is not easily broken."

"Yeah," Lank said. "Ecclesiastes 4:12. My parents had that verse engraved inside their wedding bands."

"If it gets serious, you have another hurdle to cross also—you gotta ask me for her hand in marriage." Buck grinned.

"We're not even close to talking marriage yet. If it gets to that point, maybe you could walk her down the aisle since Carli never knew who her birth father was. You're the closest person she has to fill that role."

"You gotta make me a promise, Lank. You'll never hurt or abandon Carli, you'll always love her and want the best for her. If this is what God has planned for you, then you'll know it's right. Your marriage will be strong, with God at the center."

"I won't forget, Buck. And I promise to always take care of Carli."

"You know what happens if you don't, dontcha? I'll hunt you down and it won't be pretty." Buck shoved Lank and punched his arm.

"Okay, old man, take it easy on me."

"No way." Buck laughed and put his hand on Lank's shoulder. "My mission is to make your life tough. Have you made peace with God again?"

Lank looked at him in surprise. He'd never told anyone about his doubts. About the nights he'd cussed the Almighty who had allowed his mother to suffer like she did. "I'm working on the God thing. It was hard after my mom passed."

"I know. And then Ward left us. I know he meant

a lot to you. But you know it's easier to go through trouble with God, right? He's not the one that brings us trouble. Sometimes the greatest blessings come in times of our greatest despair."

Lank clenched his jaw. "I don't understand why He took her." No matter how old he got, Lank would never get over the death of his mother. Buck was dragging up past pain and it made Lank feel like he was that scared little boy again. The one who'd taken the dare to stick his hand into a badger den.

"Lank, ya gotta go back to basics," Buck advised. "You've got to realize that life on this earth is not going to be easy. This is not the same as the Garden of Eden. Bad stuff happens. People live and die. We have no control over it. God wants the best for us but this world is flawed with sin and the Enemy's attacks. He's the one who wants to mess up our lives. But us humans blame God."

"I understand. It's something I need to think about."

"Well, Lola and I will keep praying for you and Carli. Prayer can change things. You might want to try it yourself." Again, Buck gave a grin and his eyes sparkled.

"Guess I'd better get back to mowing."

"You're just trying to get in good with the owner by working seven days a week. Making sure she sees you're loyal to the brand." Buck slapped Lank on the back. "Keep at it. It just might work."

Lank ran out of the barn laughing. No doubt he was dedicated to the Wild Cow Ranch. One thing was for certain. He was determined to figure out what was going on in that pretty head and why she was avoiding him. The ranch owner was going to take notice of him and then they'd have a talk. A talk about their future.

Chapter Thirty-Four

After meeting Raven and Lexi at the windmill, Carli eased Beau back towards the house. She didn't want to put any stress on his hurt foot, but she needed to call Angie and tell her what she'd found out from Raven. Of course, she'd left her phone behind.

As they got closer to the barn, she noticed Buck leaving the saddle house. She heard the mower before she saw Lank coming around the side of the cookhouse running at full throttle. He slowed to make a circle around an elm tree, and then continued on next to the corral fence. He glanced up and saw her but didn't wave. She didn't either.

That confused her, the fact they couldn't even acknowledge each other. This whole Lank thing bothered her. At first it was her being the employer and him the ranch hand which made for a good excuse. She had no intention of ever dating an employee, but she had to finally admit the attraction. There were sparks she couldn't deny. After he had been hurt at the rodeo and she had seen his face so pale, his body so lifeless, she realized he was an important part of her life. And there was that kiss that still burned her lips when she thought about it. Then she had blurted out those three words. Whatever had possessed her to say them? In the light of day everything was different. She was still the boss lady and he was still the ranch hand. Awkward.

No doubt that she was drawn to him. He never left her thoughts. And the few times they'd kissed had rocked her world. Her boyfriend in Georgia, the one and only for the rest of her life guy, or so she had believed, never kissed her the way Lank did.

Beau seemed anxious to be done with the ride. She unsaddled, put the tack back in its place, and hurried to her house. She could hear the roar of the mower far away on the other side of the compound.

She wanted to run and catch up, jump on the mower behind him, and hang on for dear life. She wanted to tell him about the meeting with Raven. She wanted more kisses.

Guilt stung her heart at the way she had lied, maybe stretched the truth earlier, and ridden off alone. She'd never forget the look on his face. "You can act really awful sometimes," she told herself out loud. Beau's ears pricked. She stroked his neck. "No, not you. You're a good boy."

The truth was she missed Lank's friendship too. It wasn't just the physical attraction, but much more. If anything happened, he was the first person she wanted to talk to. If he was anywhere near, her heart beat faster. She wanted to confess all of her thoughts and desires, but she never acted on those feelings. She was the problem and she was going to ruin things before they ever got started. At one time Lank had promised her he'd be patient, but now she wasn't sure how long he would wait.

Carli pushed Lank from her mind and focused on the here and now. She hurried to the house and texted Angie. Can you meet me in town?

After several minutes, there was no answer but Carli grabbed her purse and got in her truck. With or without Angie, she had to talk to the sheriff, even if it was Sunday. She knew where he'd be. Everybody in the county knew where Sheriff Anderson was on Sunday afternoons.

Mozelle's Diner sat on the outskirts of Dixon nestled under giant elm trees. The two-story Victorian seemed out of place in the middle of the prairie, with a covered porch that wrapped around three sides and intricate latticework. In keeping with tradition of the architecture, it was painted in three colors. White walls with yellow trim, and around each window a bright, robin's egg blue.

Carli followed the winding dirt drive to the front yard that now served as a crowded parking lot. Where are you? A text from Angie. Carli called her as she walked to the back door, because nobody used the front entrance.

"I'm at Mozelle's. Raven agreed to meet with me earlier and I think they're planning something for the next full moon. I'm here to find the sheriff. Can you get here soon?"

Angie was already in her pickup truck heading for town and would be joining them within the next five minutes. Carli decided to go on in. She walked in the back through the roomy and very busy kitchen where a few tables were already occupied. Weaving her way through the crowded dining room and into the front parlor. The smell of fried foods mixed with yeast rolls was exactly how she imagined her Grandma Jean's kitchen must have been like if she'd ever known her—the aroma, the warmth, the feeling of belonging.

It seemed sad really that Carli lived in her grandparents' house now, but the kitchen would never smell like that again. Maybe she should learn how to make yeast rolls.

She spotted Sheriff Will Anderson at his usual back corner table, under a large metal sign that read Eat Butter to Feel Better. He was in the process of tucking a snow-white cloth napkin into the top of his starched white shirt. Before him sat a plate piled high with fried chicken. He glanced up as Carli walked his way and a frown settled on his face. Carli swallowed the lump in her throat and pulled out a chair.

"May I join you?" She sat down and propped her chin in her hands. She waited.

The sheriff briefly nodded before biting into a golden-brown crispy thigh. He closed his eyes and chewed. Then swallowed before he looked at her again.

"Any reason why you're interrupting my Sunday dinner?"

"Yes, sir. A very important reason." Before Carli could explain, Angie whizzed around the corner in a vibrant burst of energy, shiny blonde hair and a green paisley shirt. Feather earrings fluttered when she walked.

"Oh no," murmured Sheriff Anderson.

"There you are. Howdy, Sheriff." She plopped down at the table, a beaming smile across her face. She turned to Carli. "I can't believe Raven agreed to meet with you."

A waitress appeared. "What can I get you ladies?"

At the same time, Carli and Angie both replied, "Sweet tea."

They all laughed except for the sheriff whose frown deepened.

"Coming right up." The waitress disappeared into the kitchen.

Angie looked at Carli and nodded. Carli cleared her throat.

"Sheriff, as you know we are very concerned with the sudden increase in rustling. Angie and I have been considering leads."

"Except I told you to let us handle it." He never looked up, instead focused on a pile of creamy mashed potatoes covered with gravy.

Carli's mouth watered as she watched him eat, and then she cleared her throat again. "Yes, sir, you did."

Her iced sweet tea appeared just in time. She

took a long drink, gaining courage with each swallow. She knew the sheriff was more than a little aggravated at their intrusion, but she also knew they were hot on the trail of the criminals. She had no doubt in her mind that Raven and his uncle were involved.

"But we've seen them," Angie said. She unwrapped a straw and drained half of her glass in mere seconds.

"And they're planning something big on the next full moon," said Carli.

"I knew it." Angie slapped her hand on the table.

That got his attention. "How do you know this?"

"I spoke to Raven, uh John Gibbons." Carli folded her arms on the table and leaned closer. "We should set a trap and catch them in the act."

"First of all, these guys are good at what they do. They know your schedule. They've been watching you for months and they sit and wait. The likelihood that they'd tell the kid anything is slim. And then if they do pull something off, odds are there's another rancher involved who pays in hard cash or drugs to take the stolen property. If they run 'em through an out of state auction, we'll never be able to track the stolen livestock. Plus, they're good at altering the brands."

Carli's heart sank. One more person reminding her how ineffective she was against criminals and at running her ranch, protecting her property.

"We've seen their truck. We can make a positive ID," argued Angie.

"I did check out your story from the auction," the sheriff said, "and that truck that the eyewitness, Mr. Gallagher, saw was a dually pickup. The tracks Derek measured and included in his report from Vera's pasture were single back tires. Not the same vehicle."

"What if they took off the outside tires?" asked Angie. "It's possible."

He leaned back in his chair and wiped his mouth with the napkin before taking several swallows of iced tea. "Surely you girls can find something better to do with your time. Maybe have a bake sale? Ride your horses?" He raised his hand and caught the waitress's eye. "I'll have a piece of apple pie, please."

A bake sale? Carli fumed. She did not appreciate being talked to like she was in grade school and she could tell he wasn't going to listen to anything they had to say. She stood. "Thanks for your time, Sheriff Anderson."

Angie looked at her in surprise as Carli spun on her heel and left through the front entrance. Angie hurried to catch up and stopped her on the porch.

"You're giving in that easily? We're right ya know."

"I know, but no one believes us." Carli turned to look at Angie as they walked back to the parking lot. "What if we could set a trap?"

"Go on, I'm listening."

"Let me think on it and I'll call you later."

They both drove away, Angie offering a quick wave as she passed.

Some way or somehow, Carli was going to prove to the sheriff that they had the right guys. Together she and Angie would put an end to this soon. Bake sale? Hmpff.

Chapter Thirty-Five

Before heading back to the Wild Cow after talking to the sheriff at Mozell's Diner, Carli stopped by the B&R Beanery. She needed a strong coffee with lots of sugar. She was still stinging from the bake sale comment.

The bell tinkled as she pushed the door open and made a beeline to Belinda who looked up and smiled. "Caramel macchiato, double shot and double whip," Carli said as she slapped a five-dollar bill on the counter.

"Whoa, now. Having a bad day?" Belinda laughed.

"You could say that. You could also say that nobody in this town takes me seriously. While I appreciate the macho Texas male as much as anyone, sometimes they really get under my skin."

"Like for example?" Belinda asked before turning on the coffee grinder.

Carli fumed and didn't answer for a minute. After she paid and settled into a bar stool at the back table where she and Belinda usually talked, she took a few sips. Her friend sat down, waiting.

"Cattle rustlers are a huge problem this year," Carli began.

"So I've heard. That's all they do, some of them. That's how they make their living."

"Angie and I have a bead on a group of them, but we can't get the sheriff to hear a word we're saying. He suggests we hold a bake sale." Just telling Belinda about his comment enraged her all over again.

"He did not say that." Belinda's eyes widened when Carli answered with a nod of her head.

"We have a positive ID on their pickup truck and—"

"How in the world would you know their truck?" Belinda asked.

"Angie and I have seen it twice now. Once driving through the Wild Cow and again at the auction. We saw Raven but we couldn't get a good look at the other men with him."

"So, what are you going to do?"

"I don't know what to do." Carli let out a big sigh. "There's got to be a way to catch them in the act, but we're talking thousands and thousands of acres between the Rafter O, the Wild Cow, and Crazy Vera's in between. Plus, all of the neighboring ranches in the county. It's a lot of ground to cover. How can we figure out where they'll strike next?"

"You can't draw flies with vinegar, as the saying goes."

Carli sat up straighter, stared at Belinda for a few minutes, and then said, "That's it. You're a genius.

Let's give rustlers what they want most."

"And what would that be?" Belinda tilted her head.

"Cows, of course."

After going over her idea with Belinda, which turned into a lengthy discussion, Carli stopped by Frank's Grocery to pick up a few essentials before heading back home. She needed to call Angie for help. They had a few days, give or take, before the next full moon. Carli would check the weather app on her phone to determine which night exactly.

She recalled an isolated set of working pens in the far southern portion of the Wild Cow. Just off a county road and straddling the fence line between two sizable pastures, it would be the perfect place to leave the bait. She could drive a few pairs in to the pens, and if what the sheriff said was true about them watching ranch activity, it wouldn't be long before the rustlers would take notice. If they picked a night before or after the full moon, then she would have given away valuable cattle, but maybe her luck would hold out.

Carli pulled into ranch headquarters just before dusk. Lily Jane came bounding over the grass and met her vehicle as she turned into the drive. She didn't see Lank anywhere, which was unusual since his dog usually trailed on his heels. Lily Jane wagged her tail so hard her entire body did the shimmy when Carli stepped out of the pickup. The dog immediately sat.

"Good girl, but I don't have any treats with me."

Carli reached for the two bags of groceries and walked to the front door. Lily Jane followed but then stopped on the front porch and raised her head. Her tail came up and then she cut loose in a frenzy of barking which soon turned to growls.

"What is wrong with you, girl?" Carli balanced one bag of groceries on her arm and cautiously reached for the doorknob. Lily Jane was beside herself. She refused to go inside, instead standing at the threshold growling, low and mean. "Good grief. Move over, Lily. I'm about to drop this."

Carli side-stepped around the dog and walked through the dark entry hall towards the kitchen. She should have left some lights on, but she hadn't planned on being gone so long. She placed the bags on the bar and turned to find the light switch.

"Don't bother," a man's voice said, but it was more of a growl than a comment.

Carli's heart jumped out of her throat and she couldn't hold back the gasp as she turned back around.

He sat at the far end of her dining room table, with black biker boots propped on the edge. In front of him was a can of her cola.

A possible scruff mark on her grandmother's table only made her mad and she forgot the fear. "Make yourself at home, why don't you?" And just because she could, Carli turned on the light.

The man wore a black bandana, silver hair hung from beneath it to the bottom of his ear. And ears incidentally that were rimmed with earrings.

Both forearms were tattooed, solid with images that Carli couldn't make any sense of their design. Black eyes that terrified her, but she'd never let him know. Dark and staring under bushy brows, empty sockets where a soul should be.

"Why are you in my house? And take your boots off my table." Carli managed to keep her voice calm, but she imagined he could hear her heart beating. She tried to show anger in her eyes and not fear.

He removed his boots from the table and leaned forward. "What did my nephew tell you?"

Was he talking about Raven?

"I don't know you and I don't know your nephew," Carli said. Should she sit down at the table, like she didn't have a care in the world? At the last minute she decided she didn't want to be any closer to him, so she spun around and started emptying the grocery bags. As she opened the refrigerator door her hand trembled.

"What are you doing?" he grunted, his voice gravelly. Probably from smoking.

"Putting away my groceries. I have milk and coffee creamer I don't want to spoil." She gave him a look like he was the biggest idiot in the world. It worked. She saw annoyance cross his face, and his eyes narrowed.

"I'll only ask one more time. What did you tell Raven?"

"That's between him and me," Carli said.

"I know he met you earlier today. I want to know what you talked about."

Carli stepped into the pantry out of his sight, put several cans of soup on the shelf and then leaned over with her hands on her knees. Breathe in. Breathe out. If she passed out right now, she'd hate herself from now until eternity. Her entire life she always detested showing any kind of weakness. She never let her guard down and never allowed her emotions to gain control. This was not the time to start. Give me strength, God.

She took a few more breaths and walked out of the pantry only to bump into the man's chest like a brick wall. She looked up into those black eyes. He gripped the tops of her arms and squeezed. "This isn't some joke and I don't like people who waste my time."

"We talked about him and Lexi. His girlfriend is one of my riding students. I think he's too old for her, but she likes him and I keep trying to advise her to drop him."

What possessed her to ramble on and on, she'd never know but once she started talking Carli couldn't stop. Her brain kept yelling, shut up, but her mouth had diarrhea. "She needs to finish school first before things get too serious. He's a good kid, your nephew. He has plenty of smarts. Why don't you let him find his way and stay out of his life?"

That did it. The annoyance on his face turned to rage. He removed one hand from her arm and pointed a dirty finger close to her face.

"You stay away from my family and out of my business, or I will destroy everything you hold dear. Do you understand?"

Carli couldn't form any words although seconds before she couldn't stop talking. A head nod was the only thing she could manage. She was frozen in one spot with fear.

He let go of her arm and walked to the back door. Before he left, he turned and looked at her.

"Melvin is my name. I left you a little surprise so you'll know I'm serious."

"The gates. That was you." Carli remembered the mess they had sorting cows back to their pastures after someone had left gates open in almost every pasture.

"That was nothing. I want you to understand. Stay out of my business." His deep voice was crisp and clear.

Fear gripped Carli's heart again, her legs and knees went weak. Before she could answer, Uncle Melvin had gone. The slam of the back door made her jump. Beau was her next thought. She ran out the house and to the barn as fast as she could. Not her horse. Please, not Beau.

Chapter Thirty-Six

Lank Torres gritted his teeth against the pain, closed his eyes, and focused on contorting his wrists free from the rope that bound them. It was no use. The greasy rag across his mouth didn't help any. He couldn't get enough air through his nose and he needed to sneeze.

He stopped struggling to catch his breath.

Pieces and images were starting to come back to him. He had been out cold; he knew that for sure but for how long he couldn't figure out. He remembered stepping back into the saddle house to put the brush back on the shelf, he turned, and a blow to his neck came out of nowhere. He remembered a stocky man, a bandana, but he didn't see a face or hear a voice. Just wham.

He came to leaning against the hay bale with an old grease rag in his mouth and his wrists tied so tight his hands were getting numb for lack of circulation.

A clank of the fence latch caught his attention.

He stilled and listened. Not sure if he should make a noise or not. By now the corral was in pitch black. He heard boots crunch on dirt clods, soft and slow. Whoever it was took their time, cautious and careful.

Then he heard the whispers. "Beau. Come here, boy." It was Carli.

In the dark Lank tried to remember if there was something he could make a noise with. He leaned over and scooted like a worm across the cement, closer to the shelf unit. With his boot he kicked. It rattled. He wanted to call her, but he couldn't. He wanted to say her name more than anything in the world.

He kicked again but didn't think that maneuver through. There was only one place for the shelf to fall. Brushes and curry combs fell all around him as the shelf came down with a crash. Surely, she heard that.

Slowly and silently the door to the saddle house opened. Without any warning the light switched, its sudden glare blinding him. He squinted.

"Lank." Carli gripped the shelf with both hands and set it upright. She kneeled at his side and worked on the rope at his wrists. "Oh, sorry. Let me get that out of your mouth first."

As soon as the rag was gone, he licked his lips, spit and coughed, trying to get rid of the grimy taste.

"What happened?" she asked.

He still couldn't speak.

She continued her work on the ropes behind him. "These are tied really tight. I don't know if I can work them loose."

"I never saw him," he finally managed to say, his voice coming out scratchy and coarse.

"There," she smiled at her success.

He jerked his arms loose and worked his fingers trying to regain circulation.

"We've got to call Sheriff Anderson," Lank said.

"No, wait. I know who it was. He was in my house too."

"Who? What's going on, Carli?" Lank leaned forward and untied the rope around his ankles. He never imagined his good ropes would be used against him.

"It was Raven's uncle."

"Who?" He had no idea what she was even talking about.

"Raven. Lexi's boyfriend. His Uncle Melvin is fresh out of prison and I think he's been rustling our cattle."

"What's that got to do with you and why was he here?" The realization of what she'd said suddenly hit him. "He didn't hurt you, did he?"

"No. I'm fine. His way of being a bully and tying you up was a message."

"What message?"

She hesitated. Lank glared at her. "What are you not telling me, Carli?"

"Angie and I saw his truck drive through the Wild Cow. And then we found it again later parked at Vera's. We saw it at the auction, too. Now I know for certain he's rustling cattle because why else would he come here unless we were right? He must feel threatened."

"Buck and Lola!" Lank jumped to his feet but Carli blocked his way before he made it to the door.

"I'm sure they're all right. We can't tell them, or the sheriff. It might make it worse."

"How can it get any worse? I got tied up! You found someone in your house. He could have hurt you."

"I think we should keep this just between us. I don't want anyone else to be threatened." Carli placed a hand on his shoulder.

"Now would be the time to tell me everything. Not just about the rustlers. About us too. You've been pushing me away since that night in the hospital. I didn't dream up our conversation, did I? You said you loved me, but it's like we're strangers. Why can't you trust me, Carli? Did you mean what you said?"

She hesitated. Longer than he would have liked, and her standing there avoiding his eyes made him furious. He could tell things were a turmoil inside her mind, but yet she refused to talk. She must have been terrified to find that monster in her house. He wanted to hug her and fix it, make things better, take away her fright but he held back. He couldn't do this relationship all by himself. Give and give, with nothing in return. She had to meet him halfway or there would be nothing between them. The thought that they couldn't make this work made him miserable.

He wanted her to know that he hadn't even looked or thought about another girl since he dreamt he might have a chance with Carli. He wasn't interested in anyone else. Never even considered a one-night party with an old girlfriend for old times' sake, and there'd been many opportunities. That kind of life held no appeal for him, now that he could even hope for a life with Carli.

"What's going on in that head of yours?" Lank moved closer and put his hands on her shoulders. "Carli. Please. Talk to me."

She finally raised her eyes to look at him. "Angie and I can stop them. We don't need you men to save us from the big, bad ex-con. If he knows I'm scared, he'll only make things worse. I've been on my own for a long time, Cowboy. I know how the world works and I can take care of myself."

Anger glinted in her eyes and he had no idea why. She turned to leave, but then turned back around. "I'm glad you're okay." The streak of a tear shined on her cheek. With that, the night swallowed her and she was gone.

Gone for tonight or really gone? Did they just break up? He still didn't know where they were headed. One thing for certain, she could not face these criminals on her own. She had mentioned Angie too. Those girls were up to something. He needed to question Travis Olsen. He might have overheard Angie talking. And he needed to call

Colton who had connections on the seedier side of town. Colton knew everybody. Maybe he could find out something about this Uncle Melvin and what they were up against.

Lank's first instinct was to wake up Buck and Lola to make sure they were all right, but then he had to agree with Carli. That would set Buck into action, maybe overreaction, and Lola would be upset if she knew there was a man waiting inside Carli's house. But what if they were tied up too? He couldn't leave them that way all night.

Lank made his way across the dark compound, Lily Jane suddenly appearing at his heels.

"No, girl. Home." Of course, the dog ignored him, so he picked her up and hurried to his trailer. Opening the front door, he deposited her inside before making his way back to the cookhouse.

Using his key, he silently opened the door and was relieved to see the kitchen light on. He could hear Lola and Buck talking in soft voices. Relief washed over him and he started to leave, but stepped inside and his spur jangled. He forgot he still had them on.

"Lank?" Buck called out. "Is that you?"

"Yes sir. Sorry to bother you. Are there any cookies left?"

Lola laughed. "Of course. Help yourself." She set the clear jar on the bar filled halfway with neat stacks of oatmeal raisin. Not his favorite, but he was trapped now.

Buck walked closer. "There's grease on your

face. And why are you so dirty?" He exchanged a glance with Lola but didn't say anything else.

"Oh, just sweeping out the saddle house." He walked to the sink and washed his hands, helped himself to three cookies, and turned to leave. "Goodnight, y'all."

"Goodnight, Lank," Lola called out.

"Night," said Buck.

Lank stepped outside and noticed Carli's lights were off. Guess she had already turned in. He wondered how she could sleep after finding Uncle Melvin waiting for her. That had to have creeped her out.

Chapter Thirty-Seven

Carli couldn't go back inside her house. She stood alone on the dark porch wishing Lily Jane was still there because once again she'd forgotten to leave the light on. Where had that dog gone? Back to Lank's? At least Lily could warn her if Uncle Melvin came back in the night. Surely he wouldn't, would he? She tried to still her heart and tell herself there was nothing to be afraid of.

She looked through the window. The glow from the light over her kitchen sink created shadows across the front room. She couldn't see anything clearly. The edges of the room stood in darkness. The image of that man sitting at her kitchen table caused her fear to clutch, close her throat, and make her heart race. Maybe she could use the back door, but then she'd have to walk around the house in the dark. She'd forgotten her phone too.

A slight noise caught her attention, and she turned to watch Lank leaving the cookhouse and walking towards his trailer. She gritted her teeth and wondered if he'd told Buck anything after she had clearly asked him not to. She hadn't lived here long but had come to understand the power of a small-town gossip mill. That's all they needed, word that Carli and Angie were chasing down the rustlers. It wouldn't be shed in the light of how capable they were, but more like the joke of the week. She did not want to hear anyone else remind her how it couldn't be done and to let someone else handle it. She clenched her fists in frustration. If everyone would just lend support instead of criticism.

Carli could see Lank open the door of his trailer and Lily Jane jump straight up like a jack rabbit and into his arms. His chuckle echoed across the dark compound. They disappeared inside and Carli was alone again.

In the next second, she wanted to run towards Lank. She could crash on his couch. Maybe they'd have that talk he seemed to think they needed. Maybe she'd tell him everything. About how he made her heart race. About the idiot boyfriend in Georgia who still brought tears to her eyes. About the reasons she couldn't go through anything like that ever again. She sighed and eased into one of the rocking chairs at the end of her front porch. She just needed to sit down for a minute and then she'd go inside her house.

Carli wanted to talk to Lank about her idea for setting a trap, but she wouldn't. It left her feeling disgusted and irritated at herself. Which was the reason she was still alone. There were so many people throughout her life who she'd never fully trusted. Friendships that she'd turned her back on instead. She probably needed therapy. The realization hit so unexpectedly that it caused her to gasp. Lank was different. She had to trust him or it might mean a life without him. She was throwing away their love before they'd even begun. The fact she loved him was without question. She was beginning to understand the difference between infatuation and deep love, but with deep love came trust and she just wasn't there yet. The thing about trust, it has to work both ways.

Carli woke with a start and a crick in her neck. That rocking chair was not made for sleeping. She blinked against the night, stood, and stretched. She hesitated at the door, then pushed it open and went inside her house with a heavy sigh. Without turning on any lights or locking the door behind her, she fell on top of the covers with her clothes on. Before closing her eyes and giving in to the exhaustion that made every bone in her body ache, she sent a quick text to Angie. Come over ready to ride. I have an idea.

The sound of pounding on her door jolted Carli from a deep sleep. Uncle Melvin's face flashed through her brain and she sat upright with a gasp. Angie's voice broke the silence. "Carli? I'm here."

"Back here," Carli answered, her throat was dry making her voice scratchy and coarse.

Angie appeared in the doorway of the bedroom. "You're still asleep?"

"Had a rough night," Carli replied. "Uncle Melvin paid me a visit."

"What? He didn't hurt you, did he?" Concern covered Angie's face.

"Hang on. Let me get dressed and I'll tell you about it. Would you mind making coffee?"

"Sure. But hurry, Mom made you some cinnamon rolls," Angie said as she left the room.

The smells of freshly brewed coffee beans soon drifted to her nose making Carli get dressed even quicker, and came to the kitchen.

"When I got home last night Uncle Melvin was sitting at my table."

"That means he knows we're on to 'em," said Angie. "Good."

Certainly not the response Carli had imagined, but then she hadn't told her about Lank yet.

"I admire your grit," Carli said, "but he also tied up Lank. Told me he'd left me a message to stay out of his business. I thought he'd done something to Beau."

"I cannot believe that. He had the gall to walk inside your home? I guess the sheriff was right, they are watching the targeted ranches. They know our schedule."

"He knew that I had talked to Raven and Lexi." Carli reached for a mug of coffee. "But I think I have an idea. You've been by that set of working pens in the far pasture? Why not drive a few pairs down there as bait, and on the next full moon we'll be waiting?"

"It might work," Angie agreed. "That's not far off the county road, assuming they'll be driving around checking things out beforehand."

"And hopefully it's the night of the full moon and not the night before or the night after. It's a gamble either way, but we have to try something." Carli checked her weather app. "Cloudy the night before, if that prediction holds out. We need to make a ruckus though. Make out like we'll be somewhere else."

"I have a feeling the Olsen family might need to host a cookout that night." Angie smiled. "I'll spread the word and ask Mom, except I won't be there."

"Let's go drive those pairs into the pen then. I'll have to figure out a story for Lank and Buck in case they notice what we've done."

"This is going to work, Carli. We're going to stop those guys."

That evening Carli told a bold-faced lie to both Buck and Lank, and she felt bad for a second but she had to keep in mind the greater good. Besides, it could be counted as a half-truth.

Lola had invited her over for barbeque and of course, Lank was there too. He didn't smile when she walked in and certainly didn't kiss her hello or sling an arm around her shoulder. She missed his touch.

After they got seated, Buck turned to Lank. "Any reason you have those pairs in the pen down south?"

"No sir. I was going to ask you the same thing. Is there something you need done?"

"It wasn't me that put them there."

Carli cleared her throat. "It was me. Angie helped. I'm working with Beau some more. He's still not used to cows and I thought a smaller enclosure might work better. I'll make sure the water tub is full."

Buck and Lank both looked at her like she was crazy, but neither said anything. She hurriedly ate her dinner and then excused herself. Lank caught her eye, a suspicious look on his face like he wanted to say something but changed his mind. She had worried that he might bring up the Uncle Melvin incident, but he didn't. At least while she was there.

Chapter Thirty-Eight

Lank Torres eased around a group of parked cars at the Rafter O compound for a cookout, his heart heavy and his thoughts on Carli. He was not making any ground with that girl and he couldn't figure out why. She'd avoided him despite his efforts to cross her path. He had watched her saddle Beau and ride off. Come back and leave in her pickup truck. Come back and disappear inside her house.

Fine with him if she needed space. So, he decided to leave her alone until the time was right. And then he'd lay his heart on the line and see how that worked. She was a mystery, unlike any girl he'd ever known but that was part of her appeal. So independent and distant. But it sure did drive him crazy. He wanted to know her secrets. He needed to know everything about her. He craved her touch.

Lank heard chattering from the crowd, so he opened the side gate and went around back to the patio. Mr. Olsen had burgers cooking on the grill; the smell of mesquite and cooked meat made Lank's mouth water as he walked closer. He offered a hand in greeting which Skip Olsen returned, and then he saw Colton and Travis in the far corner and walked over to them.

"Lank, my man!" said Travis. "Can I get you something to drink?" The Olsens were the epitome of welcoming hosts. That's why no one ever turned down an invitation. He scanned the crowd for Angie before answering.

"I'm good for now, thanks. Is Angie here?"

"Haven't seen her yet." Travis turned his attention back to Colton and continued his story about a new horse. Lank barely listened. He leaned against a stone pillar and looked for Carli. He'd bet his last nickel that she and Angie were together, wherever that was.

Lank walked over to the beverage bar and filled a tall glass half full of sweet tea and the other half lemonade. Took a sip and wandered into the spacious family room. Several people talked in small groups. Some gave a wave and he nodded in return. He made his way to the kitchen. A handful of ladies were busy cutting up vegetables. He gave a nod to Lola.

"Hello, Lank. Glad you could make it," said Mrs. Olsen. She gave him a hug. She looked at him curiously. "Can I get you something?"

"Wondering if Angie might be about."

"I haven't seen that girl all day, and this little get-together was her idea. I'm not happy with that young lady. She was supposed to help me."

Lank wandered back outside just as Mr. Olsen took the burgers up and asked everyone to bow their heads for the blessing. The smells wafted around his head and Lank realized he was hungry. He got in line, filled his plate, and stood under an oak tree.

"What's with you, man?" Travis asked.

"You're jumpier than a new colt at a rodeo," added Colton.

"Nothing. Just hungry I guess." Lank took an oversized bite so he wouldn't have to answer any questions.

Colton kept them entertained as usual with his stories of horse mishaps as the sky turned from a bright orange and faded into a blue-gray when the sun disappeared on another day. Lank turned to fill his tea glass and that's when he caught a glimpse of a full moon. Big and bold, it was a perfect circle.

At that exact moment the calf pairs in the far pasture crossed his mind, and he knew exactly what Carli was up to. He chided himself for not thinking of it sooner.

Lank grabbed Travis by the arm. "Did Angie say anything to you about the full moon tonight and going somewhere with Carli?"

"I don't pay no attention to what she's doing." Travis shrugged. "I don't really care. Got my own self to worry about."

Lank explained to them both what he thought might be going down. "We've got to go."

In several minutes they were piled into Lank's

truck and headed back towards the Wild Cow. "We'll have to drive part ways without lights and then we're going to have to hotfoot it in. We can't let them hear or see the truck. I know of the place to park, and then we'll have to come in from the creek bottom."

"Sounds like a plan," said Colton. "I can't imagine those girls doing anything like this. You can't bait cattle rustlers and set a trap. The odds of them being out on the same night are like a gazillion to one. Stupidest idea I've ever heard of."

"There's no such number as a gazillion," said Travis. "And don't underestimate my sister. When she sets her mind to something, you might as well move out of the way."

"I'm learning that about Carli, too," Lank said. "My mother was a force and totally devoted to my father, but I don't think she would have gone after criminals without taking him along."

And that's what stung so much, but Lank didn't say it out loud. Carli hadn't trusted him enough to take him into her confidence and tell him what they had planned. He should be by her side, sitting out in the middle of the pasture under a full moon. Why couldn't she trust him? He loved the Wild Cow Ranch just as much as she did.

"Dang it," said Colton. "I forgot my .22 with rat-shot. It for sure works at stopping a fella."

"I guess we're taking fists to a gunfight, boys." Travis sighed.

"When it comes to Carli, I'm never surprised.

She is a mystery to me," said Lank. "But if there's any chance at all that something is going down, I'd never forgive myself if she got hurt."

Lank pushed the gas and his pickup roared into the night.

Chapter Thirty-Nine

Carli and Angie sat side by side, cross-legged in a plum thicket. Their pickup truck was parked about one hundred yards away on a lesser used pasture road that crossed a dry creek bed. Carli had stopped it there at the dip in the road where it was hidden. From their spot they had a clear view of the working pens that straddled the fence line between the South End Pasture and Pasture Five. Carli tried not to think about the creatures that might be crawling around in the wild sand plum bushes.

"Hand me a water, would ya?" Angie whispered. "I'm thirstier than a wild dog chasing a rabbit for his supper after that walk up the hill."

"Why are you whispering? There's nobody around for miles. We might be here all night."

"I hope not. Did we bring anything to eat?"

"Oh, shoot," Carli said. "I left the snack bag on the table in my kitchen."

"What are we gonna do to pass the time if we can't eat?"

Carli could hear the impatient annoyance in Angie's voice. It amazed her how much that girl could put away and still stay slim.

A cow bawled softly to her calf. The four pairs shuffled around in the working pens, settling in for the night. They'd done a good job of eating the belly high weeds and grass that'd been trampled during branding.

"I hope this works," Carli said. "Do you think the rustlers noticed these cows we moved here? I sure hope the moon comes out."

"All forecasts indicated it will," Angie said. "And yes, I think they spend a lot of time driving around area ranches every day and they've probably seen this small herd of cows and their calves several times. They know how isolated this pen is."

Angie set her water down and hissed as she grabbed Carli's arm. "I see lights."

Carli's heart beat a little faster as she strained her eyes in the gray dusk until she saw a flash of vehicle lights on the far horizon. The beams moved up and down with the bumpy road and then disappeared again. The girls watched in silence as the headlights drew nearer.

"Who knows we're out here?" Carli asked. She couldn't tell how far away it was. As the vehicle drew closer the moon suddenly burst from behind one lone cloud, big and glowing gold, casting a soft light over the grass.

"Travis blabbed to somebody, I'm sure. I'm going to beat him bloody. That boy cannot keep his mouth shut." Angie sounded steamed.

"How could he know what we're doing, unless you told him? He doesn't mean any harm in it," Carli said. "He worries about you."

At the same time the dark colored vehicle topped the nearest rise. "Do you think rustlers drive minivans?" Angie asked.

Carli squinted. Angie was right. That definitely was a minivan and it was headed straight for the pens. It rolled to a stop, and then turned in a slow circle as the beams shone over the pen before stopping again facing the opposite direction. The ding, ding of the door as it opened broke the silence of the evening and a lady stepped out.

"Carli. Angie," she called out.

"Belinda?" Carli stood up from her hiding place. "What are you doing?"

"You didn't think I'd let you girls stay out here by yourselves and that I'd miss all the fun, did you?' She giggled.

"Your voice would drive a coyote to suicide," shouted Angie. "Can you please be quiet? Park your van down the hill next to the truck and hurry back."

Carli tried not to chuckle. Angie was just as loud as Belinda.

Before long Belinda shuffled through the plum thicket using her phone as a light. "This is a bit too snaky for me," she whispered loud.

"I'm packing my pistol and Carli brought a shovel. If you hear a rattle, let us know," Angie said.

"Between the two of you and all that yelling,

I'm sure you've driven them all away by now," said Carli. "What'd you bring?"

Belinda set a cooler on the ground between them. "Coffees and blueberry scones. Thought you might need something to keep you awake."

"Yeah, great." Angie grabbed a tall coffee and sniffed the aroma from the vent in the top. "Thank you. Did I ever tell you that you're my favorite coffee shop owner?"

"That's because I'm the only coffee shop owner you know." With a smile Belinda took a breath. "That walk up the hill was something else. Now what's the plan?"

Carli couldn't answer, her mouth full of the flakiest scone she'd ever tasted. The blueberries were plump and juicy, and she could taste the powdered sugar dusted on the top. She swallowed and washed it down with coffee.

"That's not your SUV," she said.

"You mean my big, white SUV? Thought a dark colored vehicle might be less conspicuous. I borrowed it from my neighbor," Belinda answered.

"How did you explain that one? Excuse me, I'm taking your car to a major crime scene at the Wild Cow. Be back in a few." Carli leaned closer to Belinda as they both laughed.

"No chit chat, girls. This could go down any minute." Angie half-scolded. With that, they sat in silence.

Carli covered a yawn with her hand. If she could just close her eyes for one minute. Maybe she could lie back on the dirt. Her coffee was empty, she'd put away two scones, and her water bottle was only half full. Plus, she had to go wet a bush. She couldn't hold it any longer. Easing to her feet, she whispered, "Be back in a sec."

Belinda and Angie both nodded their heads without saying anything. Carli made her way out of the bushes and stretched. She didn't even need her cell phone light. She could see perfectly fine under the sky's expansive glow.

The moon-bathed night stretched out in front of her. So peaceful and still. She could hear a cow tear grass and then the suckling sounds of a calf as it found nourishment.

Just as she squatted, she heard the sound of a truck engine. Every so often the rattle of what sounded like a trailer as it bumped along the county road. She held her breath and stayed low. The beam of lights showed over the next rise and sure enough, a pickup truck pulling a livestock trailer curved along the road and headed her way. So much for wearing dark clothes. Her bare butt most certainly would reflect the full moon. She would've giggled at the joke, if she hadn't been so scared.

The truck didn't stop but veered off the caliche road slightly so that the lights cut across the pen, slowed, and then turned back on the road and eased past.

Carli let out a sigh of relief, finished her business, and hurried back to the girls.

"A white truck. That's Uncle Melvin," said Angie,

her voice high and breathless.

Carli remained silent. She could still hear the truck engine not entirely fading as it got farther away, and then maybe the night winds deceived her ears but it sounded like it was getting closer.

"Is it coming back?" asked Angie.

Belinda gasped and hugged her knees. "This is exciting."

The vehicle and trailer appeared again from the opposite direction and this time they backed the trailer up to the gate.

Carli didn't move a muscle but sat stone still holding her breath. She sensed the other girls were doing the same.

"What's the plan?" asked Belinda.

"What'a we do, Carli?" asked Angie.

"I don't know," said Carli. "Any ideas?"

"You mean to tell me you had this all set up and you girls have no idea what happens next?" Belinda's voice was tinged with frustration and a bit of fear.

"I never thought that far," said Carli.

"Shhh. A door's opening." Angie hissed.

Carli watched three men step from the truck. As the cab light came on, she thought she could see another head but wasn't sure. Raven she recognized immediately, and the stocky build of Uncle Melvin. Seeing him again sent chills down her spine. The other man must be Raven's father.

They seemed proficient around the cows as they walked into the pen and herded them towards the waiting trailer. Raven stood behind the trailer gate, ready to swing it shut as soon as the last cow stepped up inside.

Carli got to her feet. She had no idea what she was going to say or do, but she had to act now before they drove away.

Suddenly, a voice growled from the dark, sharp and mean. "You're trespassing." Lank appeared on the top rail of the fence and walked across the pen towards the rustlers.

Carli gasped and she heard Angie and Belinda do the same.

From one side of the truck, Colton appeared and not far from where the girls sat, Travis walked out of the shadows of the plum thicket.

"Step back, boys. We'll be unloading those cows now," Colton said to the rustlers.

That's when the scene turned ugly.

Chapter Forty

Angie Olsen's adrenalin coursed through her veins. Eyes wide, her head darted right and left. The full moon shone like a giant movie premiere spotlight on this crazy scene. She hustled to her feet to stand next to Carli as they both watched Lank, Colton, and Travis surround the rustlers.

If she'd been a betting gal, she would never in a million years think this plan of Carli's would work, but she hated to discourage her. She seemed so determined to catch the rustlers. It hadn't been that long ago when Belinda had shown up in her minivan like a hippy dippy flower child bringing coffee and muffins into shark-infested waters. And now here they all were in the middle of a pit of venomous criminal cattle rustlers, hell bent on stealing what was not theirs, probably capable of murdering for their cause if it came to that.

Without so much as a shout of warning, Uncle Melvin lunged for Colton punching him square on the nose, and the other older man jumped on Lank.

Carli burst out of the bushes and Angie followed.

"Wait for me," Belinda shouted.

They ran towards the men.

Uncle Melvin slammed Colton against the trailer, the impact causing it to rattle loud in the silent night. The other man, probably Raven's father if she had to guess, had Lank on the ground and was pounding his face. The older men, ex-cons trained in prison brawls no doubt, were solid and stout and no match for the skinny cowboys, although the younger men got in some good punches.

Travis just gave Raven a mean, dirty look and the kid backed down.

"Stop it," yelled Carli as she hurried closer to the rustler's truck. "Raven, tell them to stop."

Raven climbed into the truck and sank into the back seat of the cab, leaving the door wide open. Carli got in his face. Angie followed and heard her gasp at the sight of Lexi huddled in the corner.

"Lexi?" Carli asked.

"What's she doing here?" Angie demanded.

Angie felt sorry for the kids. By the look on Carli's face, Raven would be lucky to survive the night.

In the next instant Lank let out a loud hmpff from a solid punch to his gut. Carli reached in the rustler's truck, grabbed a rope from the floorboard under Raven's feet, and ran to the men next to the livestock trailer. She swung it overhead, roped the man, and yanked him clean off Lank like he was a runt calf. Lank was then able to get a few punches of his own in while Raven's father fought the rope.

"Belinda, help me," Carli yelled. They both tugged hard and pulled the man away from Lank.

Carli and Belinda hurried over and sat on the criminal but he pushed them off. Raven's father made a run for it to the dually truck and yelled to Melvin. "Let's go."

Travis appeared out of nowhere and tackled the man. They both landed with a thud on the ground.

Angie searched for Colton.

There was so much going on it was like a three-ring circus. Gotta keep my wits about me or this whole crazy party could go south in a hurry.

Scuffling and cursing caught Angie's attention as Uncle Melvin grabbed a hold of Colton's jacket and threw him to the ground. Colton's mouth and eyebrow were bleeding. Punch after punch from Melvin was turning Colton into a limp ragdoll. His face was becoming an unrecognizable mess.

Angie had to do something. She couldn't let these lowlife criminals get the upper hand. Or hurt the guys anymore. They had to be stopped, one way or the other.

And then Angie saw Uncle Melvin land a solid punch to Colton's jaw. He collapsed to the ground and Melvin made a dash to catch up with Raven's father at the dually. Carli stood at the back door of the cab still pleading with Lexi to get out of the truck and come with her. The man yanked on Carli's arm and threw her several feet away from the pickup truck. She landed with a thud, the momentum causing her to roll over several times.

Can't let them get away. Angie quickly pulled her firearm from her shoulder holster, clicked off the safety, and took a deep breath. Extending her right arm out straight, Angie cupped the gun hand with her left. She had to be careful not to hurt anyone—Lexi was in the dually and Carli was nearby—so she said a quick prayer, aimed low to the ground at one of the back tires, and hit the mark on her first try. Her ears stung from the crack of gunfire. The tire hissed as the air escaped. Lexi screamed.

In the next second the sound of a siren split the air and red and white lights popped up over the rise. The sheriff's cruiser was coming in fast.

"Stand still," Angie shouted as she stared down the two men. "Nobody move."

Lank stumbled to Carli who had rolled over to her back on the ground. He helped her to her feet.

Lexi and Raven emerged from the backseat, his arm around the frightened girl. "Carli, please don't let them take Raven to jail. Please."

"You kids hurry down the hill and hide in my truck," Carli said. "Do not make a move or utter one word. I'll deal with you later."

Lank shouted. "No. He's a criminal."

"I can handle this, Lank," Carli argued.

"Do the right thing, man, or you'll regret it the rest of your life." Lank leaned on Carli's shoulder and stared at Raven.

"Lexi, go," said Raven. "He's right. I'm just as guilty as they are."

Lexi burst out in tears. Belinda put a comforting

arm around her and said, "Come with me, honey. Let the sheriff sort it all out."

The cruiser came to a stop and a cloud of dust followed, sifting over their heads. The siren beeped one last time and clicked off, but the blue lights were blinding them, they were so bright.

"What's going on here?" boomed Sheriff Anderson. He pulled his sidearm, with a steely glare at both Melvin and Raven's dad. "Everybody flat on the ground. You too, Raven."

Carli leaned against Lank, as they both offered support to each other. "Welcome to the bake sale, Sheriff."

He was not amused, but Angie had to giggle.

"Don't do anything stupid, Dad," pleaded Raven as he lay flat on his stomach.

The sheriff and a deputy clicked handcuffs on the three of them in no time.

"How'd you know we'd be out here?" Angie asked.

"Got an anonymous tip," the sheriff said. "Decided I might mosey out and see for myself. Looks like you have a mess on your hands."

And then Angie remembered she held a gun in her hand and Colton still was on the ground out cold.

Angie carefully placed the gun on the ground and held her hands up high palms facing outward. Another truck pulled up and stopped.

"Daddy?" Angie watched her father reach for his cowboy hat before stepping out.

"Dad!" Travis said.

"Got it under control, Sheriff?" Mr. Olsen asked.

"We're good. Thanks, Skip."

He walked closer to Angie. "It appears you are capable of running a ranch," her father said with a bit of a smile.

"Yes sir, I am," she replied, but Angie needed to get to Colton.

She turned away from her father and knelt on the ground. The pesky cowboy had taken a bad beating. She gently patted his cheeks, and his head rolled to the other side. A couple Texas cowboys were no match for jail-hardened criminals. Fear gripped her heart as she looked at his bloody face. Maybe she really did have feelings for this joking, full-of-himself cow puncher. Life would never be dull with him around, she told herself. He'd always keep her laughing.

Carli made her way to Angie's side. "Great work, shooting out the tire. Just like Annie Oakley. Next time, give me a little warning."

Angie looked up at her friend. "Yeah, well, somebody had to do it. These guys were gittin' the snot beat out of 'em."

Colton's eyes fluttered open at that moment. "My angel. I guess I lost."

"You should see the other guy's face," said Angie.

"How's he doing?" Carli leaned over and placed a hand on her shoulder.

"I think he'll make it. And you take care of Lank. Seems we both have fellas that need some extra

302 | NATALIE BRIGHT & DENISE F. MCALLISTER

TLC."

"Really? Is Colton your fella now?" Carli's eyebrows arched as her mouth smirked.

"Whose gonna take care of me?" asked Travis.

Colton was holding his side and struggling to stand.

"Just a minute, Cowboy, let me give you a hand." Angie put her arm around his waist, and with his over her shoulders they worked to get him to his feet. Colton moaned, coughed, and spit.

"Thanks, Angie. I guess this is the only way you'll let me get close to you."

"Well, I've got a weak spot for the underdog." She smiled at him. "You should go to the hospital."

After securing the prisoners in his vehicle, the sheriff walked over to them with a stern look on his face.

He glared at Angie. "And I want to have a few words with you, young lady, about firing that gun."

Skip Olsen spoke up. "Now, Will, you've gotta agree. My girl saved the day. She shot out those rustlers' tires. Or else they'd be long gone. Probably to the next county by now."

Angie was in shock, her mouth slightly gaping open. She never thought she'd ever hear her father say anything in support of her. Actually defending her. Pretty much saying she was a hero.

She went up to him and said, "Thanks, Dad. That means a lot." They both hugged each other for a long couple of minutes. Any ill feelings just washed away. She had missed his hugs. This was a new beginning.

Her little brother Travis sidled up next to her and in a low voice only she could hear said, "Yep, she's a regular Rambo." He shoved into her some but she didn't mind.

Sheriff Anderson cleared his throat and nodded to Skip Olsen.

Angie was still holding on to Colton and he seemed to be pretty comfortable with the arrangement. She steered him next to the truck and he leaned against the tailgate.

"Ow! Be careful, girl. Ya tryin' to kill me?"

"Good grief. Did you say you used to ride broncs? You're not that tough, are you?"

"C'mon, Angie. Take it easy on me."

She hesitated a few seconds, stared into those gorgeous eyes, and said, "Well, just this once." The moonlight was definitely getting to her.

He gave her a look that made her feel uncomfortable like he was appraising not only her body but might even be reading her mind.

Fire flashed in his eyes and she thought he might kiss her, but instead gave her that sparkly smile of his. "I like it when you're sweet to me, Angie. I'll need somebody to take care of me while I heal."

"Don't push it, Cowboy. I ain't nobody's nursemaid." That kiss would have been nice and she'd hold him to it another time, that's for sure.

Chapter Forty-One

Carli watched the sheriff and his deputy drive away with Uncle Melvin and his gang of rustlers. Behind them followed Skip Olsen with Angie and Travis. She stood for a minute watching the taillights of Belinda's minivan, thinking of Raven. He was on his own now but she would tell Sheriff Anderson how he had cooperated and told her about the plans for the next full moon. She hoped they would give him a second chance with some leniency, and she would keep him in her prayers.

"He'll be all right." Lank came up behind her and placed an arm around her back, giving her a tight squeeze. She leaned her head against his shoulder.

"I hope so," she whispered.

"I need to take Colton to his truck, and then I'll see you back at the ranch."

She nodded in the dark and walked down the hill to her pickup truck. Just as she slipped into the seat, Lexi sat up in the back. The dome light reflected on her face, tears glistened on her cheeks. Peering at Carli with red-rimmed eyes, Lexi sniffed and wiped her nose with the bottom of her T-shirt.

"There are consequences for the decisions you make in life, Lexi. Raven did the right thing by owning up to what he did, even if his uncle more or less forced him. I'll make sure the sheriff knows that."

Lexi nodded and remained silent.

"I'm calling your mother to come get you."

"No. Please." The girl's voice was barely audible, her throat scratchy sounding from crying.

Carli started the engine and gripped the steering wheel with both hands. The dashboard clock showed three o'clock. "I'll take you home."

They drove in silence through the pasture, headlights bouncing along the rough road. There wasn't much to say that hadn't already been said. The silence was broken by an occasional sniffle from the backseat. Carli couldn't help but feel relief knowing Raven would be involved in legal proceedings; that way he wouldn't be able to see Lexi. With time, Lexi might realize the choices he had made and how they would affect her future. But girls in love are so blinded, even broken.

Carli knew from experience. She realized that too late. On reflection, she was sure there had been signs that her boyfriend in Georgia was being unfaithful, but she never saw them at the time.

By the time she got back to the Wild Cow, Lank was sitting on her front porch. Even from the dim glow from the porch light, the appearance of his handsome face bruised and swollen made her chest ache. The events of the night suddenly drained her, and she took weary steps towards him. Giving in to her instincts for once, she ignored her usual defensive boundaries. She eased onto his lap and leaned against his chest. He put both arms around her. They remained like that for several minutes, maybe hours; she wasn't sure until his stomach growled.

"I'm hungry too. Come on. I'll cook." Carli stood and tugged on his arm. Without a word, he followed her inside.

Under the harsh light of the kitchen, she gasped at the sight of his face. A trail of dried blood ran down the side of his head. One eye was completely swollen shut.

"We should clean you up first," she said.

He sat on the barstool as she wet a rag with warm water. Standing between his legs, she gently cleaned the blood from his face. He flinched when she touched his bloody nose.

They exchanged glances but didn't speak. The yearning in his eyes told her all she needed to know. Her cheeks warmed. Her whole being seemed to be filled with this moment in time. Why was she holding back? Lank was nothing like her boyfriend in Georgia. What was she afraid of?

She cleared her throat and backed away. "I'm out of eggs. Let me see what else I've got besides cereal."

She opened a plastic container and sniffed. Leftover taco meat from several days ago that she had used on a salad. She started the coffee pot, then

found a package of tortillas, and warmed everything in the microwave. She handed him a plate
and he gave an uncertain look.

"Do you have any grated cheese?"

"No."

"How about salsa?"

"Nope."

"Lettuce and tomato?"

She hesitated a minute. "Sorry. Ate it all several
nights ago."

Lank slowly wrapped the ground meat into the
warmed tortilla and took a bite. "This is pretty
good. Thanks."

Carli's heart fluttered and she cleared her throat.
Lank looked at her and smiled. Dang those dreamy
blue-gray eyes. Well, only one eye at the moment.

"His name was Josh and I caught him kissing my
biggest competitor at a horse show. I hadn't realized we were broken up."

The Adam's apple on Lank's throat bobbled as he
swallowed. Their eyes met but Carli looked down
into her mug of coffee.

If she had to look into those eyes again, she
wouldn't be able to continue. "I thought he was the
one. It's hard for me to trust, and, after that, even
more so. I'm sorry. It has nothing to do with you."

"Thanks for telling me," Lank quietly said.
"Where does that leave us?"

"I don't know. I'm tired. You should probably go."

Surprise showed in Lank's eyes, followed by a
hint of sadness before he turned, put on his cowboy

hat, and walked towards the door.

"Good night," was all he said, without turning around.

Carli stood at the door watching Lank walk across the compound towards his trailer house. The sun wasn't up yet, but a faint glow appeared behind the cottonwoods that lined the creek. It would be morning soon.

A deep feeling of remorse washed over her like a queasy stomach. She had just rejected a good man. Not in so many words, but, basically, she had told him to get lost. She should run after him. Carli even went so far as the end of the porch but stopped. She crumpled on the front steps. She knew in her heart of hearts that her future had just walked away and she had done nothing to stop him.

Why couldn't she find the courage to trust and believe in Lank. Take a chance again, Carli.

Chapter Forty-Two

The next morning Lank's mind swirled with details, scenarios, what-ifs. First, he thought about the past. Carli coming to the Wild Cow Ranch from Georgia. What he had thought of her back then. What she thought of him. Even though she had seemed irritated at the time, he couldn't deny the instant spark. They had sure butted horns more times than he would have liked. But they'd also been through so much together—the hay barn fire where his horse, Blackie, had died, the winter snowstorm that almost claimed Carli and her horse, Beau, when she got lost in it. Then there were jealousies and misunderstandings, petty fusses. Definite trust issues on both sides, but mainly hers which she had admitted. Through it all they'd become close friends, and then more than that. He knew she felt the same way.

He was head over heels in love with her and if he didn't do something quick, he'd lose her forever. He knew she felt the same about him, but he felt her pulling back. It was time he told her. Clear. Direct.

Just lay his heart on the line. Then maybe he'd stop tossing and turning and seeing her face every waking moment.

If she rejected him, so be it. What would she want with a down and out cow puncher anyway? She could do better.

Lank was proud of his Hispanic ethnicity but he didn't always think about it or advertise it front and center. Now though, as he contemplated a future with Carli, and hopefully starting a family together, he wondered if his heritage might be a problem for her. But it was a part of him, coursing through his blood vessels. He wished his mother was alive. She would know what he should do about Carli. One thing he was certain of, the pride he felt for his family and ancestors.

Then, because he was human and his mind was darting here and there, he had a few doubts. Was this the right time to propose? Just last night they had faced cattle rustlers and all that danger, with Angie and Carli showing fierce independence to stop the crime ring. In their future together, Lank was certain he wouldn't be the only one wearing the pants, so to speak. Carli had shown everyone that she could stand on her own two feet and take charge. She never appeared to be a damsel in distress. As a couple, they would need to learn how to balance this since his maleness always wanted to rescue and protect her.

He should tell her how he felt. He should propose. At this point he wasn't sure what her answer might be. So how should he propose, Lank wondered. Make a grand gesture at sunset up in the pasture? Take her to a nice restaurant in Amarillo?

No, that wasn't who they were. They were fun, quirky at times, and often kept each other guessing. They had a push and pull kind of relationship. However, in the end, they had to make sure they were together in whatever they faced.

He opened a dresser drawer and took out a ring box. His grandmother's wedding ring. Simple. Small diamonds that burned like fire. His mother's ring had gone to his sister, but before she died his mother had given him this ring. "Make sure she loves you as much as I do, mijito."

Lank had some ideas about how to get his plan off the ground. But he'd have to enlist the help of others. Maybe Buck and Lola. They could keep a secret.

He envisioned something romantic, a table on the hill where they could look down over the Wild Cow. Champagne or wine. Music. He'd get down on one knee. No. Maybe he should play his guitar. Serenade her with the song he'd been working on the last few months.

What if he only made a fool of himself and she said no? He knew she was unwilling to give in completely. She was so guarded, but she had finally told him about her boyfriend back in Georgia. That was progress, and maybe he was moving too fast for her. She frustrated him to no end.

He'd bring her back to the cookhouse where

Buck and Lola could talk some sense into her. Maybe that would be unfair if they all ganged up on her, but he wasn't taking any chances. She had to see a future with him and he wanted everybody to know how much she meant to him.

Before he could ask for Buck and Lola's help, a knock on his front door startled him. He opened it to find Carli standing before him.

"Feel like riding? We need to talk," she said, a half-smile on her face which didn't reach her eyes.

Lank's heart dropped to his feet, but he masked his emotions. If she told him to get lost, he figured it could mean the end of his job too. He knew there was a war going on inside her, but if she'd just listen to reason.

"Sure. Give me a sec. I need to tell Buck where I'll be."

"I'll meet you at the saddle house." She turned and walked away.

Carli saddled Beau and waited on Lank to get back from the cookhouse. When he walked in, she noticed the frown on his face, but didn't say anything. Her heart thudded in her chest and she felt nauseous. They needed to talk and she had no idea where to begin. Their eyes met and, somehow, she got lost in the depths of the love she saw there, and then suddenly she knew. Her future was in his hands. Lank was the one.

All this time he had patiently been on the sidelines, waiting, but when she really needed someone, it had always been Lank. So many wasted days arguing with herself and pushing him away, when the true desires of her heart had been right in front of her all along. God had known, but she had refused to listen.

A wide smile spread across her face as joy filled her heart to overflowing and her mind reeled with full clarity.

They got on their horses, took off in a lope side by side going in no particular direction. As they emerged on top of the hill, Carli stopped Beau and Lank reined up next to her. A somewhat panicked expression came across his face, but she just smiled.

"Let's get married," she said.

The look on his face was pure gold. Carli laughed out loud. First his eyes bugged out and his mouth opened; his jaw worked up and down but no words came.

She smiled. "You heard me right. I've been thinking. I guess we both have been thinking. The same thing, I hope. We just haven't said it out loud. I know I can be difficult and that I have trust issues. I also know that I love you, Lank Torres. And I'm pretty sure you love me. So, let's get married. Only I'm not getting down on one knee. That's your job, Cowboy."

White as ghost, he jumped off his horse and pulled her off Beau.

Without a word, he kissed her gently at first, then stronger, deeper, more demanding. Her knees went weak, and her head grew light.

"Follow me," he said. Lank jumped back on his horse.

Carli hurried to get on Beau, and then prodded him into a run to catch up. In a way she was panicked because he hadn't said yes or no. The kiss might have meant yes, but why would he jump on his horse and ride away? Maybe she should stop following him. Perhaps he didn't feel the same and she had read the signs wrong. Wouldn't be the first time, but this felt different. It felt right. For once in her life, she was at peace and in no way apprehensive about the decision she had made. She had prayed about Lank for many months, and this had been her answer. This is where she belonged. She urged Beau to run faster and catch up.

They stopped in front of the cookhouse where several cars were parked. Lank grabbed her hand and led her.

Inside, Lank whistled and little L.J. came running to him. Lexi had been holding onto the dog at the back of the crowd. Carli was surprised to see a small group of friends and neighbors—Angie and Travis, Crazy Vera, Colton, Buck and Lola, Lexi and her mom, Belinda and Russell. All standing still with big smiles on their faces.

Lank scooped the dog up into his arms and gazed into Carli's eyes.

"Carli, looks like L.J. has brought you something," he said. "And she and I each have a question for you."

Carli petted the squirming, licking pup and immediately saw a ring affixed to her collar.

She shook her head and smiled at Lank. "Oh, my."

As Carli held the dog, a tear slid from her eye and she said, "Her name is Lily Jane."

Lank loosened the collar, retrieved the ring, and got down on one knee. Carli let the dog go and Lexi was there to pick her up.

Holding the ring in two fingers, Lank looked up, and said, "Carli, I love you with everything in me and want to spend the rest of my life with you. Will you marry me?"

Carli tilted her head from one side to the other, seemingly stretching out the seconds in a playful way as though pondering her answer.

Finally, Lank blurted out, "For heaven's sakes, will you?"

"Yes, yes, yes, I will."

He jumped to his feet, put the ring on her left hand, and kissed her soundly on the mouth.

Carli grabbed Lank's arm. "You said Lily Jane had a question for me too."

"Oh, yeah, she wants to officially be adopted by the both of us and she wants her name to be L.J. once and for all."

Carli shook her head. "No chance of a name change. She's my Lily Jane." They'd have to call a truce on that one and agree to disagree on the name for their dog.

Still a bit stunned by the group of people, Carli

looked around the room.

"You know I proposed first," she said. "How did y'all know he'd say yes?"

"We knew," said Lola. "But if he hadn't, and if you hadn't, we'd still have a little party anyway. You know there's always food here." Everyone laughed.

In unison the group said, "Kiss, kiss, kiss," and Lank complied, kissing Carli sweetly.

Then he said to her, "I have one more surprise for you."

He walked to the wall where his guitar was propped, and sat down in front of her. "I wrote this for you. It's not quite done. It's a work in progress. Like us."

Carli seemed to be glowing and her eyes glistened.

Lank strummed and sang his heartfelt words.

> *"You were a girl from Georgia*
> *And I was just marking time.*
> *You came into my life*
> *All on your own, no place to call home.*
> *We love the same things*
> *You can see it was meant to be.*
> *God is on our side*
> *So how could we go wrong?*
> *Please say 'I Do'*
> *And make me the happiest man ever.*
> *Let's do life together.*
> *Will you marry me, Carli Jean?"*

Even though she had already said yes, this song, these words, this love was private, between the two of them, even in a crowded room.

Lank put the guitar down and Carli took both of his hands in hers.

"Yes, a thousand time yes. I will always say yes, Lank."

"I love you, Carli."

His arms drew her into a tight embrace. "I love you too, Lank."

The roomful of friends clinked their glasses in unison, celebrating love.

Lank kissed her again.

A loud knock on the door broke the spell and Sheriff Anderson's voice boomed through the dining hall. "Are we too late?"

"Yes, and you missed the song too," said Lola as she wiped her cheeks and sniffed, which made everyone laugh.

Behind the sheriff followed the cattle brand investigator, Derek McKinney, and another man. Carli couldn't help but notice the way Derek's eyes scanned the crowd and landed on Angie. Colton was quick to put his arm around her shoulder which she shrugged off. Derek's face showed a flash of disappointment.

"Come in, Sheriff. You didn't miss the celebration," said Buck.

"I brought these guys along. You remember Derek, and this is his boss."

Buck shook the other man's hand and clapped

him on the shoulder. "It's good to see you." They smiled at each other and talked in low voices for a few moments then walked closer to Carli.

"Carli, I'd like you to meet Derek's regional boss with the Texas Ranchers' Association. He used to work at the Wild Cow Ranch when he was a teenager."

"Yes, sir. How are you? I'm Carli." She barely noticed him. Her head was swirling with wedding plans and more kisses from Lank, and the ring that seemed odd on her finger. But it was a perfect fit and she loved what it stood for.

The man hesitated for just a second, as if studying her face. "Good to meet you. I'm Taylor Miller."

Carli's breath left her, and her head suddenly went blank. Lank introduced himself and shook hands. She would have fainted dead away if he hadn't been standing next to her.

How in the world would she ever tell her new fiancé about the birth certificate she'd found in her grandparents' house? The one she'd never seen before that listed the name of her birth father. And how in the world would she ever explain to this stranger named Taylor Miller that he had a daughter?

Acknowledgements

Thanks to the readers and fans who have read, posted reviews, and sent us emails and texts about how much you love the Wild Cow Ranch. Your comments mean more than you'll ever know. Thanks to the Wolfpack Publishing family for making this series a reality, and for your hard work and dedication to the Western genre. Meeting you all at the 2021 Western Writers of America convention assured me that our books are in good hands. Looking forward to our continued collaboration. Thanks to my husband Chris for his unwavering support. Sometimes you have to accept the journey without questioning the why. Thanks to our Heavenly Father who brought us together on this path.

- Natalie Bright

Acknowledgements

While co-writing this book, a health blip inter-rupted my life for a short time. My wonderful co-author Natalie Bright and I continued to ponder the plot about Carli and Lank's lives. Through it all, Natalie was encouraging, understanding, and hardworking (and she sent me really funny cards!). She also prayed for me. I can't thank her enough.

Gratitude goes to our loving God for staying by our sides in a topsy turvy world and on this jour-ney of life; to our many friends with the Western Writers of America; Wolfpack Publishing and CKN Christian Publishing; and to so many others who are there for us.

- **Denise F. McAllister**

Take a look at A Place Called Destiny by Emma Easter

Twenty-five-year-old Rachel, nearing the end of her pregnancy, makes an urgent dash to flee her polygamist husband Mike Caldwell and his embittered first spouse Olivia. Pregnant with her first child, a product of her troubled forced spiritual union with Mike, Rachel knows if she doesn't escape her unholy relationship both her and her child will never be free.

She has been unable to accept this way of life and feels it is not right for her to act as a barrier to Mike and Olivia and the sanctity of their marriage. Her escape plan fails, due to Fallow Creek, the polygamy commune she lives in, employing a security detail of young men who guard against escape.

With help from the unmarried pastor Keith Thorn, of nearby town Destiny, they are reminded that with faith, love and trust in God's plan they can achieve anything.

AVAILABLE ON AMAZON

About Natalie Bright

With roots firmly planted in the Texas Panhandle, Natalie Bright grew up obsessed with the Wild West and making up stories. The small farming community where she lived gave her a belief in hard-working, genuine people and a firm foundation of faith. She is the author of books for kids and adults, as well as numerous articles.

This author and blogger writes about small town heroes with complicated pasts and can-do attitudes, who navigate life's crazy misfortunes with humor and happy endings. A passionate supporter of history and libraries, Natalie loves exploring museums and collecting old books. Her ranch photography is featured in a chuck wagon cookbook. She lives on a dirt road with her husband, where they raise black and red Angus cattle and where the endless Texas sky continues to be her inspiration.

About Denise F. McAllister

Lovers of the West can be born in the most unlikely of places. For Denise F. McAllister, her start was in Miami, Florida, surrounded by beaches and the Everglades.

After being in the working world for some years, Denise F. McAllister decided to apply her life experience and study for her B.A. in communications and M.A. in professional writing. She loved going back to college "later in life" and hardly ever skipped a class as in her younger years. Growing up in the suburbs of Miami, Denise credits her love of horseback riding and showing in Atlanta, Georgia (15 years) for her heartfelt connection to all things Western.

Denise's faith is important to her and she loves to write about characters' journeys as they navigate real-world challenges. She prays that readers will enjoy her books, but most importantly experience a blessed connection with their Creator and Heavenly Father.

CPSIA information can be obtained
at www.ICGtesting.com
Printed in the USA
LVHW030622220921
698416LV00003B/203